Lucy is a professional medical w...
in cell biology (and has got used...
doctor" to anyone who asks). S...
and horses, listening to 1980s so...
me?), and binge-reading uplifting, happily-ever-after stories.
The Hot Henry Effect is Lucy's first novel and was as much a
surprise to her as to anyone who knows her, but now that
creative writing has turned out to be a lot more fun than it was
in GCSE English (sorry about that, Mrs Caswell), hopefully the
first of many.

www.lucychalice.com

instagram.com/lucychalice.author
x.com/LucyChalice
tiktok.com/@Lucychalice

Also by Lucy Chalice

The Hot Henry Effect

FUNDAMENTALS IN FLIRTING

LUCY CHALICE

One More Chapter
a division of HarperCollins*Publishers* Ltd
1 London Bridge Street
London SE1 9GF
www.harpercollins.co.uk
HarperCollins*Publishers*
Macken House, 39/40 Mayor Street Upper,
Dublin 1, D01 C9W8, Ireland

This paperback edition 2024
1
First published in Great Britain in ebook format
by HarperCollins*Publishers* 2024
Copyright © Lucy Chalice 2024
Lucy Chalice asserts the moral right to be identified
as the author of this work

ISBN: 978-0-00-864621-9

Printed and bound in the UK using 100% Renewable Electricity
by CPI Group (UK) Ltd

To the science girls, the nerdy girls, you're absolutely bloody brilliant just as you are.

Playlist

We Are Never Ever Getting Back Together - 🤍
Taylor Swift
As It Was - Harry Styles 🤍
Risk - Gracie Abrams 🤍
Bags - Clairo 🤍
teenage dream - Olivia Rodrigo 🤍
Good Graces - Sabrina Carpenter 🤍
'tis the damn season - Taylor Swift 🤍
positions - Ariana Grande 🤍
People You Know - Selena Gomez 🤍
I know it won't work - Gracie Abrams 🤍
Love Again - Dua Lipa 🤍
Astronomy - Conan Gray 🤍
Landslide - Haley Klinkhammer 🤍
What Happens Now? - Dasha 🤍
Diet Pepsi - Addison Rae 🤍
Vertigo - Griff 🤍
Wish You The Best - Lewis Capaldi 🤍
mirrorball - Taylor Swift 🤍
I Had Some Help - Post Malone 🤍
West Coast - Lana Del Rey 🤍
All My Love - Noah Kahan 🤍
There She Goes - Sixpence None The Richer 🤍
invisible string - Taylor Swift 🤍

Chapter One

As a first kiss it was pretty devastating, actually.

I mean, it wasn't my first kiss ever, just the first time I'd been kissed without wanting to throw up in the other person's mouth. Usually, I was put off by too much tongue, or saliva, or lips that suctioned on in a wholly uncomfortable fashion, like a toilet plunger to the face. In fact, in my fairly limited teenage experience of kissing, it had felt more like my mouth had been subjected to the turbulent effects of snogging a washing machine drum, rather than the seductive and emotionally satisfying experience I had hoped kissing might be. Who wants to have to wipe spit off their whole face when you pull apart? *Gross.*

But kissing Teddy Fraser at his eighteenth birthday party, on a bench at the edge of the rugby club field, was an enlightening occasion. The evening was surprisingly warm, bright stars blanketing the sky above, the steady thrum of the bass from the disco a distant noise reverberating through the club building behind us, the heady smell of Lynx Africa filling my nostrils. But it was Teddy's languid technique, unhurried yet thorough, large hands featherlight on my face, threading into my hair, that made me feel like I was the only person in the whole world who he wanted to kiss.

We were alone and a bit tipsy, and I thought for a few brief moments that I might truly be in love.

Until he pulled away and huskily uttered the following words, "Shit, Hannah Havens, I never thought someone like you would kiss like that."

It took me a minute to register what he had said. Someone like me? What did that mean? We were still quite close together, noses almost touching, the orangey hue of the lamppost casting a shadow over Teddy's face, but even in this light I could see that his pupils were blown, his ragged breathing fanning over my lips.

"What?" I asked, confused, my mind still a little slow after the three generous rum and Cokes that I had consumed. And the mind-altering kiss that I was still reeling from.

"You kiss like a porn star," Teddy laughed, stroking a finger lazily down my cheek, leaning back in for round two if I wasn't mistaken.

"*A porn star?*" I replied incredulously.

In that moment, I think it dawned on him what he'd just said, and he lurched away sharply. "Er, well, that's not quite what I meant. It's just that you're a surprisingly good kisser."

"Surprisingly good?"

"Shit. What I meant to say was *unexpected*. That was unexpected." He was flustered. I could see that, but I wasn't about to let him off the hook. Not Teddy Fraser, one half of the infamous Fraser twins, and cocky, confident, arrogant heartthrob of the upper sixth form.

"Unexpected? What were you expecting when you followed me out here and kissed me then, Ted?" Because he had most definitely instigated this kiss, not me.

I'd come out to get some air, my head pounding with the incessant drone of cheesy pop music. All my friends were either getting off with, or attempting to get off with, someone on the dance floor. Even my best friend, Betsy Okoro, who I knew wasn't really into guys at all (although, I was the only one she'd tearfully admitted this to over our biology homework one evening), was snogging geeky Rob Parsons rather passionately by the girls' loo. I'd been blissfully alone, and enjoying the peace, when Teddy had taken me by surprise, casually sitting next to me, even though there were at least half a dozen other benches he could have chosen. We'd spoken briefly – irrelevant chit-chat about his birthday and whether we were enjoying the party, then he'd leant in, close, tucking away a stray piece of hair that had blown across my face, his fingertips brushing my skin before slowly moving even nearer, lips hovering over mine.

With a soft exhale, he had said, "I'm going to kiss you now, if you want me to?"

I'd nodded. And in that second, I definitely had wanted him to, wondering if this would be the moment that finally lit up my eighteen-year-old brain with passion and longing for another person. Or if I was just in line for another wet-faced disappointment and would have to employ awkward avoidance techniques in the sixth form common room from now on.

But no, the kiss had been spectacular, and I was feeling wholly awkward for an entirely different reason now. And pretty bloody annoyed, actually.

In a practised move, Teddy ran his fingers through his floppy hair and gave me a wry grin. "If I'm honest, Hannah, I wasn't expecting you to let me kiss you at all."

"So why did you even try?"

"Because I really wanted to kiss you. Didn't you want to kiss me too? It certainly seemed like you did," he replied smugly, knocking his knee against mine.

He was infuriating. And gorgeous. But mostly infuriating.

I was in maths with both Teddy and his twin brother, Henry, and they were insanely good at it. Henry was pleasant and charming, kind to a fault really, and a few times he'd helped me get to grips with some particularly tricky homework. But Teddy spent more time chatting up the bevy of girls that followed the twins around than actually working, seemingly able to pull out eighty or ninety per cent on all the tests we'd had, without even having to try, like some sort of super genius. How was that even fair?

Yes, being around Teddy Fraser annoyed me greatly, and I should have remembered that before snogging his face off.

I shifted a little on the bench to give myself some more space. "It was an ok kiss, I suppose."

"Just ok? Are you sure? Because you made this seductive little moaning noise, which made me think that you were enjoying it, Hannah," Teddy murmured, glancing sideways at me.

My face heated a little as my mind flew back to a few moments ago, a time when I'd been lost in the feel of his lips and tongue, in the soft and insistent way they'd caressed me, the gentle nips and the feeling of his hands in my hair, warm breath over my skin as he teased his mouth down my neck.

"I've had better kisses, Teddy," I lied, noticing with some

satisfaction the slight slump to his shoulders. "But things definitely took a nosedive when you compared me to a porn star."

I got up from the bench and smoothed down my slightly wrinkled top. This was the last party I'd be attending before knuckling down to revise for my A levels followed by a summer packed with the hours and hours of placements that I'd committed to since being offered a conditional place at vet school. There was no other option, no plan B for me. I'd wanted this for as long as I could remember and was on the cusp of realising my dreams. Boys were not on the agenda and I fully intended to get away from this particular one as soon as I could.

"I'm sorry I said that. It was meant to be a compliment. A fucking shit one, granted, but please don't go yet." Teddy reached out to take hold of my hand.

But I pulled it away. "Why? You'll be missed inside and there are plenty of other girls who'd welcome some attention from you."

"I don't want to kiss anyone in there," he said, angling his head towards the rugby club main building. "I want to kiss you. Again. Please stay."

"Why me?"

Why me, indeed. I was a million miles away from anything special. In fact, my bell-bottom jeans and baggy T-shirt were a far cry from everyone else's fancy dresses and figure-hugging outfits. Looking away, I let the curtain of my long strawberry-blonde hair fall across my cheek, hiding me from view. It was a shield against the world, a distraction from my flawed and imperfect face. A face I struggled even to look at in the mirror most days. A face that had left me wide open to ridicule from my classmates. A face that I despised. Perfection – that's what everyone strived for. Symmetrical features, clear skin, tanned and gorgeous. Just like Teddy Fraser.

"Because as infuriating as you are, I like you, Hannah," Teddy said. Then, turning his face away, he whispered so softly that I could barely hear him, "And you're the most beautiful girl I've ever seen."

It was so quiet, in fact, that I was left wondering if I'd made it up, merely manifesting my subconscious yearning for someone to say those things to me. But really knowing that no one ever would. Well, not say it and really mean it. I was cursed with the looks that I had, and surely it was better to focus on my brains and ability, to get by without being the pretty one. God knows I was reminded of this fact every day by the popular girls in my year. I knew I should embrace my geekiness because I was on much safer ground there.

The doors of the clubhouse opened and Teddy's brother, Henry, appeared, stopping short from walking over to us.

"Ted, are you coming back in?" he called over, hands in his pockets, looking away to give us some privacy, I supposed.

"Yeah, yeah, in a minute," Teddy shouted back before glancing at me again and smiling. "Goddamn geek hates being the centre of attention. He just wants me to take the flack for him."

My heart hurt at the insult. Being a geek was what I was good at, and here he was, ridiculing it. Balling my fists, I went to follow Henry back inside.

"Right, us geeks should just hide away in the corner, shouldn't we?" I replied, purposefully allowing a sharpness to creep into my voice.

"Wait, Hannah, please," Teddy muttered, taking hold of my hand and not letting me pull away this time.

"What is it?"

"About tonight ... I just wondered, well, if maybe you'd ... or if we could..." His voice drifted off as a gaggle of girls appeared around the corner of the building, lit cigarettes in their hands. Mandy Shaw – gymnast, beautiful elite, sociology student, my tormentor and least favourite person at school – was heading up the group and making a beeline for us.

"What, Ted? What do you want me to do? Keep quiet about what just happened?" I whispered acerbically.

"What? Well, er..." he stuttered, getting more and more uncomfortable as the gang of girls approached, the curious slant of their heads indicating that they had seen us and were wholly intent on finding out what was going on.

"Listen, don't worry. I'm not going to tell anyone. It's not like I'm proud of myself either." I hissed, "I know what this was – a drunken snog, a mistake. I'm not expecting you to announce that we're boyfriend and girlfriend. I know better than to expect anything chivalrous from you, Teddy Fraser. It's not like you're Henry, is it?"

The air around us turned frigid in an instant, Teddy's demeanour shifting, defensive and something else ... hurt, perhaps?

"No. I'm definitely not Henry," he practically growled at me, dropping my hand as if my touch was burning his skin, and stepping away.

"No, you're not," I said, equally tersely.

In the soft glow of lamplight, we glared at each other, just as Mandy neared.

"Teddy," she whined, "what are you doing here with her?"

"Nothing," we both said at once, and Mandy looked sceptically between us.

"Chatting about the extra maths revision sessions he needs," I added sourly and Teddy snorted in disbelief.

"You're such a weird fucking loser, Hannah. Why on earth would Teddy want to talk maths revision at his eighteenth birthday party?" Mandy laughed unkindly. In my mind I had a dartboard with her face on it, and I took great pleasure in mentally lobbing pointy implements at it, with alarming regularity. And now was no exception.

I shrugged. "He needs some help with the fundamentals," I answered evenly, stalking away from this group of teenage arseholes that I was most definitely going to leave behind in a few months' time. And never think of ever again.

Chapter Two

Fifteen years later

I angled my head in a different direction to see if this made the sight in front of me any easier to comprehend. Nope. There were still too many legs peeking out from under the covers of the bed, too many bodies writhing about beneath the duvet, accompanied by the distinct grunting, gasping sound that Jonathan made when he was getting really close to climaxing.

It was difficult to know what to do. My awkward British sensibilities made me want to back out of the room, close the door quietly, and pretend I'd never seen this. I wanted to make a strong cup of tea and have a sit down. Maybe even eat a whole packet of bourbon biscuits and have a little cry.

But the honey badger part of my brain was having none of it, was rising from slumber, acutely and furiously awakened. And she was most definitely not going to let this apocalyptic transgression slide.

"For the love of God, Jonathan, why did you have to turn out to be such a total and utter bastard?" I said. Loudly. I was proud that my voice didn't waver or wobble. I was rationality personified, even if my intestines were looping the loop and sickening bile was rising in my throat as my love life crashed spectacularly down around me.

All writhing and grunting stopped. A corner of the duvet was lifted and his face came into view, all flushed skin, panting obscenely, and sandy hair dishevelled.

"Hannah?! It's not—"

"If you're about to tell me that it's not what it looks like, I will legitimately get the phenobarbital from the car and draw up enough to kill a horse," I interjected. An angry self-righteous violence, likely from my Viking ancestry, was rearing its head in the face of the dreadfully clichéd way in which our relationship was going to end.

A dark-haired head appeared next to his, her eyes wide, fearful. Christ, this was even worse. Totally humiliating and disgusting. On all levels.

"You're shagging your PhD student, really, Jonathan?"

"We're in love," he muttered.

I stared in disbelief, his once familiar and attractive face now like a blob of vomit in my brain. Initially I had found him confident and charismatic. I had been amused by his slight condescension that was thinly veiled as humour. Impressed by his innate ability to ingratiate himself to all around him with an affable, upper-class charm. He had been so pleasant and helpful, championing my burgeoning career and always quick to offer his contacts or knowledge to further my research and allow me to flourish. And when he'd told me that he wanted me, that he loved me, so early on in our relationship, I'd felt like I'd won the romance lottery and would get my happily ever after. But now, seeing this betrayal first-hand was a hideous punch to the guts, the cold realisation, the sudden stark acceptance, a slap in the face. I really had meant nothing to him. He had, in fact, just been a cheating and disingenuous wanker all along, and I had fallen for him, hook, line, and sinker. How stupid was I?

"Love? Is that what this is?" I directed my furious gaze at the young, impressionable woman who was desperately looking everywhere but at me. "Well, I sincerely hope he can make you orgasm, Daisy, because he's never been able to do that for me in the entire two years we've been together."

Meeting my eyes briefly, she shook her head slightly.

"What?!" Jonathan spluttered, turning an incredulous stare down at her.

"You've never made me come, Jonathan. I usually go home after and sort myself out," she said, somewhat awkwardly.

Folding my arms, I leant against the doorframe to see how this would unfold, immensely enjoying his discomfort despite the nausea still bubbling in my stomach.

"What?!" he repeated. "Why didn't you say anything?" He looked up at me. "Why didn't *you* tell me?"

I shrugged. "I thought you might have noticed."

Jonathan rolled over and sat up, rubbing his hands over his face while Daisy, his PhD student (and possibly now ex-lover), scooted out of bed and began gathering her clothes together.

"I'm so sorry, Dr Havens," she said to me. "I was in real danger of failing my first year and he said he would help me."

I shot a disbelieving look at Jonathan, who had the grace to look suitably ashamed.

"That's appalling behaviour from your supervisor. You

should definitely report it to the Dean of the Graduate School. No student should be coerced into having sex with a professor to improve their grades, or for any other reason whatsoever."

Dressed in record time, Daisy nodded and skirted around me and out of the door, leaving me staring at the person I'd thought I knew – the person I'd fallen in love with but who was now so unfamiliar and repulsive to me that it was like looking at a stranger. A dirty, libidinous stranger. The sort of person who made you feel as if one look would cause your skin to crawl entirely off your body.

"I think I'll just go," I said. This was his very grand house after all. He was the senior lecturer and professor of veterinary medicine here while I was just an academic research fellow and still paying off my student debts. I wasn't exactly flush with cash. And even after two years together, he hadn't even let me move in with him. Instead, I'd been renting a poky little room in a dingy house near the vet school with some other research fellows and PhD students. The true and heady heights of success in my thirties.

"Hannah, don't go! We can work through this."

"But you're in love with her, Jonathan, and I don't want to be anyone's second choice, least of all to a sexually coercive prick such as you."

"Hannah, please," he begged.

"Perhaps you've done me a favour. I might actually have a chance of finding a guy who can satisfy me in bed now." I was still scarily calm; a picture of cold indifference. I had the temperament of a complete bitch. It was a bit like having an out-of-body experience, watching this cool and collected ice queen laying into this man as if she couldn't give a crap. Yet inside, my emotions were in turmoil: rejection, disgust (at

12

myself as well as him), and failure swirling in a sour mix that boiled under my skin.

"I am sorry," he whispered, head bowed in dejection.

My resolve faltered for a moment because, despite how I appeared outwardly, I was still wishing that this could all be undone somehow, unseen, unknown, my uneventful little life returned back to its normal status quo.

"Jonathan, I..."

His expression changed, like a lion spotting the weakest member in a herd of antelope. "You know you still need me, Hannah. You know you still want me. I want you too. Don't throw this away because of one silly mistake."

"I..." The niggly little unkind gremlin who lived in my head had thrust herself forwards, reminding me that there was zero likelihood that anyone else would want me, and that it was a miracle someone as good-looking and successful as Jonathan still wanted me. But then the sound of the front door closing at the bottom of the stairs – presumably Daisy hot-footing it out of here – reminded me of the "silly mistake" I had just witnessed. My blood began to boil all over again. A life of spinsterhood was calling.

Someone get me a cat. Or twelve.

"I no longer want you. It's over."

Jonathan's expression darkened, and I knew what was coming, knew where this would likely head. I was familiar with the usual pattern of angry denigration that he spewed when embarrassed or when he felt he had been wronged. I'd seen it from him before, but had often felt that he was justified. I had forever taken his side in all things, blinded to his fuckwittery by my own devotion. But now I needed to ready myself, to be prepared.

Come on ice queen, brace yourself in case of extreme bastardliness. And don't fucking crumple, whatever you do.

"I would never have gone elsewhere if you'd shown me even an ounce of affection. What did you expect? You've essentially forced me into the arms of other women."

Women? More than one.

What a fool I was.

"Plus, you're so cold and unresponsive in bed that it's like having sex with a corpse. If you'd been enough of a girlfriend, this would never have happened."

"So this is all my fault? Wow." I slumped back against the door frame. This was a low blow. I'd tried to spice things up in the bedroom more than once, but he was the one who'd decided it was missionary or nothing. I levelled a stony fuck-you glare at him.

"If you tell anyone about this, I can make things very difficult for you in the department. You know that, don't you?" he carried on, his tone now a touch desperate. "Your academic career will be gone, just like that." He clicked his fingers theatrically.

What an arsehole.

"You'd have to start all over again and I'd make damn sure every door was shut in your face," he carried on smugly.

I remained mute. Sadly, I knew he was right. I knew he could gather the old boys around himself and make any chance of success impossible for me. I also knew that he would threaten Daisy in exactly the same way, and she would buckle and keep all this to herself so as not to jeopardise her own fledgling career.

"But we can turn this around. I can forgive you for not being affectionate, you can work on it – have some sex therapy or something – and we can move on," he said, his voice taking on a persuasive lilt. He smiled and patted the duvet next to him, his expression deceptive and slippery. "Come on, Hannah. Think about your future. You know I'm the only one who can help you be truly successful in the veterinary field."

Screw this.

With a saccharine smile, I walked over to the bed, watching his face sag with relief, believing that his threats and posturing had weakened my resolve; that he had got his own way. As he usually did. Leaning down so that our faces were level, I surreptitiously reached out and grasped the full pint glass of water that he always had on the bedside table but never drank.

"Do you know what, Jonathan? You're absolutely right. I *am* thinking very carefully about my future, and I've recently decided that my life needs to take on an entirely new trajectory. One that is a fucking million miles away from you."

And I poured the whole glass over his head, and stalked out of the room.

Chapter Three

The steady beat of Pluto's hooves on the compacted earth was like a drum, a hypnotic rhythm as we cantered along through the dappled sunlight illuminating the woodland, my mind free of everything but the breeze on my face and the evocative floral scent of wildflowers in early summer. This was me-time, time to be free of the pressures of work, time to be present, in the moment, enjoying all that was offered in this gloriously beautiful part of England, my worries melting away. Escaping the hold Jonathan had had on me was the best thing I'd ever done. My life had settled into a new normal, my resolve hardening to my forced spinsterhood, even if embracing the dramatic U-turn in my career aspirations had been a tougher pill to swallow. But it had definitely been a relief to come home and release myself from the shitstorm that had been the last few months.

I let out a contented sigh and patted Pluto's neck gratefully.

"Good boy, steady now." I applied a touch of pressure on the rein, sitting up a little in the saddle to encourage him to slow as we turned the corner of the bridleway we were following. It was wonderful and peaceful and cathartic.

But then, just like that, all hell broke loose.

Pluto screeched to a halt and swerved violently to the right as a mountain biker came careering off the bank straight towards us, accompanied by a string of expletives. And before I knew what was happening, I was sailing through the air like a missile, heading for certain destruction into the ditch in front of me. A loud bang, like a gunshot, resounded as my inflatable body protector went off, and Pluto and I parted company to the dramatic sounds of someone groaning (me), and someone else continuing to swear (the bike-riding bringer of doom, I assumed).

Eyes screwed tightly shut, my body encased in the suffocating vice of my fully inflated air jacket, I lay still for a moment, surrounded by wild garlic and lightly perfumed flowers. My backside, meanwhile, simultaneously squelched into a soft bit of ground, mud oozing right through to my underwear.

Lovely.

"Shit, are you ok? I am so sorry. I didn't see you there."

How anyone could miss a five hundred kilogram, predominantly white animal travelling at about twenty-five miles an hour was beyond me, but, you know, a lot of people were really unobservant. Like this dickhead, clearly.

"Is my horse ok?" I whispered, my body contorted and partially hidden by the undergrowth, and from my depressed position in the ditch I could see very little other than the tree canopy above. I squeezed my eyes shut again.

"Erm, how would I know?" The voice was male, uncertain.

"Can you see him?"

"Yes."

"Is he standing up?"

"Yes." The voice was growing in confidence with these easy-to-answer questions.

"Has he got all four feet on the ground?"

"Yes." This time the voice was triumphant, like he'd just scored a win on *University Challenge*.

"So, none of his limbs are waving in the air or dangling loosely or look weird?" I tried, upping the difficulty level slightly.

"Er, nope?" Uncertainty had crept back in.

"What's he doing?" I was starting to get some feeling back now as the air jacket slowly deflated.

"Erm, he looks like he's eating the hedge." A pause. "Is that a good sign?"

"Yes. Can you see any blood on him?"

There was another tension-filled pause. "Nope." The voice had gone a bit trembly.

This all sounded promising and I began moving my arms and legs, one at a time, to check my own body for broken bones. I was subconsciously aware that the man was now leaning over me, quite closely, but I kept my eyes tightly shut, concentrating on my own body inventory. I knew that if I looked at him, I was probably going to launch into a strongly worded diatribe and I needed my full breath back before I could do it with any kind of conviction.

"Can you open your eyes?"

Reluctantly, I cracked my eyelids open a fraction and squinted up into the shadowed face of quite a tall man in a cycling helmet, backlit by the sun and crouching on the edge of the shallow ditch. Gingerly, I carried on testing each of my limbs with my hands. Everything seemed to be moving and reacting as it should – no weird tingly feelings or absence of vital appendages – so I started to sit up and grunted in discomfort.

"Woah, wait. Are you ok?" Large, warm hands reached for my shoulders, clasping the tops of my arms firmly. "Should you be sitting up? Do I need to call an ambulance?"

"I'm fine, honestly. No need for an ambulance." I began undoing the toggles of the air jacket and its torso-crushing hold on my body lessened, so that I was finally able to breathe normally again.

Looking up and out of my position in the ditch, I could see Pluto was eating the hedge nearby, just as goddamn Evel Knievel here had said, and seemed totally fine. My horse was watching me with faint equine interest between munches, as if to say, *Not sure what you're doing down there, lady, but I'll be all right snacking here until you're ready to go home.*

Smiling at my goofy horse – I really did love him – I took off my riding hat and glanced over at the cause of this untimely dismount. He was stooping over me, concern etched on his face. His oddly familiar face. His gorgeous, infuriating face. His bloody-hell-you're-a-blast-from-the-past face. His I-really-hoped-I'd-never-see-you-again face.

Shit.

I groaned in despair. No, this could not actually be happening.

"Are you ok?" he repeated, leaning down towards me and touching my shoulder gently, staring into my eyes.

"Yes, I'm fine." I wasn't going to acknowledge him if he didn't know who I was. This could be ok. I could get away anonymously and he'd be none the wiser. All fine and dandy, dignity intact. Hoo-bloody-ray.

"Hannah Havens?" A hint of stunned disbelief coloured the tone of his voice.

Bugger.

"Yes, hello, Teddy Fraser," I replied, cringing, before muttering sarcastically, "Fancy, quite literally, running into you today."

"Oh my God," he whispered and rocked back on his heels, studying me intently.

"Right, well, since we're both uninjured, I'll be going."

Uncomfortable with his scrutiny, I started to get to my feet, a wave of dizziness causing me to pitch forward and stumble into Teddy, but his hands caught me easily, holding me briefly against his chest. Christ, he seemed so much broader and more potent than I remembered at school, the muscles of his arms bulging as he righted me before ducking his head down to look into my face.

"Hannah, I think I should take you to hospital," he said in a gravelly voice, running his hands down my arms and lacing his fingers with mine.

"That won't be necessary. I'm fine." I pulled away from him, his proximity and tenderness causing a ripple of unwelcome desire to course through me. My libido already annoyingly optimistic at this most basic of touches.

Teddy stood up and stepped back in contemplation, a frown on his face. "Are you far from home?"

"No, the stables are about ten minutes away."

"Right, well, I'm accompanying you back there," he said, his tone allowing no room for negotiation.

I snorted. "Who are you and what have you done with the smug, self-centred guy I went to school with?"

He raised an eyebrow and chewed his lip thoughtfully, before muttering, "I can be chivalrous too, just like Henry, you know."

For a moment we stared at each other, a strange crackling intensity to the air. Charged particles seemed to be zipping between us, invisible protons of weirdness that were holding me captive in his gaze, until with exaggerated annoyance, I plonked my riding hat back on my head and stalked over to Pluto. His reins were broken, but otherwise he was unscathed and I was grateful for that. Taking a few calming breaths, I hung onto his reassuring bulk and familiarity, grounding myself by pressing my nose into his soft grey coat and inhaling the comforting aroma of horse.

Meanwhile, Teddy had disappeared into the undergrowth and was retrieving his bike from a particularly vicious-looking patch of brambles. When he reappeared, I noticed a trickle of blood running down his leg where his baggy shorts were now fairly tattered, exposing an indecent amount of thigh, which I had to make a conscious effort not to ogle.

Overactive libido be gone, what the hell are you thinking, Hannah?

But nothing looked as tragic as his poor, crumpled bike. The front wheel was no longer round – more sort of D-shaped – the front forks horribly bent, frame a little twisted, and he stared forlornly down at the mangled wreckage.

"Can it be fixed?" I asked.

Glancing up, he sighed and shook his head slightly. "I think it might be toast."

"Oh." I felt a little sad for him, then remembered that he

had been hurtling down a steep bank at speed, and I felt my eyebrows knitting together in consternation. "Maybe you'll be a little more careful with your next bike."

Teddy scowled in response. "You were going at quite some rate yourself, Hannah. I had to take pretty evasive action not to hit you or your horse."

I glared. He glared. Pluto munched happily on some sticky grass that was stuck to Teddy's T-shirt, oblivious to the glare-off going on next to him.

"Is this yours by the way?" he asked, holding up a bent horseshoe and I looked down to see only three of Pluto's feet still appropriately shod.

Well, isn't that bloody fantastic.

"Yes, thank you," I said, snatching it from his hands.

"You're welcome." Lifting up the front of his bike onto its back wheel, he started to push it along. "Which way are the stables?"

Grumbling, I reluctantly pointed down the hill and set off after him, definitely not watching the muscles of his back and arms flexing as he marched off ahead of me.

Nope. No siree. Most definitely not.

Chapter Four

Teddy followed me into the livery yard where I kept Pluto. It was a busy Saturday morning and the hive of female horse owners turned in unison to watch him wheel his broken bike along beside us, staring open-mouthed like I'd just brought some international rock star back with me. I didn't need to look at him to know that he was flashing knicker-dropping smiles left, right, and centre, as the appreciative expressions from all around told me everything I needed to know. Why did he still have to be such a flirt?

"You never told me that the stables would be such a hot bed of women, Hannah," he said over the stable door, as I put Pluto away and began taking off his saddle and bridle, checking him over again for any injuries or anomalies, other than the lost shoe.

Not dignifying that comment with an answer, I busied myself with making my horse comfortable, flicking a brush over his body and ensuring he had enough hay and water. With my back turned, Teddy had left his bike outside and come into the stable, and was now cautiously stroking Pluto on the neck.

"Right, Teddy, you can see I'm fine so you don't need to hang around here any longer. Don't you have a home to go to?"

Irritation bristled with every word. I couldn't put a finger on the exact reason this unexpected encounter had rattled me so much, but I was more on edge than I had been in a very long time, and desperate to be alone so I could work my way out of the whole-body funk he was subjecting me to.

"He feels so soft. I've never touched a horse before," Teddy whispered distractedly. Pluto turned his head, blowing warm, sweet breath over Teddy's face. It made him laugh and he stepped back slightly. "Is that him telling me he likes me? Or that he wants to eat me?"

"Pluto likes everyone – he's not discerning," I muttered, teeth gritted.

"Pluto? You're pretty nice, huh?" Teddy said quietly, gazing at my horse with a sort of reverential expression.

"So … home? You do have one, right?" I ground out, ushering him from the stable and back into the bright sunshine.

"I do, yes, but I'm quite a long way from my house. I don't suppose you could give me a lift, could you? Since you're the one responsible for my broken bike?"

"Me?!" I retorted with an incredulous snorting, equine-like noise.

"I'd say so, yes. A lift is the least you can do." He had crossed his arms over his chest, which was fairly expansive in the Lycra T-shirt he was wearing. Was he intentionally flexing his biceps?

I mirrored his stance, narrowing my eyes at him. "I'd say you were one hundred per cent the cause of the accident, actually."

Teddy bit his lip, clearly trying not to laugh at my haughty tone.

"I'd say it was more like sixty–forty, in favour of me," he countered smoothly.

"Maths was never your strong point."

He just grinned in response.

"You're not going to make me walk all the way home, are you? I'm bleeding, and town is miles and miles away. Especially since I've been such a gentleman and escorted you and Pluto back safely." Then he pouted. A full-on Victoria Beckham pout. It should have been ridiculous, but it just made him more gorgeous.

How is that even possible? Infuriating man!

"Fine," I replied, purposefully turning my back on him and marching around to where I'd parked my car.

What else could I do? Because, even though every cell in my body was screaming that I should be getting away from him as quickly as possible, and that being around him was dangerous and foolish, he did have a point. I couldn't leave him stranded, could I? I'd just have to reawaken my inner ice queen, which shouldn't be too hard if I let myself think about my school days and how miserable I'd been the last time I'd seen him. I could do this; I could be around Teddy Fraser again and not succumb to his overt charm and epic levels of sexual potency, right? I bloody hoped so.

"Hannah, what is all this stuff in your boot? Do you live in your car?" Teddy was scratching his head as he stared into the cavernous, yet overflowing recesses of the back of my car. "Where will I put my bike?"

"I'm a veterinary surgeon, Teddy. This is all the equipment that I have to cart around with me in order to treat sick or injured animals," I replied, accompanied by an exaggerated and decisively condescending eyeroll.

Oh yes, the ice queen has cometh.

He looked over at me. Was that admiration on his face?

"You're a vet?"

"Yes."

"Wow. Ok, well, I guess I can take my bike to bits and put it on your back seat?"

"Fine."

Taking a small multi tool out of the zipped pocket of his shorts, he began to quickly dismantle the bike. His deft fingers made light work of the nuts and bolts, muscular forearms flexing as he stacked the bike's component parts into a more compact heap. He dusted himself off then neatly loaded everything on top of a plastic horse feed sack inside my car, looking altogether very pleased with himself.

Sliding into the driver's side, I glanced at Teddy as he made himself comfortable, shooting the passenger seat backwards to make room for his long legs. I couldn't help but stare until he caught me, his face breaking into a mischievous grin. The car suddenly seemed very small and stifling.

"Since you're a medical professional, have you got anything in your supplies to treat my injuries?" he asked, now twisting his upper body to look at me as I put the key in the ignition.

"I'm a vet. I don't treat humans."

"Oh, ok. But you could just patch me up a bit though, right?"

"No."

"Please, I think I may need stitches."

"You don't need stitches."

"See, you know what you're talking about, Hannah. Please? I'd be really grateful? And imagine how bad you'd feel if I died of leg gangrene."

"Leg gangrene?"

"Yes, or whole-body sepsis."

"You're so dramatic." I paused and observed the pleading look he was giving me, complete with puppy dog eyes and a lopsided, impish smile. His whole demeanour was completely disarming. And something else too, something I didn't want to admit to, if I was being totally honest.

"Please?"

"Fine. There's a human first aid kit in the glove compartment," I said eventually, wrinkling my nose.

Why am I letting him coerce me into this?

I got out of the car and went round to the passenger side. Meanwhile, Teddy had rifled around until he found the little green case and handed it to me. I cleaned up all the scrapes with antiseptic wipes, using tweezers to pull out some embedded thorns and gravel. It was difficult not to react to the warmth of his skin under my hands, particularly as I worked my way up his thigh, trying to ignore his penetrating focus, which was seemingly directed solely on what I was doing. But I refused to acknowledge it, forcing my mind into professional mode and disengaging all thoughts of anything remotely personal. Especially kissing.

Shit, now I'm thinking about kissing.

Mind on the job, Havens. Come on!

Eventually, after applying a couple of plasters and ignoring the little "ouchy" noises he made occasionally, I chanced a look at his face.

"You're done."

"Thanks."

I finally allowed myself a good look at his face and realised a small trickle of blood had dribbled down and dried on his chin.

"Oh, wait, you've bashed your mouth as well."

"Have I?" His voice was unusually quiet as I leant in closer to examine his split lip.

Against my better judgement, I started to clean up his face, my fingers grazing the stubble of his jaw to steady him. His breath was a soft caress against my skin, taking me back to a certain rugby club field on a balmy summer night, and the taste and feel of his mouth on mine, his hands in my hair, a quiet, seductive moan against my neck. The memories rumbled through my mind, like it had happened fifteen minutes ago instead of fifteen years. I wondered, as I had so many times, why he had kissed me that night, and why I'd never experienced anything even remotely like it since.

And now kissing him is all I can think about. Dammit!

Distracted, I not-so-gently dabbed at the cut on his lip with hand sanitiser rather than the antiseptic cream I had meant to pick up.

"Owww!" Teddy winced, his long fingers encircling my wrist and jerking my hand away. "I think that one's ok now, Hannah."

"You're being an almighty wuss about a few scratches, you know."

Standing up, I pointedly avoided the bright, clear gaze of his eyes. Categorically *not* noticing how his irises sparkled as if they were made of summer skies, surrounded by a darker ring of midnight blue. I was totally *not* having to calm my thumping heart rate as I got back into the driver's seat. Nor did I have to wipe my clammy palms on my jodhpurs so I wouldn't leave sweaty marks on my steering wheel.

This is ridiculous.

I was a grown woman who would not be derailed by flowery, romantic notions. I had succeeded in life because I had always made sensible, logical decisions every single time. And I would do so again, even when the face of a Greek god was mischievously grinning at me across the interior of my car.

"I was pretty sympathetic when I thought you'd broken your back in that ditch," he said, arching a brow.

"Overreact much, Teddy?" Pushing my driving glasses upwards on my nose, I started the car and we drove in silence for a few moments.

"I like the glasses, Hannah. They make you look like a hot librarian," Teddy said, nonchalantly taking a bite of a protein bar that he'd pulled out of his pocket.

I hit the brakes hard, sending us both lurching towards the dashboard. All my medicine bottles rattled in the back, my fingers gripping the steering wheel so tightly that my knuckles were white, the skin almost translucent. Luckily, we were still in the country lanes and my impromptu emergency stop hadn't caused anyone to crash into the back of my car.

"What?!" I looked at him in open-mouthed horror and disbelief.

"What?!" Teddy replied at the same time, a shocked expression on his face, his mouth slightly twisted in mid-chew.

"A *hot librarian*?" I muttered under my breath, starting the car again.

"It was meant as a compliment, Hannah," Teddy said, wiping crumbs off his crotch where the protein bar had ended up.

"I suppose it's better than being likened to a porn star."

"Ah, now, I was young and foolish in those days. My comments weren't always well thought out."

"But you really thought long and hard about *hot librarian*?" I asked incredulously.

Teddy leant back in his seat and sighed. "Forget I said anything to you, ever."

"Good idea."

My brain was fried. I needed to not hold on to this comment. I needed to not allow myself to breathe it in and process it, because it was nothing. It meant nothing. He was a terminal flirt – I knew this from school days – and becoming a fully fledged adult didn't seem to have improved this aspect of his personality. He must just use throwaway comments about being "hot" as another way to dazzle and befuddle poor, unsuspecting women. He didn't mean it, not about me. The mean gremlin in my head, the one who crept in whenever I felt a shred of confidence, poked and prodded her way to the front of my mind, reminding me that looks were not something I should concern myself with; that men like him were not attracted to women like me. Men like him, like Jonathan, cheated on me with young, beautiful women. More than once.

Briefly leaning back against the head rest I caught sight of my face in the rear-view mirror. My own startled green eyes gazed back at me, large and round and full of anguish, the freckles that bridged my nose and mottled my whole face as overly prominent as ever. I looked back at the road, disgust brewing like a bitter potion in the cauldron of my stomach, before putting the car back into gear and setting off again

"Where's your house?" I asked Teddy as we entered the small town of Chipping-on-the-Water, the town where we'd both grown up and gone to school.

"Abbots Lane."

"Abbots Lane?" I repeated in surprise. This was where the veterinary practice was, along with my little flat above the surgery. It was a sleepy, out-of-the-way place on the edge of the countryside.

"Yes."

"Which house?"

Please don't say The Old Rectory.

He couldn't live in the beautiful crumbling rundown house that I could see from my window, the one I fantasised about living in on a regular basis.

"The Old Rectory."

Damn.

Of course it would be him who'd just bought it. The law of sod was working in full force for me today.

Excellent.

"What are you planning to do with it?" I asked, trying to sound casual, but he turned from gazing out of the window, his attention focussed on me again.

"Why do you want to know?" he replied, suspicious.

"I work at the surgery next door."

"Oh, do you?"

"Yes, and I'm currently living in the flat above it."

Why did I tell him that?

"We're neighbours?" He grinned widely, making my breath hitch a little.

Havens, get a grip. It's just a face.

Only a unique composition of muscles and skin and teeth. Nothing extraordinary to see here.

Except, who am I kidding. His is anything but ordinary.

And that was entirely the problem.

"I guess. So what are you going to do with it?"

"I'm not sure. I've just taken a partner role in my dad's architectural practice in town, so I might use it as my first big project to showcase my ideas."

"You're an architect?" I tried to hide how impressed I was, but his telling look convinced me he'd heard it.

"Yeah. See, I'm not just a pretty face," he teased. And winked.

"Oh." My mind had suddenly emptied.

Shit. Think of something else to say, Hannah. Stop him grinning at you in such a villainous way.

"What's Henry up to these days?" I blurted out.

Teddy's face fell.

"He's some bigshot engineer with a PhD and his own biotech company," he muttered darkly.

Wow, cool.

I was genuinely pleased for him, having always thought deep down that he would do well and fully deserved to.

"That's great! It'd be lovely to see him. Where's he living now?"

Teddy let out a long breath and glowered at me from under lowered brows.

"He's living in Oxford with his impossibly beautiful and

intelligent fiancée, and shaming us all in how he's winning at life. He's even got a fucking cat."

We turned into Abbots Lane and Teddy huffed another exasperated breath. Clearly there were some issues between him and Henry, which was sad, but I'd barely brought the car to a stop when he jumped out and grabbed the pieces of his bike from the back seat.

"Thanks for the lift. Maybe see you around some time."

And with that he slammed the door and stalked off through the rickety iron gates of The Old Rectory, quickly disappearing from sight amongst the overgrown foliage.

Chapter Five

The screaming that was coming from the surgery waiting room was chilling. Like something straight out of a horror film, the sort of noise that raised all the hairs on the back of your neck and sent an involuntary shiver down your spine. And it was loud. Really, really loud.

"Hello, Mrs Ryan. Bentley." I crouched next to the ginger and white cavalier King Charles spaniel and the screaming stopped instantly, his expression turning ecstatic as he panted and wriggled his way onto my lap with delight. "Let's get you seen to, shall we?"

I carried his obese little body along the corridor and into my consulting room, his decidedly prim owner following in our wake. I murmured soft words into his floppy ears, rubbing my fingers against the silky fur as he grunted in pleasure, his eyes partially closed.

"I don't know why he makes such a fuss in the waiting room." Bustling in and closing the door behind her, Mrs Ryan shifted her designer handbag onto her shoulder and unclipped the lead from Bentley's collar as he settled onto the table. "He screams when anyone he doesn't know tries to touch him or if we go anywhere new. It's rather embarrassing, actually. Is there something physically wrong with him?"

Taking the stethoscope from around my neck, I raised my eyebrows as I looked at her, and was met with a stern and matronly expression, so I continued my examination in silence for a moment, avoiding her gaze while trying to keep my features impassive.

"No, I don't think he's got anything physically wrong with him. I think maybe he's just anxious, Mrs Ryan. Does he have a favourite toy?"

"Yes. A rather tatty tennis ball, but I won't take it out of the house. It's disgusting." She wrinkled her nose, creasing her immaculately made-up face and causing deep lines to form around her pouty pink mouth.

"I see. Why don't you keep this ball with you, in your handbag, and offer it to him whenever he starts to get worked up."

"I don't see what good it will do." Mrs Ryan eyed me sceptically, patting her obviously expensive handbag protectively, while I administered Bentley's annual vaccination and gave his portly little frame a quick once-over.

"Anxiety in dogs often comes from the owner." I couldn't help but notice her horrified little gasp, but I ploughed on regardless, keen to get her out of the door as fast as possible now. "That's his vaccination all done for another year, Mrs Ryan, but he is still horribly overweight so we do need to reassess what you're feeding him."

The grossly obese dog panted and grinned up at me from

the examination table, pushing his head against my hand for more stroking, seemingly very relaxed in my presence.

"But I don't give him very much as it is, do I, darling?" Mrs Ryan crooned at her dog, her slight side-eye in my direction alerting me to yet more animosity.

I considered the old lady in front of me carefully. It was quite clear that she did give this dog too much food and too little exercise, but how to broach this in a sensitive and tactful way? This was the most difficult thing about my job, and something that I struggled with every day. Plus, I was probably already on the back foot with my anxiety comment, so this might be a case of too little too late.

Shit.

"You must be feeding him the wrong type of food then. Have you been sticking to the prescription diet I ordered for you?"

"Oh, Bentley won't eat that awful stuff, Dr Havens. It smells like old socks!"

"Right." I knew I was fighting a losing battle here. "How about we try a bit longer with it, and don't give him anything else if he doesn't eat it?"

"Let him starve?"

She was horrified, which suggested to me that she was giving him all sorts of other things rather than the light dog food he was supposed to be eating.

"We could try a different brand."

"Well…" Her resistance was palpable, her demeanour most definitely a bit put out.

"There are other flavours to try – turkey, perhaps?" I suggested, starting to feel a bit desperate here.

"We could do, I suppose," Mrs Ryan begrudgingly agreed, and I decided to leap on this small concession.

"Excellent. I'll look up some alternatives and ask Betsy, our brilliant veterinary nurse, to get some in. You'll need to bring him to her weigh-in clinic once a month to see how he's doing. It's important that you bring him along, Mrs Ryan, no excuses. It's his health at stake here." There. A healthy dose of owner guilt should help things along.

Mrs Ryan looked doubtful, but I was already ushering her out of the consulting room. She was my last client in this evening's surgery and I was ready for my dinner and a sit down after a very busy day.

"Ok. Well, if you're sure?"

"Yes, totally sure. We'll be in touch, and make sure you keep his ball with you!" I replied brightly, rearranging my face into what I hoped was a genuine smile, and promptly closed the door behind her.

I typed up Bentley's notes and shut the computer down, but when the door opened again, my boss and the practice owner, Giles, appeared, standing awkwardly behind the consulting table. A little groan of annoyance accidentally slipped from my mouth and he twitched, looked briefly at me, and then down at the floor, his countenance exhibiting extreme discomfort.

Giles was stout, about my height, and had a crop of thick, unruly greying hair. He was a particularly rosy-cheeked and cheerful individual, and the older female clients loved him. But right now, he looked like he was about to euthanise his favourite labrador. This was bad.

"I've just seen Mrs Ryan outside, Hannah."

"Yes?"

He shifted uncomfortably on his feet again. "She said that you were a bit dismissive of Bentley's needs. And, um, well, rude…"

Urgh.

I thought I'd tried really hard this time. "I just suggested that she needs to change his diet because as you can see, he is grossly obese."

Giles sighed and scratched his head. "I know that, and you know that, but to Mrs Ryan, Bentley is her entire world and she doesn't want to be made to feel as though she's not doing her best."

"Right."

"Plus, telling her that she makes her dog anxious is a bit insensitive," he said with a wince.

"Got it."

"Hannah, you are an extremely well-qualified vet and an exceptional clinician, but if you're going to stay in first-opinion practice, you need to work on your bedside manner."

Giles was starting to back away from me ever so slightly.

"I see."

When I'd left my research position at the referral practice in the vet school at Bristol, I'd thought it would be easy to step into general practice – less pressure, less stress, and the perfect antidote to get over my failed love life and doomed academic aspirations.

Seems I was wrong.

"You're sometimes a bit, well, prickly. Perhaps you could work on that side of things?" he added, cringing even more.

"Right," I said again.

Giles scratched his head, his go-to gesture in times of extreme awkwardness, and tapped his fingers on the top of his hair absently. He shot me an uneasy tight-lipped smile. "Excellent. Ok, good to have had such a productive chat. Excellent. Brilliant. Thanks."

And with that, he practically ran from the consulting room as if being chased by a marauding stampede of bullocks, while I stared after him trying to compute my way through the thinly veiled verbal warning with which I had just been issued.

Betsy came bustling in from the dispensary, wiping down the table and raising her large dark brown eyes to look at me, a mixture of apology and amusement in her expression. I wondered if she'd overheard Giles's comments.

"Do you think I'm prickly?" I asked her.

"Noooo. No," she said, not quite meeting my gaze. "Perhaps a bit?"

"Tell me the truth. I can handle it."

"Truthfully? You're about as prickly as a hedgehog in a blackberry bush."

"Oh."

Dammit.

The best thing about returning to Chipping-on-the-Water had been reconnecting with Betsy Okoro, the only true friend I'd ever had at school. Her personality was the exact opposite of mine. She was always smiling and joking. A force to be reckoned with, a soul so beautiful and vibrant that she immediately swept you up with her zest for life. Growing up in a small Cotswolds town had not been easy for her, and she'd worked hard to overcome the kind of prejudice and difficulties that I would never know, yet she was the most positive person I'd ever met. We'd kept in touch over social media since leaving school, and it was a Facebook post that she'd shared that had alerted me to the position here at the practice, and she'd encouraged me to apply. And, if I'm being honest, probably strong-armed Giles into giving me the job.

Today, her hair was styled in corn rows and bleached at the ends, and her trendy make-up and oversized glasses made her appear effortlessly cool and glamorous, even in her nurse's tunic and shapeless uniform trousers. Compassionate and excellent with the clients, while clinically capable and caring with the variety of animals we dealt with on a daily basis, she was the best veterinary nurse that I'd ever worked with, and my most loyal and trusted confidante. I knew I could always rely on her in every way, especially her ability to tell me the absolute truth.

"By the way, there's an emergency in the waiting room and Giles has said you'll deal with it." As she went out to call the emergency in, she turned and added, conspiratorially, "And you'll never believe who it is, Hannah."

"Who is it?"

"I'll let it be a little surprise for you."

"Er, thanks. I hate surprises."

"I know," she laughed evilly.

"Are you heading out now?"

"Yes, unless you need anything?"

"No, I'll manage. See you tomorrow."

She gave a little wave and headed down the corridor to the waiting room. A few moments later I heard the door open again, just as the computer finished booting back up.

"Ah, thank God you're here, Hannah."

Nope, absolutely bloody no. Nope, crapping-well bloody nope.

I didn't even turn around. It had been almost a week since

43

the bike incident, and I'd only just managed to find my inner equilibrium again.

"Teddy," I said with a sigh, finally glancing in his direction.

"I just found it like this, stuck in the outside loo." He sounded breathless and desperate.

Teddy was covered in dust and dirt, only the impression of having worn some goggles leaving any hint of his normal skin colour visible around his panic-stricken eyes. He was wearing a tight grey T-shirt and ripped jeans that were also caked in dust.

In his arms was a wide-eyed and beautiful tortoiseshell cat.

"Like what? Is this your cat?"

"No! I don't have a cat. It's got a big bloody lump on its head, Hannah. I think it might be dying," he whispered dramatically.

"Ok, well put her on the table and I'll have a look," I replied, barely repressing a tut at his overly theatrical assessment of things.

The cat was surprisingly calm and sat quietly while I performed a quick examination of her vital signs. There was a large sticky, weepy sore behind her ear, and a huge bulbous bubble of infection straining the skin.

"She's got an abscess, likely from scrapping with another cat. She's not dying, Teddy."

"Oh thank God. Can you treat her?"

"Yes, but you'll have to help me by holding her," I replied, putting on some gloves and gathering swabs and warm water in a stainless steel kidney-shaped bowl.

Teddy stepped forwards and gingerly put his hands around the cat's middle.

"She's probably not going to like this so, you know, hang

44

on, ok?" Our faces were quite close together as we both leant over the examination table and near to the cat.

"Ok," he whispered.

His blue eyes were stormy with worry, his stance rigid and tense, while my own body was bamboozled, yet again, by his intoxicating maleness and charisma, which was hitting me like a sledgehammer to the chest.

Concentrating all my effort on the cat and blocking Teddy out for a moment, I started to ease the oozing scab from the lump behind the cat's ear with a dampened swab, unmatting the sticky fur and looking for the entry wound. Suddenly the abscess ruptured like a mini volcano, the pressure of the infection exploding upwards in a thin jet, and I quickly whipped my head away to avoid being hit in the face by this impressive pus fountain.

"Holy-mother-of-all-that-is-shitting-well-holy!"   Teddy yelled, leaping backwards and dropping his hold on the cat. "What the actual fuck even is that?!"

His pallor was a little green, even beneath the layer of dust, while the cat decided to make a break for it, yellowy pus and blood oozing like a river down her neck.

"Bloody hell, Teddy! You had one job – hold the cat!" I reached under the table and retrieved the unimpressed feline, placing her back on the rubberised surface.

"What is that smell?" he whispered, his eyes tightly shut, body bent double, leaning against the wall in the corner, hands on his knees. He made a faint gurgling, groaning sound.

"It's the infection – sometimes they get a bit whiffy. Ted, can you come back over here and help me, please?"

"I'm sorry, but I feel a bit unwell, Hannah."

"Don't you chuffing well faint on me. Get over here and

hold the sodding cat," I ordered sternly. I wondered if I should call Betsy and get her to come back in, even though she'd probably already be halfway across town by now.

His eyes snapped open, comically wide, and he shakily walked over to the table again, putting his hands back around the cat but purposefully looking at the ceiling. He was breathing unsteadily, his lips moving silently. Was he counting?

"What are you doing?"

"Calculus in my head. It helps to keep me calm."

"Who's the geek now?" I muttered under my breath as I worked quickly to tidy up the wound and extricate as much pus as possible before flushing it with sterile saline and administering some pain relief to make her feel better.

"I'll grab some antibiotics. You'll need to give them to her every day and try and keep the wound open and clean so it drains," I said, typing into the computer and printing out a label.

"I have to do what? Can't you just keep her here, in the hospital, and do it?" he replied, horrified.

"Not really. It's not life threatening, Teddy."

"Can't you have her? I'm just not great with animals. Or blood. Or large amounts of oozing gunky shit. Or smells."

I considered him steadily. "Let's see if she's got a microchip. We might be able to find her owner and reunite them."

"Yes! Yes, let's do that!" Teddy was still gripping the cat quite tightly and she let out a little protesting yowl. But when the microchip reader didn't pick up anything, we both slumped our shoulders in disappointment.

"Fine, I'll keep her here in my flat for a couple of days. But you have to try and find her owner, agreed?" He nodded. "If you can't find anyone, I'll give the cat shelter a ring and they can rehome her, ok?"

"Ok. They won't, you know…" He gave the universal sign of death by running his finger across his throat, before giving the cat a concerned look as if she might know what we were talking about. "Will they?"

"They'll try and find a new home for her first. She's pretty and fairly friendly, so I'm sure they'll find someone."

Teddy was now absently tickling the chin of the cat, a loud rumbling purr building up inside her body while she closed her eyes in total bliss.

"She likes you. You should keep her."

"Er, no. My place is a building site – no good for a cat," he protested, before adding softly (as if we were naming our firstborn child), "What should we call her?"

"I've logged her as 'Fraser' in the system," I said, cleaning up the consulting table and chucking the used swabs into the clinical waste bin.

"You can't call a girl cat Fraser," Teddy admonished, and the tortoiseshell minx purred loudly as he crooned softly down at her.

"What do you suggest?"

"How about Hannah?"

"Hannah Fraser?"

"It has a ring to it, don't you think?"

"Yeah, like a death knell, Ted," I muttered, and he laughed, the deep luxuriant sound causing a ripple in my mind. I smiled in return. We stared at each other until I dropped my head away to look in the cupboard for a plastic collar to stop the cat scratching at her wound.

"It's nice when you smile, Hannah," Teddy murmured, almost tenderly, from somewhere above my head.

I'd lost count of the number of times I'd been told to smile more, or how much better I'd look if I just smiled. And when the universally awful phrase of *"Smile – it might never happen"*, was uttered in my presence, I could feel myself getting more than a little bit murdery.

"Do not come up with some ill-thought-out simile, Teddy, whatever you do."

"Would I?"

"Yes, you really would." Straightening, I gave him a pointed look. "We're not calling her Hannah. How about Tramp, as she has no fixed abode?"

"No!" He looked aghast.

"Lady?"

"Fine."

"Right, I'm starving and I should get her ladyship upstairs. You can pay your bill with Jenny on reception."

"Ok, I can do that. But why don't I help you get her settled and then buy you dinner in the pub?"

I stared blankly at him for a moment.

"As a thank-you for dealing with my first highly traumatic veterinary emergency, and to apologise for being a crap cat wrangler," Teddy added. His smile was coy, seductive, enticing. Dangerous.

"You don't have to do that," I responded uncomfortably, twitching. I was itching to run away.

"I know, but I'd like to. Plus, I'm really hoping that I'll be able to bribe you into not telling anyone that I nearly passed out in your consulting room."

It was tempting. I had a frozen macaroni cheese ready

meal waiting for me, but an awkward, intimate dinner with Teddy Fraser was most definitely the last thing I needed right now.

"Come on, Hannah. I'm not that bad. I can be charming, and I'm pretty funny," he coaxed. "I promise not to liken you to any dubious professions and I'll be on my best behaviour, Scout's honour."

He did the Scout Association salute. I remained mute.

"I'll pay. You can have whatever you want…" he added in a persuasive whisper.

"Ok, fine, but I'm on call tonight so I may have to dash off if I get called out," I replied, my resolve weakening at his genuine smile, and the promise of something other than a tasteless pasta dinner for one.

"Great. Let's get Lady Fraser into your flat then." He grinned and scooped the cat off the table, being careful to keep his face away from her still slightly oozy ear.

Teddy followed me through the surgery and into the back hallway, past the operating theatre, and outside to the entrance and stairs that led to my private flat. It was small and poky, and it looked out over the surgery car park and to the orchard of The Old Rectory that was nestled just in view from my windows.

"Ah, now I know why you want to know what I'm doing with my place. You overlook it. I can probably wave to you from my bedroom window," Teddy said, putting the cat on the floor.

I fitted the cone of shame around Lady's neck to stop her scratching and placed food, water, and a litter tray in the kitchen area, draping a couple of old towels on the two armchairs that furnished my sparse living space.

"It's a beautiful old house, Teddy. I hope you're not going to do anything hideous to it."

"I do have some taste, Hannah, so, no, I'm not going to do anything *hideous* to it," he said grumpily. "I'm just trying to live in it as I do it, but it's a bit of a wreck. I don't even have consistent hot running water yet." He paused and gave me a sly glance. "I don't suppose there's any chance I could shower here? I could nip home and get a change of clothes and pop back? Please?" he begged, dropping to one knee in front of me and clasping my hands. "Otherwise, I have to wash in an old tin bath tub in the garden with cold water from the hosepipe."

A frown wrinkled down my forehead, encompassing my whole face, like a disapproving, cutaneous Mexican wave.

"In fact," he said standing up and ushering me to the window, "if you look over there, you can see my temporary bathroom from here." He winked. "You don't want to have to witness me getting naked and freezing my balls off right in front of you now, do you?"

He was like some romance novel anti-hero. An actual real-life dastardly duke or villainous viscount, teasing and charming his way through life. But I wouldn't fall for this. He could take a running jump if he thought I was going to let him use my shower...

"All right, fine, help yourself." My mouth formed the words without permission from my brain. Which really was rather excellent.

"Great, I'll just be a couple of minutes. You're the best!" Jumping up he kissed me gently, his beard grazing my cheek before he rubbed his nose over my skin. "Oh, sorry, you've got a little something on your face."

Then he winked (again) and raced out of my front door,

leaving me and Lady Fraser staring at each other. Curiously, I reached up and ran my fingertips over my face, looking at the plaster dust that he had just marked me with.

"This is such a bad idea, isn't it?"

And with a gentle chirrup, the dainty little cat disappeared off to make herself comfy in my bedroom.

Chapter Six

I'd spent the whole time he was in my shower trying not to think about the fact that he was in my shower; trying to avoid the glaring fact that Teddy Fraser was naked in my bathroom. *Totally naked.* But when he appeared, dark hair damp and curling slightly, freshly washed in a checked shirt and dark blue jeans, it was all for nought, because my filthy mind just jumped straight back to the imaginings that I'd tried so desperately to tamp down. This was highly unacceptable and would only lead to more disgruntlement on my behalf.

Teddy Fraser fantasies are not on the agenda, horny Hannah, wind your neck in.

"Ready?" Teddy smiled, oblivious to my internal chastisement.

"Yes, as I'll ever be."

He laughed and put his arm around my shoulders, and I was engulfed in his spicy citrus scent, which was disturbingly evocative. I was suddenly imagining sun-kissed orange groves in Valencia and sipping on cool margaritas by the pool. Teddy

Fraser no longer smelled of Lynx Africa. No, this was far more potent, far more masculine, far more delicious than that.

Bugger.

"That's the spirit, Hannah. Nothing like going out of your way to make a guy feel special."

"I think you feel special enough without my input," I said, raising an eyebrow and extricating myself from his grip. "I'll drive. Come on."

The Three Crowns was old, the ceilings so low that Teddy actually had to duck in places, with wobbly mismatched tables and chairs, and rustic stone-flagged floors. It was a place I was familiar with, having regularly attended many family dos here because it was a favourite of my parents. While Teddy got the drinks, I found somewhere near the bar to sit and perused the blackboard, which was awash with delicious, mouth-watering offerings, and I realised just how hungry I was.

"Chosen what you want?" Teddy asked as he sat back down opposite.

"You're paying, right?"

"Yep," he replied, taking a sip of his pint and eyeing me with amusement over the rim of the glass.

"I'll have a burger and chips then," I said, knowing that I could easily get them to put this in a box for me to take away and eat on the hoof if I got called out.

"Good choice. I'll have the same."

I had expected an uncomfortable silence while we waited for the waitress to take our food order but Teddy seemed relaxed, and my usual twitching and discomfort around people began to ebb away. We chatted a bit about our experiences at university – me at Bristol, him at Edinburgh – and how things had been since we'd left school. He seemed impressed that I'd got a PhD and pursued an academic fellowship, but I decided to leave out the disastrous last few months. It was still pretty raw and humiliating and I was trying not to think about Jonathan on a regular basis.

"Why did you come back here, Hannah?"

Teddy looked at me speculatively, fiddling with his cutlery, long fingers turning over the stainless steel fork hypnotically.

"To be near my parents. The job at the surgery came up and it seemed like a good choice as Giles is looking to retire in a few years."

This was all true. Well, mostly. I hadn't at all wanted to move nearer to my parents because I found them difficult and overbearing, particularly my mother, but inside I was craving some sort of comfort and familiarity. Plus, after reporting Jonathan to the Dean of the Veterinary School, my options had become somewhat limited. True to his word, he had made my position untenable and then thwarted all my attempts at getting another research fellowship at any of the UK vet schools, so I was left with finding a job somewhere he had no influence. Daisy, as predicted, had not complained about his behaviour, and the dean had seemingly ignored my emails, so Jonathan's life had remained entirely unaltered.

Why is it that crap always seems to float to the top?

The door to the bar opened with a creak and I heard a group of people enter, their soft laughter and chatter adding to the already cosy atmosphere of the pub. I had my back to them but I watched Teddy's face go from recognition to horror, and I turned in my seat to see the unmistakeable figure of Henry

Fraser enter the bar, accompanied by an extraordinarily beautiful blonde, and Mr and Mrs Fraser following behind.

"Shit." Teddy turned to me with a look of panic in his eyes, then whispered, "Should we make a run for it?"

"Ted?" Henry's deep voice called out, puzzled, glancing quizzically to me and back to Teddy.

"Too late," Teddy groaned.

"Edward!" Mrs Fraser had always been impossibly sophisticated and glamorous, and today was no exception. Her diminutive frame was clad in designer clothes, her beautiful, lyrical French accent soft and subtle as she continued to speak, while looking curiously at me. "And who is this?"

"This is Hannah Havens. We used to go to school together," Teddy said uncomfortably. He was clearly as upset as I was that his family might think we were a couple.

"Oh, how lovely!" Mrs Fraser was clearly more delighted than us about this encounter.

"Hannah?" Henry's voice was all surprise. "Oh my God."

"Hi, Henry, how are you?"

Well, wasn't this bloody awkward? I could see exactly what this must look like to Teddy's family and I was both mortified and annoyed to be thought of as his latest conquest. Where was an emergency cow caesarean when you needed one?

"Wow! It's been such a long time. How are you? And why are you sitting with Ted in the pub?" Henry was genuinely disconcerted. He rubbed a hand up the back of his neck uncomfortably and shook his head slightly. "You hated him when we were at school, as I recall?"

"We accidentally bumped into each other again recently and he's trying to buy my silence," I replied, shifting in my seat and glancing at Teddy, who narrowed his eyes.

"Is he?" Henry laughed delightedly.

"Are you eating?" Mrs Fraser asked, before adding, "We could all eat together?"

"Er, well, Mum, no, Hannah and I were just grabbing a quick bite," Teddy tried desperately, and I noticed Henry seemed to be enjoying his discomfort, before wincing as the beautiful blonde pinched his arm sharply and tutted at him. I liked her already.

"Nonsense. I'll ask Bob if he can put two more places at our table," Mrs Fraser declared, marching over to the barman in a no-nonsense way.

"I'm Clara, by the way," the woman at Henry's side said, reaching out and shaking my hand warmly as I stood. "Nice to meet you, Hannah."

"Henry's fiancée," Teddy added helpfully.

"Right. Nice to meet you too. Congratulations," I murmured, carefully watching Henry, who was gazing at Clara with slightly nauseating eyes, his arm around her waist, holding her tightly to him. They were a poster couple for being in love, if ever I saw one. I briefly wondered how it would feel to have someone look at me like that, before swallowing such a ridiculous notion away.

The Frasers began to mill around while we waited for the table to be readied. It was getting crowded in the bar, and we were already pushed quite closely together when another couple entered. And I felt my body begin to shut down, system by system.

There was no way we could hide because the presence of both Fraser twins had always drawn the eye. This latest couple was no exception, turning as one to gape at the film star looks of this small gathering and then catching me in the midst, looking like a blob fish caught in a net of mermaids.

"Hannah?" My father's voice was like the foghorn on the QE2 coming out of the mist, and all the Frasers turned as one to look at him. Meanwhile, my mother was running an appraising glance over the cast in front of her, eyes lingering on Teddy, who was standing really quite close to me.

I gave a small, feeble wave as they strode over to us.

"Hello, darling, what are you doing here?" my mother asked. Her voice sounded sickly sweet but I knew it was dripping in accusation because she hated to be caught on the back foot in any situation. She gave me *the look*, the one that had withered the soul right out of me as a child, the one she always gave when she was displeased with me, as she so often was.

"I-I-I…"

Shit, why do I always become such a stuttering mess around her?

"I asked her to dinner, as a thank you for treating an injured cat I found," Teddy said, stepping forwards and getting a comedy double-take from his whole family at that little revelation. "I'm Ted Fraser. We went to school together."

"Oh." My mother studied him carefully, eyes briefly flitting back to the rest of the beautiful people that had now assumed a protective circle at his back.

"Yes, and my family happened to drop by unexpectedly. My brother, Henry, and his fiancée, Clara. My parents, Fiona and Jim Fraser." Teddy did the introductions swiftly and politely and then looked expectantly at me.

I stared back at him over my shoulder, and he raised his eyebrows, clearly wanting me to do something. But I was out of ideas, my tongue stuck to the roof of my mouth, dry and immobile. In reality, I was unable to see my way out of this horror show, wishing that someone would just put me out of my misery. What I wouldn't do right now for an injection of phenobarbital to end things quickly, a kindness that we offered to suffering animals. And I was definitely experiencing some extreme suffering right now.

Teddy coughed and angled his head at my parents and finally my one functioning brain cell kicked in.

"Sorry, these are my parents, Linea and Peter Havens."

When all the handshaking was done, a weird, cold-eyed stand-off began. My mother had a lot of questions burning a hole in her skull, obviously. I knew my father was trying to work out if he could get any business out of the men in the room and that he was also itching for a drink. Jim and Fiona were glancing awkwardly around the pub, while Henry and Clara were wrapped up in gazing at each other. Teddy had stepped closer, his body just a hair's breadth from mine, warmth radiating from him. My fingers twitched involuntarily, accidentally brushing his, but he didn't flinch or pull away. He kept them close – it was the briefest of touches, barely a touch at all really, yet it was there, like lightning up my arm.

Finally Fiona broke the silence and addressed my parents. "Are you planning to eat? We're all having dinner and I'm sure we could squeeze two more on the end."

No. No. No.

This was turning into an absolute disaster. My head whipped around to look pleadingly at my mother, but she was already smiling and wandering away with Fiona, her lithe figure disappearing into the crowd. My father and Jim Fraser, who had struck up a conversation and were laughing good-naturedly, also headed for the bar. Henry and Clara were still drowning in each other's eyes. Teddy seemed like a beaten man, and I just looked at the floor, dread and the inescapable feeling of doom swamping my whole being.

When the mothers came back with Bob, the cheerful bearded barman, and ushered us to the table, I sat heavily, sandwiched between my own mother and Teddy.

"If you're going on a date with such an attractive man, Hannah, the least you can do is dress up a little," my mother hissed at me, her mouth so pouty with disapproval that I couldn't help but compare it with a cat's anus. A snigger escaped from me and her eyes narrowed to slits, looking with disdain at my polo shirt and jeans, before sighing dramatically at her lost cause of a daughter.

"I'm on call tonight, Mum, and this is not a date," I muttered back.

"Well it should be. His mother says he's an architect, so a good match for you."

"What does his profession have to do with anything?"

"Everything, Hannah, everything, especially since you blew it with Jonathan who was a *professor*," she murmured, enunciating "professor" as if she were announcing that he was the actual King of the Universe, and not a slimy two-timing sleazebag.

But my mother was big on social standing. She was an inveterate climber of the society ladder and a complete and utter hypocrite. My grandparents had come over from Sweden in the 1960s, liberal and hippy, living a nomadic life and selling their Viking-inspired art and jewellery to get by. My mother had been home-schooled and given an amazingly free and wonderful childhood – my grandparents were avid nature lovers, with keen, intelligent minds. But she shunned all this, and while I was away at university had placed my ailing *mormor* in a home when my *morfar* died, her once free spirit encased in a soulless pink bedroom with a view of a car park, her memories and her mind slowly rotting, until she too had died, alone, a few months later.

"So, are you going to tell us about this cat of yours, Ted?" Henry asked from across the table, making Teddy shift uncomfortably in his seat next to me.

"Oh yes, tell us about your cat!" Clara agreed excitedly.

"It's not my cat. She's a stray and is at Hannah's place now." Teddy shifted a glance in my direction, before taking a sip of his drink. "She's excellent with animals."

"She's a vet," my dad said loudly from across the table, so that everyone turned to look at him, as he nodded and necked the red wine. "Always been excellent with animals. Really understands what makes them tick."

My mother hissed a low sound, the universal family signal to shut up and not embarrass her. She knew, as did I, where this would go, and for once I was in complete and utter agreement with her. But my father was oblivious, pouring more wine into his glass and smiling around at the rapt attention of the Frasers.

"A vet. How marvellous," Mrs Fraser said with a genuine smile.

"Oh yes, she's extraordinarily in tune with animals, particularly horses." My dad was already in his element.

"Peter Havens." My mother said, bringing forth the warning use of his full name, a deadly calm to her voice. It was the voice that still, to this day, struck fear into my heart, even if it wasn't *my* full name she was uttering.

"Very, *very* in tune…" he said, followed by a wink and a smirk and another mouthful of wine.

"All right, Dad," I muttered, feeling the blush start to creep up my neck.

Please let him shut up, now.

Because when he started on this topic, it only went one way. And it never ended well for me.

"In fact," he carried on, loudly, my prayers clearly going unanswered, "she spent most of her formative years *being* a horse."

And there was his punchline, the cork of the bottle of fizzy confessions from my youth violently unstoppered, ready to spew forth with significant mortification for me. Excellent.

"Oh yes?" Teddy was staring at me with undisguised amusement.

"Yes, from about three to twelve years of age, wasn't it, Linea?"

"I don't remember." My mother was so tight-lipped now that it was a wonder any sound came out of her mouth at all. This was as embarrassing for her as for me – I knew this for a fact. How she hated for anyone to see anything other than the vision of the perfect family unit she had so carefully constructed. I remember at the time how she used to shake me, ordering me to stop playing, to behave, to be a "normal" little girl and dress up the endless string of dolls she'd bought for me. She begged me to stop humiliating her with my unbridled (pun intended) imagination.

"Do you remember when you were in the supermarket, Linea, and an old lady tried to cut in front of you at the till and Hannah kicked her, hard, in the leg, then neighed and ran off?"

My dad was actually guffawing now. "That took some explaining, didn't it?"

My mother had gone impossibly still next to me, whereas I was shrinking into my seat, hoping the world would open up in a big fiery chasm and kill me now. I didn't care if it was painful as long as it was quick. Eternal flaming damnation would be better than this. I didn't look at anyone, but felt an awkward chuckle reverberate around the table.

"We even had to take her to the hospital once when she was seven and we caught her eating grass, just in case she'd consumed anything poisonous from the garden." He raised his glass to me. "How many times did we have to take you to A&E to have your stomach pumped, darling?"

I held up three fingers while continuing to look down at the table. The ensuing silence was excruciating. Despite being someone who rarely drank, and who got pissed on a thimbleful of alcohol, I had the sudden urge to grab the half-drunk bottle of red wine and down the lot.

Teddy picked up the menu that was lying between us on the table and said, ever so casually, "Do you remember that time in that posh hotel when we were seven, Henry, and you stuck those balloons down your T-shirt and pretended to have an enormous pair of boobs?"

"Actually, Ted, you put some down your T-shirt first, but you fondled yours so hard they burst," Henry answered smoothly.

Teddy smiled at me, waggling his eyebrows, and then said, "I always was the best at fondling boobs."

I choked a little as I swallowed a mouthful of lemonade, while my mother gasped in shock and my father slapped Henry on the back with a roar of laughter.

"Oh, boys, stop it, please. We're in company!" Mrs Fraser admonished, and both Henry and Teddy had the grace to look a little contrite. For a moment, anyway.

"Do you remember that time at our eighteenth birthday party when I found you two outside, alone, by that bench? What were you up to?" Henry said, giving Teddy a challenging look.

Teddy opened his mouth, and the fear of what he was about to say consumed my brain in such a fiery haze that I panicked and gripped his thigh under the table like a bird of prey capturing a rabbit, talons digging into flesh.

"Owww! What the hell, Hannah?!"

"Teddy nearly passed out in my consulting room today because of a stinky cat abscess," I blurted out desperately, practically screeching this information and flapping my free hand wildly so that the nearby bottle of wine was flipped onto its side, spraying the ruby liquid all over the table and turning it into a scene from the *Texas Chainsaw Massacre*.

Frozen to the spot, my death grip on Teddy's quadriceps still in full swing, I stared in horror at the slow motion scene of devastation unfolding across the table. My mother dropped her head into her hands with an audible groan as Mr and Mrs Fraser jumped to their feet to avoid being splattered. Meanwhile, my father remained seated, staring forlornly at the lost wine as it dripped onto the floor.

Well, at least no one was thinking about me and Teddy alone and kissing anymore, right?

Chapter Seven

"Give me your phone number," Teddy whispered in my ear as carnage ensued all around and I finally let go of his leg.

"W-w-what?"

"Give me your number so I can call you and pretend to be a client and we can get away from this car crash. That's if you want to…?"

Teddy's lips were so close to my ear that I could feel his softly spoken words on my neck as well as hear them, their teasing caress and promise of rescue nearly my undoing.

Shakily, I rattled off the digits out of the side of my mouth and he replied with, "Got it." And then, more loudly, addressing the whole table, he said, "I'll ask Bob to come and clear this up and order another bottle."

Getting to his feet and striding off across the pub, Teddy disappeared from sight, and this loss of his comforting presence left me feeling exposed and surprisingly vulnerable, an unpleasant jolt to my system which I tried desperately not to notice.

Moments later, Bob appeared with a large roll of blue paper towel from the kitchen and another bottle of wine, much to my father's unrestrained delight. He started to mop up in earnest just as my phone began to vibrate on the table, an unknown number coming through on the screen.

"I should take this."

"Really? Can't you let it go to voicemail?" my mother asked, so irritated it was rippling off her body like an army of poisonous ants.

"No, I absolutely cannot," I said, swiping to accept. "Hello, Chipping-on-the-Water Vets, Hannah speaking."

"All right there, Haaaannaaaah, it's Farmer MacDonald here and I have a right poorly cow," Teddy's voice came through the speaker into my ear, his attempt at a West Country accent the worst I'd ever heard. The way he was elongating the vowels of my name to fairly epic proportions made him sound more like a deranged pirate then any farmer I'd ever met, and it took all my willpower not to burst out laughing.

"Mr MacDonald, what seems to be the matter with your cow?"

"Oh, erm…" Teddy seemed flummoxed for a moment. "He's got a verra poorly leg?"

"Is it an emergency?"

"Yes! Definitely an emergency. He can't walk on it, my lover," he replied in a strangled voice, trying not to laugh. I could hear his voice echo from the toilet cubicle he was in and sincerely hoped that he was the only one in there. I snorted and tried to cover this with a cough as I heard Teddy continuing to snigger down the line.

"I see. Is she weight-bearing, Mr MacDonald?"

"Yes! I mean no, I don't think so."

"Is she down?"

"Down?"

"Unable to get up?"

"Oh! Yes, definitely not able to get up."

"Ooh, that does sound worrying. Do you need me to come and take a look?"

I glanced up and the whole party on our table had gone quiet, even Bob who was still mopping the spillage up had slowed his actions and was watching, everybody clearly listening to my side of the conversation with a mixture of expressions. Henry and Clara seemed fascinated, Jim impressed, and Fiona a bit misty-eyed, if I was honest. Probably best not to dwell on that. My dad looked proud, and was mouthing "She's a vet," to anyone who'd look at him. My mother's face was pinched and angry. No real change there then.

"That'd be grand if you would," Teddy's accent had slipped a little further north, to the Yorkshire Dales, if I wasn't mistaken.

"Ok, I'll see you in about half an hour then," I replied.

"That you will. I cannae wait." Old MacDonald's native Scottish ancestry was now shining through. Badly.

I hung up the phone and cleared my throat. "I'm so sorry. It's an emergency call-out to a cow with an injured leg. I really have to go."

At that moment, Teddy sauntered back in, trying to act nonchalant, but his grin was something to behold.

Bloody hell, Teddy, play it cool or you'll give the game away, I urged him silently.

Henry was looking at us both suspiciously, and gave Teddy a pointed eyebrow lift, which he dutifully ignored as he slid into the seat beside me.

"I'm so sorry, Teddy, but I'm going to have to go. I've been called out to a verra poorly cow," I murmured into my glass as I took a sip of lemonade.

"Have you indeed?" he replied, sounding overly surprised and really hamming up his part.

"Yes, I'm so sorry to cancel dinner." I couldn't look him in the eye now because I knew I'd start laughing. The giggles were already starting to bubble in my chest, and I could feel them threatening to spill over, my face hurting from the effort of not smiling. This was a jubilant feeling, carefree and uplifting, so that a lightness seemed to seep into my soul, something I couldn't remember feeling for a very long time.

"Right, well, we should go then. Best not to keep this poorly bovine waiting." Teddy quickly finished his pint and made to get up as well.

"But surely Hannah doesn't need your help with this cow with the broken leg, does she, Ted?" Henry asked, scepticism in his voice. "You almost fainted at a cat with an infection so I'm not entirely sure you'd be any actual use in this case, would you?"

Teddy glowered at Henry but didn't sit back down. I got to my feet, grabbing my jacket from the back of my chair. "I drove so I should probably drop you home on the way."

"We can take Ted home after dinner," Henry persisted.

Clara leant towards him and with a mischievous smile whispered something in his ear. He went a little pink and coughed a few times. She looked to us with a subtle wink and said, "But you're going to make sure Hannah gets back safely, right, Ted?"

"Right!" Teddy beamed gratefully at Clara, before turning back to me. "Plus I still owe you dinner, so I can do this after you've sorted the cow out, can't I?"

I nodded as Teddy helped me into my jacket. "I'm so sorry to bail. It was really nice to meet you all. Sorry about the wine," I said feebly, giving everyone a small wave, and going over to kiss my parents on the cheek.

"Come on, Hannah, we've got a cow to cure. Bye, everyone," Teddy said, his hand on the small of my back. He guided me towards the exit, accompanied by an obvious and disapproving tut from my mother as we left the devastation that I had caused in our wake and headed for the door.

"Let's hope you're a better architect than you are an actor," I said when we were outside, and I started to snort-laugh as I thought about his performance. "That was the worst collection of accents I've ever heard."

Teddy squeezed my waist lightly before letting me go and chuckling.

"I don't know what you mean. That was a flawless execution of a series of regional dialects. Shall we get some fish and chips and go to Coatley Park to eat them?"

Coatley Park was a tucked-away tourist hotspot with panoramic Cotswolds views and scenic leisurely walks. It was also known locally as Dogger's Drive, for, well, obvious reasons, and it was best avoided after dark unless you wanted to see something that you maybe weren't quite ready to see. It had been an eye-opener for sure when I'd pulled in there to take a call after a late-night check on a colicky horse last week. It had left me wanting to burn my eyeballs with a blowtorch.

"All right, but we leave before it gets dark."

Teddy laughed. "Spoilsport."

I dropped him at the fish and chip shop to put our orders in, while I parked up in a side street opposite. Through the window, I could see him leaning against the counter. He seemed relaxed and was smiling at the woman in a hairnet and white hat who was scooping chips into cardboard trays. She seemed familiar, and as I pushed the door open and she glanced up, I suddenly found myself staring into the surly face of my teenage nemesis, Mandy Shaw.

Urgh! Would this bollocks of a trip down memory lane never end?

"There you are, Hannah," Teddy said pleasantly, "I was just telling Mandy how we'd run into each other again."

"Were you, now," I muttered.

"Wow, it's so good to see you, Hannah! How are you?" Mandy asked, her voice falsely cheery and bright, but she couldn't disguise the undercurrent of meanness that I recalled from our schooldays.

So, she hadn't changed much then. How lovely.

"I'm fine, thanks, Mandy. You?"

"Better now I've seen Teddy again," she said gustily, batting her eyelashes at him, and he grinned in reply.

It was a stark reminder that he was the biggest flirt known to man (or woman), seemingly able to schmooze his way around anyone he chose. It was a fact I needed to remind myself of whenever he levelled the full force of that charisma at me. I was definitely not going to let myself fall for that, because another overtly charming but adulterous man was definitely not what I needed in my life. I needed to remember once bitten, twice shy, and likely to commit murder, in my case.

"Ted says you're the new vet at the practice down the road?"

"Yep."

Teddy shot me a puzzled expression at my clipped answers, clearly picking up on my reluctance to speak.

"Wow, that's cool," she said in a tone that indicated she thought it was anything but cool.

"But Ted is an architect, and that really *is* cool," I said sarcastically.

"Oh yeah, that really is cool," she breathed and gazed back over at him, but he was scowling at me, clearly trying to work out what on earth was going on here.

"And you work in a fish and chip shop, Mandy, so that's really, *really* cool." Ooh, horrible Hannah had rocked up today, and both Teddy and Mandy gawped at me, open-mouthed. This was monumentally petty and nasty, not really like me at all, and I was suddenly ashamed of myself for being such a cow. "Sorry, I didn't mean that."

Mandy finished wrapping up the food with a flourish, placing the packages into a bag and handing them to Teddy, her fingers accidentally (on purpose) brushing against his. "It's been so lovely to catch up again, Ted. Why don't we go out for a drink sometime?"

Teddy smiled and gave her some cash. "Sure. I'll let you know."

Without waiting for the change, he firmly ushered me out of the shop and towards my parked car.

"What was that about?" he asked when we were driving out of town and up towards Coatley Park.

"What?"

"Why were you so rude to Mandy when she was being nice?"

It still amazed me that he had never picked up on her inherent nastiness. Were boys really so unaware of the digs and bullying that girls – and she in particular – had subjected me to every single day that we had been in school? Clearly he was still oblivious.

"I apologised, not that she'd care."

I could feel Teddy's scrutiny across the car. "You don't like her much, do you?"

I laughed bitterly. "Whatever gave you that idea, Ted?"

"Call it a sixth sense." He shrugged. "Why though? What did she do?"

Speckly skin. Mole face. Freckly freak. Blot on the landscape. Those were just a few of the names she'd called me. Then there was the day she'd held me down in the girls' toilets with her gang of cronies, and forcibly applied concealer to my whole face in an attempt to make my freckles "less offensive to look at". Or the time on our cross-country run when she'd pushed me head-first into a muddy puddle to give me a helping hand at "evening out my skin tone". These were just a few instances that had stuck in my mind, but there had been a lot more. So many more that I had eventually stopped crying, and stopped reacting to her attacks. I had remained mute and sullen as she rained down insult after insult on me, shutting down to try and survive the abuse and get through another day in the seventh circle of hell.

But no matter how hard I have tried to forget it, or how many times I told myself that looks aren't important or that there are people worse off than me, it never really helped. All I ever see in the mirror, even now, is that repulsive teenager, the ugly duckling, who never became the beautiful swan.

"Because she's a mean girl, Teddy."

"Mandy? Mean? Is she?"

He was genuinely perplexed.

"She is if you don't happen to look like a film star," I replied, gesturing at him, glossing over the true depth of my issues with Mandy Shaw – and with myself.

"You think I look like a film star? Which one?"

I parked up and turned to him with a frown. "Oh, I don't know. How about that guy they kept in the cellar in *The Goonies*?"

Teddy laughed delightedly.

"I really thought you'd compare me to Danny DeVito."

"Nah, he's way better looking than you."

Teddy continued laughing and handed me a warm package of food from the bag on his knee.

"When are you going to take her out for a drink and continue your wooing, anyway?" I asked, trying to push away the totally ridiculous hurt feeling that was skimming under my skin at the thought of them hooking up together. It's not like they hadn't done it before. Probably.

"I'm not." He shifted uncomfortably in his seat. "And I wasn't wooing her – which is a ridiculous term, by the way."

"But you told her you would?"

"I was letting her down gently."

"By telling her you'd go out with her and then not actually going out with her? How is that 'letting her down gently'?"

Teddy glanced over at me as he ate, the little wooden fork hilariously small in his large hands. "I wouldn't want her to read anything into it if we went for a drink and, if I'm honest, she's not really that interesting to hang out with. I used to avoid her like the plague when we were at school. She's a bit vacuous."

Curious.

I thought they'd been best buddies as she'd always been trailing along in his wake. "Didn't you two go out in school?"

Teddy almost choked on the chip he had just swallowed. "No!"

Oh. A smug bloom of pleasure warmed behind my ribcage.

"So why did you not just tell her that you weren't interested back there?"

"I didn't want to hurt her feelings."

"I see. So you just employed advanced level flirting to lead her on instead."

"I don't know what you're on about. I was just making small talk, being nice. Perhaps you should try it?"

He was right; perhaps I should. Not that I'd ever tell him that.

"Not with Mandy Shaw I won't."

We ate in silence for a while, gazing out at the view from the car park. When he'd finished and wrapped the chip paper up into a ball, Teddy took a sip of water, and turned his body slightly to face me. He stared intently at me for a moment.

"Urgh. This feels like you're going to say something important, Teddy," I said discouragingly. He faltered a little, just briefly, before his composure returned, and I raised an eyebrow at him. "What piece of devastatingly vital information are you about to impart?"

He gave a slight laugh and leant back against the head rest.

"Do you like me, Hannah?"

74

I paused with a chip midway to my mouth, lips parted in surprise.

"Like you?"

"Yeah. Do you *like* me?"

Teddy tilted his head, his smile a little unsure. His demeanour was a touch subdued compared to his normal swagger.

"I like you more since you fed me," I said non-committedly. Where was he going with this?

"I see. So, am I on a sliding scale of your approval then?"

I nodded, thoughtfully.

"You started quite a long way off the bottom of the scale, just so you know."

"Right, but I'm actually in with a chance of you eventually not wanting to emasculate me?"

"I suppose so, although we do have some emasculators back at the surgery for bullock castrations, if ever I change my mind."

Teddy turned a slightly funny colour, and whispered in a hoarse voice, "Duly noted."

As he continued to watch me quietly, he blew out a long and mournfully loud sigh.

"What now?" I asked, finishing my food, grabbing all the rubbish, and putting it into the bag.

"I was hoping not to have to do this, but, well, you're forcing my hand, Hannah," Teddy replied seriously, and he took the rubbish bag from my lap. "I'm just going to have to go ahead and *woo* you."

On that bombshell he got out of the car and took the bag to the bin across the car park, sauntering with his usual air of self-confidence. It left me totally speechless and staring after him (and not at all fixing my gaze on his tight denim-clad backside. Honest.).

Walking back towards the car, he had a very cocky grin on his face as he slid into his seat.

"Ready to go?"

"Woo me?" I snorted.

I really needed to spend less time with Pluto. I was beginning to sound more and more like my equine companion.

"Yep."

"I thought it was a ridiculous term?"

"It is."

"Why?"

"Well, it sounds as though you're an eighty-year-old grandmother from the Victorian era and—"

"No, Teddy, I mean why would you even want to woo me?" I cut him off with a shake of my head, exasperated and slightly alarmed at where this conversation might go.

"Because you're clearly resistant to my obvious charms and I would like to rectify that," he said casually, amusement dancing across his features.

"Why?" I felt like a three-year-old who'd just discovered this word.

"Don't you think we should try to get along better?" His expression was mischievous, reeling me in. Hook, line and sinker. Once again.

"Why?" Again.

Teddy shrugged. "It's the neighbourly thing to do."

"Is it?" I was breathless, confused, but somehow eager that he should go on.

"It is. And maybe I can even help you to loosen up a bit. Have some fun."

"Fun?"

My voice was now barely a whisper. It was croaky and didn't really sound like me at all.

"Yep." He swallowed slowly, his Adam's apple bobbing. His tone had changed and he was staring intently at my mouth. "Oh, I know lots of ways we could have some fun."

With fascination I watched his face crease into a smile, so seductive and enticing, that a faint tingle of anticipation lit up my insides. It was a buzzy, shimmering feeling, a thrilling hum of expectation, like that wonderous, frightening sensation of looking down over a precipice to a yawning abyss below. In my brain a warning alarm was sounding, but it seemed very far away, drowned out by the heady cry of excitement that was, in that moment, all-encompassing.

Opposite me, Teddy's pure magnetism was drawing me to him like a moth to a flame. And it was as though time stood still, electricity arcing between us. I began to lean in, an unspoken intention in the air. A repeat performance of our one and only kiss surely imminent. I licked my lips and his pupils enlarged to impossibly dark pools in response, his body shifting over the gear stick towards me. Repositioning myself in the seat, ready for action, I turned and my arm brushed the steering wheel, catching the volume control for the radio and sending it into sonic boom mode. The car's speakers rattled and filled the car with the sonorous notes of "We Are Never Ever Getting Back Together". And thankfully the very wise words of Taylor Swift gave my good sense a proper kicking at the very last minute.

I switched off the radio and sat back in my seat, putting as much distance as possible between us again. What had I been thinking? Well, it was pretty clear that I'd been led astray by my sex-starved hypothalamus and reproductive system, rather than listening to the logical musings of my frontal lobe.

Let's not make that mistake again, Hannah, ok?

Teddy remained in place, frozen, silent. A muscle ticked in his jaw, his hand on the handbrake lever, white-knuckled as he clenched his fist around it. He stared at me until I looked away first, fixing my gaze on the setting sun on the horizon.

"What does *wooing* entail exactly anyway?" I asked eventually, suspiciously, not really sure I wanted to know. But also, desperately wanting to know. Because in the last couple of minutes, I'd apparently developed an embarrassing crush on Teddy Fraser, and was acting like a needy teenager despite being in my mid-thirties, even though it was dangerous and ridiculous, and likely to be an emotional car crash. Because he surely did not have any feelings for me, not beyond some weird, misplaced lustiness that had clouded his judgement a moment ago.

I should stop this. I should move away, and put some distance between us to save my sanity. But I didn't seem able to.

"Ah, you'll have to wait and see," Teddy whispered after a beat, before leaning right over the gear stick and adding seductively in my ear, "But I think we're both going to enjoy it immensely."

Using his thumb and index finger under my chin, he turned my head to look at him and gently closed my gaping mouth so that I no longer resembled a gawking codfish.

Chapter Eight

It was late when I woke up the next day, being gently battered around the head with Lady Fraser's plastic cone of shame. The cat was sitting on my stomach, purring and kneading sharp claws into my chest. Groggily I pushed her off and swung my legs out of bed.

In a horrible case of coincidence and bastard karma, I had been called out at 2am by a real-life farmer called Angus MacDonald, and had spent most of the night up to my armpits in a cow, trying to deliver a stuck calf.

And now I was bloody knackered, ached like I'd done ten rounds with Mike Tyson, and had a Saturday morning clinic in twenty minutes.

After feeding Lady Fraser and taking a record-breaking super-quick shower, I bounded downstairs, pulled a white coat on over my clothes and hurtled headlong into Giles in the dispensary.

"Morning, Hannah. Are you ok?"

"Yes."

"Busy night of call-outs?" Giles queried, taking in my damp hair and the granola bar I was hastily cramming into my mouth.

I nodded and swallowed. "Yes, tricky calving, but all went well in the end."

"Good." Giles shifted on his feet, limbering up for something. "So, um, we've had another complaint. From Mrs Wainscott this time."

"Oh."

Mrs Wainscott was a po-faced old lady with a grumpy dachshund called Bridgit. She had not been happy with me when I had growled ferociously at her little darling last week and called the diminutive canine a "vicious little grotbag". In my defence, Bridgit had tried to bite me while I performed the joyous task of emptying her impacted anal glands, so she most definitely deserved the reprimand and had behaved perfectly after that. I admit that she had been a bit quivery when Mrs Wainscott had carried her out of the consulting room – or maybe it had been Mrs Wainscott who was quivering? Either way, I didn't think my actions were wholly unjustified.

"I really do need you to work on how you're addressing clients, Hannah. I don't want this to be an insurmountable barrier. Perhaps you could take an interpersonal skills course or something?"

A course on how not to be a sour-faced cow. Right. I'd be sure to look that up on the internet. I rolled my eyes and Giles opened his mouth to say something when the bell above the clinic door rang. We both looked across the reception area to see which of our clients had turned up early for their appointment, and I was met with Teddy's dazzling smile as he gave us a little wave.

"Morning, I've come in to check on my favourite feline and her amazing vet. How is everyone today?"

Jenny, Giles's wife and our indomitable receptionist, jumped up from her seat and scooted over, gushing and fawning at him, while Betsy was speculatively eyeing up the huge box of chocolates and bunch of flowers in his hands.

Giles gave me a not-so-gentle shove.

"Now's your chance to prove to me how accommodating you can be with your client."

I glared at him.

"But not with Teddy Fraser, though?"

Giles nodded.

"But—" I shot Betsy a desperate look. *Help me*, I pleaded silently at her.

"You've got this, tiger," she said with a grin.

"Yes, why not?" Giles asked.

"We have a history," I hissed.

"Then you need to show me how professional you can be, and practise being happy-to-help Hannah, rather than here's-the-door Hannah, ok?"

Giles looked inordinately pleased with his little play on words. It was nothing that a quick rap across the shins couldn't have fixed, but I resisted the very real urge to kneecap him, instead balling my hands into fists until my nails dug into my palms.

Professional, see?

"Are you serious?"

"Yes, Hannah, I am. You could learn a thing or two from this chap about how to talk to other people, *nicely*."

Teddy was schmoozing his way around Jenny who was

giggling flirtatiously in his presence, then he glanced in our direction. "Hey, Betsy, lovely to see you again."

"And you, Ted. How are the renovations coming along?"

"Good, thanks! I've still not got hot water, but at least the hole in the roof is mended." He grinned broadly. "How's Emily? Have you two managed to decide on that extension yet?"

Betsy and her partner, Emily, were planning substantial work on their house, and I was surprised that Teddy knew about it.

"Oh yes! Can we pop in to see you next week? We've ironed out the kitchen layout and could do with a few amendments to the drawings, if you don't mind?"

"Of course. Let me know what works for you, and I'll have the kettle on and ready."

I gawped at Betsy, who just shrugged and mouthed, *"What?"*.

Giles gave me another nudge and I contorted my face into a grimace-attempting-to-be-a-smile, and positioned myself next to Betsy, trying to channel her zesty presence.

"Lady's fine this morning, Teddy. Are you here to settle your bill? Because Jenny can absolutely help with that." I kept the false smile plastered on my face, like a maniac, and Teddy took a hesitant step backwards as I approached.

"Are you ok, Hannah?"

He was looking at me as if I were a serial killer. Maybe I needed to tone down the homicidal grin.

"Yep."

Giles appeared next to me. "Mr Fraser?"

"Please, call me Ted. We're neighbours," he said, with a meaningful look in my direction.

"Ah. I'm Giles, the other vet here. Have you bought The Old Rectory then?" Teddy nodded and Giles carried on: "Glad to hear it's going to be lived in. Hannah, why don't you take Ted into consulting room one and have a chat about his cat. Reassure him?" Giles beamed up at Teddy.

I stared blankly at my boss for a moment.

"Now?" Giles said awkwardly out of the corner of his mouth.

I let out a long, resigned sigh and angled my head towards the consulting room. "Come on. This way."

Teddy dutifully followed and closed the door behind him. He laid the flowers and chocolates down on the examination table with a flourish.

"These are for you."

"Why?"

"Why what?"

"Why have you brought me flowers and chocolates?"

"It's stage one of my plan to woo you. How's it working?"

Crossing my arms, I scowled at him.

I am not – I repeat not *– falling for this. At all. Ever.*

And I was most definitely not thinking about the almost-kiss in the car last night. Nope.

"What are you playing at?"

Teddy folded his arms as well, frowning slightly as he said, "I'm not playing at anything."

"Listen, I'm on decidedly dodgy ground here and there's a real risk I may be about to lose my job. So, I don't need you popping in on dubious social calls while I'm at work."

"I'm here about Lady Fraser. I made an appointment to see you because I've not managed to find her owner yet, so I thought we should probably discuss what to do with her. And anyway, my social calls are not dubious, Hannah." He paused. "What have you done to risk losing your job?"

"It doesn't matter."

"I might be able to help…"

I shuffled my feet awkwardly and looked away. "Probably not."

"Try me."

I chanced a look at his face and saw that he seemed genuinely concerned. "Fine. All right. Well, the thing is … some clients have complained to Giles and accused me of being a bit prickly to deal with."

Teddy started to laugh – a deep, rumbling belly-laugh. Some snorting was also involved. He may even have had to wipe away a couple of tears.

"Hey! It's not that funny!"

"It kind of is though, isn't it?" he said, trying to straighten his face and failing miserably.

"No! I'm on my last chance here. If I lose this job in my probationary period I may not get another one in first-opinion practice, and there's nothing else nearby, anyway. I need this job. I can't go back to my clinical fellowship at the university, so without it I'm essentially screwed."

"Oh." He abruptly stopped laughing.

"Yes, Teddy, *oh*."

I plucked at a loose thread on my shirt.

"Why can't you go back?"

Should I tell him this?

He'd probably cheated on hundreds of women in his time. He'd think I was being emotional and hysterical (just like Jonathan did). No, now was not the time, and he was definitely not the person to unload this baggage onto.

"I just can't."

"Is there anything I can do?" He looked sincere, any amusement having vanished without a trace.

With a sigh I rubbed my hands over my face. "Maybe there is one thing you could do."

"What is it?"

"You could tell Giles that I have been unwaveringly polite and professional, and that you don't think I'm prickly to deal with. Please?"

Teddy looked thoughtful and smiled. "Yeah, I can do that for you." He paused, and narrowed his eyes. "On two conditions."

"Conditions?"

Uh oh. I do not like the sound of this.

"Yep."

"And they are?" I asked, pinching the bridge of my nose with my fingers, readying myself for something entirely onerous and annoying to come out of his mouth.

"One: you accept these kind and considerate gifts that I brought for you. Graciously. Maybe even with a smile."

"Fine."

I tried to smile and he wrinkled his nose.

"Forget the smile."

I stuck out my tongue.

Excellent professional skills here, Hannah.

This was going superbly well.

"Say 'Thank you, Ted'." He gave me a pointed look and a little James Bond eyebrow action.

I glared. "Two?"

"Two: you agree to help me with my house renovations in your spare time."

"What?!"

"Only a bit of painting or helping me move stuff. I'm really struggling on my own, Hannah, and everyone else is too busy to lend a hand. You're right here, next door, and you look fairly strong."

"I have no upper body strength. These long, skinny arms are like two bits of cooked spaghetti."

I waved them around a bit like Mr Tickle to prove my point.

"I've seen the enormous horse you ride and I don't believe that for one minute."

"Honestly, Ted, I'm pathetically weak."

"Not buying it."

He was not budging on this. Dammit.

"Well, I'm useless at DIY stuff so you definitely do not want my help."

I was getting desperate now. I could not spend all my spare time with Teddy Fraser. No way. Absolutely not.

"You'll learn. Anyway, it's really just fetching and carrying stuff or holding things that I need you for. And to make me cups of tea."

I stared at him incredulously, but he just continued to contemplate me with a confident and amused expression. There was no way I was going to be any use in his house renovations, but he kind of had me over a barrel here, and as much as it pained me to think it, I really needed him to tell my boss that I wasn't always an angry hedgehog.

What he'd said last night came into my mind – *I was just making small talk. Being nice. Perhaps you should try it?* – and a brainwave began to conga through my head gaining traction as it went. What if Giles was right? What if I just needed to study techniques in being nice to people? Perhaps I could learn from Teddy's charming personality and use it to my advantage, maybe even convince Giles that I didn't need to go to some lame-ass interpersonal skills course? And it wouldn't be forever, right? I could stand to be in the same room as Teddy Fraser for a little while. I could resist his ridiculous wooing or whatever it was he was doing. I could keep it platonic. I could stamp on this ridiculous crush. I could do that, couldn't I? For the security of my own career?

"Fine, but only for a few weeks. You can't string me out as your labourer forever."

"Would I do that?"

"Yes. You absolutely would." I placed my hands on my hips and gave him my best I'm-taking-no-nonsense-from-you look. "In return for utilising my questionable brawn, not only will you tell Giles how great I am at my job and what a professional, friendly service you have received from me, but you'll also teach me how to be nice to people so that I get to keep my job, and you get to have the delightful pleasure of continuing to be my neighbour. Deal?"

Teddy smirked and cocked his head to the side. "You want me to teach you how to be *nice* to people? That's your negotiation?"

"Yes. Consider this a chance to deliver a masterclass in flirting techniques."

His smile broadened further. "Ok, let's shake on it, then I'll go and tell Giles what a great job you're doing being so *nice* to me. We can get stuck in to your first DIY skills tutorial tomorrow."

"Fine."

I took his outstretched hand, resisting the urge to pull away as his long, warm fingers firmly wrapped around mine. A little ripple built up my arm as the nerve endings fired rapidly under my skin.

With a satisfied nod, and seemingly unaffected by my touch, Teddy dropped the contact. He turned to open the consulting room door, and added, "Oh, and as part of the deal, and to demonstrate how *nice* you can be, I also get to use your shower until I have proper running water sorted, ok?"

The absolute bloody cheek of him had my mouth hanging open in shock, but he was already sauntering off towards the reception area and was regaling my colleagues with tales of my wonderful bedside manner, and not-at-all hedgehog-like tendencies.

Chapter Nine

I t was a bright Sunday morning, and I was just brushing
Pluto down after an early-morning ride when my phone
began to ring. Teddy's name flashed up on the screen.

"What is it?" I answered, phone balanced between my ear
and shoulder as I battled with a saddle, bridle, and grooming
kit while also trying to open the stable door without dropping
anything.

There was mumbling, a muffled sound, a slight squeal and
a thunk, before I heard Teddy's distant voice saying, "Shit."

"Teddy, are you there? Did you pocket-dial me, for Christ's
sake?" Pluto was watching my struggle with interest between
munching on his hay and hoping I might drop a treat or two
for him, probably.

There was a load of static and then another squeaky little
sound.

"Hannah, is that you?"

"Yes! You called me, you idiot, so of course it's me," I said
with an undisguised sigh. I'd made my way across the yard

and was finally able to put everything down in the tack room. "What do you want?"

"I need your help," he said quietly. "And calling someone an idiot is definitely not on the wooing curriculum at the Fraser Foundation for Flirting, just so you know."

"The Fraser Foundation for what? Actually, never mind, I don't want to know," I muttered, closing my eyes. "What kind of help do you need?"

"I'm in my shed and there's a sort of devil sheep in here and it won't let me out."

"A 'devil sheep'?"

"Yes."

"Sorry, you're going to have to run that all past me again." This must be a wind-up. Teddy had said a lot of really random stuff in the last minute or so, and my brain was struggling to compute it all.

"First, I am not an idiot. Perhaps you should repeat that for me, Hannah?" He paused, but when I remained silent, he sighed and carried on, "Secondly, I'm trapped in my shed." Another slightly pregnant pause. "And thirdly, I need your expertise to help me escape."

"From the clutches of a *devil sheep*?" I added, thinking that I might use this turn of phrase in the future. Some of my ovine patients could certainly be classified as devilish.

"Yes."

"Do you need me to come right now?"

"If you would, yes please, otherwise I don't think I'm getting out of here alive."

"You are quite possibly the most dramatic person I have ever met, Ted Fraser."

"Please, Hannah, I don't know how much longer I can fend

it off." There was a distinctive bleat in the background and Teddy let out a decidedly unmanly noise.

"Fine. Where are you?"

"Come around the side of the house and go straight out the back. The shed is about a hundred metres away at the bottom of the garden. Please be quick."

"I will. But I'm at the stables so may be a while." I heard him groan, but what did he expect me to do? "Be brave, Teddy, I'm coming to rescue you."

"Hurry," he hissed, and then the line went dead.

A Cheshire cat-sized grin stretched across my whole face, and I began to laugh as I slipped off my riding hat. I hung it neatly on its allotted peg with all my other stuff and headed out to my car. The images that my mind was conjuring up about this predicament were too funny. And so, with a light-hearted bounce in my chest, I drove towards The Old Rectory.

Pushing open the ancient creaking garden gate at the side of the house, I called out just in case he was lying in wait to prank me. "Hello? Ted?"

But there was no answer. Maybe this was actually happening and it wasn't a joke. Maybe all six foot three inches of well-muscled, highly educated, supremely confident Edward Fraser were indeed trapped in a shed with a terrifyingly devious demon sheep. This made me smile even more. Hilarious.

Heading down the shadowed path by the side of the house, I stepped out into the sun-dappled back garden and began threading my way amidst the undergrowth, following some stepping stones twisting between towering walls formed of overgrown bushes higher than my head on both sides. In front of me, there were some low outbuildings, at one end of which a stable door stood ajar. This looked like the probable setting for the comedy sketch I was imagining, and I rubbed my hands together in wicked glee.

"Ted?" I called through the doorway.

"In here! Where have you been?"

"I told you – I was at the stables. I came as quickly as I could." As my eyes adjusted to the gloom, a dusty, tumbledown shippen, split into several small pens by old wooden gates, came into view. At one end of the building was Teddy, pressed firmly up against the wall. There was a broken gate by his feet and a large, rotund white Angora goat gazing up at him and blocking his exit to the door. "Made yourself a friend, have you?"

"It broke down the gate to attack me," Teddy whispered, his eyes huge and round with terror, his body attempting to become one with the whitewashed stone wall behind him.

"Attack you?"

"Yes, it made this awful noise." As if on cue, the goat bleated loudly. "Just like that. Then it charged at me. What kind of animal even is it?"

I snorted and laughed. "Ted, it's a goat, and it just wants to be friends."

"A goat?"

"Yes. Latin name *Sheepimus Devilius*." I sniggered, proud of my own joke.

"Very funny. How was I supposed to know there was a goat in my shed?" He looked back down at the animal. "*Why* is there a goat in my shed?"

"I don't know, but you could just step around it and come out?"

Teddy glanced up at me and shook his head, all his usual swagger and bravado gone.

"You can do it, Ted. I promise the goat won't hurt you."

He shook his head again.

With a long sigh, I entered the building, climbing over a rickety gate and walking towards the goat, gently using my knee to push her away. I held my hand out to Teddy, who grabbed it with both of his like I was a life raft in a stormy sea, gripping on so tightly that my metacarpals screamed in protest.

The goat bleated again and Teddy jumped, scooting around and placing my much smaller body between him and the object of his fear. He pressed himself firmly against me, his fingers now digging painfully into the tops of my arms, while the goat pottered about haphazardly for a moment, bumping into the wall and bleating mournfully.

"Let's get out of here," Teddy whispered in my ear, his towering frame folding around mine from behind.

"There's something not right about that goat. I think we should check it out," I said over my shoulder.

"No, we should leave and shut the door," Teddy insisted, tugging me back towards the exit.

"No, we should mend the broken gate and check that the goat is ok," I said, shaking myself free of his grasp.

Teddy grumbled something incoherent, which sounded a bit like "Let sleeping devil sheep lie", but I chose to ignore it and stepped further into the pen. The goat was fairly elderly by the look of it, and her eyes were coated with a milky film.

She seemed unsure and bewildered, and when I waved my hand in front of her face there was no response.

"She's blind," I murmured.

"Blind?" Teddy repeated.

"Yes, I think she was following the sound of your panicky, maidenly screams and accidentally broke the gate. I think she was frightened and disoriented. I don't think she charged at you on purpose."

"Oh."

Teddy had edged closer, still behind me though, with the air of someone ready to flee. I knelt down and gently started to scratch the top of the goat's head, crooning quiet words to her, and she leant into my touch.

"See, she's a softy. There was absolutely no need for such a hulking great big idiot like you to be frightened of a lovely little goat like this, now was there, Ted?"

Grumbling, he crouched next to me on the balls of his feet, tentatively reaching out to touch the soft, curly fleece of the goat.

"I think I may already have mentioned that *idiot* is not a term we use when we're being *nice* to people, Hannah."

I glanced sideways at him with a smirk, meeting his slightly less terrified gaze, and he begrudgingly smiled back at me.

"Maybe not, Ted, but *idiot* is definitely the right term to use for a grown man who's frightened of a blind old goat."

"I'll definitely be putting all this in my report to Giles."

"Oh, I'm sorry." Then, in a sarcastic voice, I said, "What a vewy, vewy bwave boy you are, Teddy."

"You're not anywhere nearer to being less prickly, just so you know."

"I gave up my Sunday morning to rescue you from a devil sheep. A little gratitude wouldn't go amiss."

"Fine. Thank you. You're my hero."

"You're welcome. Now, let's fix this gate, check she's got food and water, and then maybe find out who owns her."

"I own her."

Teddy and I turned as one to the open doorway, where a stooped, elderly lady in a blue headscarf and matching wellies was watching us with complete puzzlement.

The goat, who had also heard her, launched herself across the pen towards us, crashing into Teddy and knocking him clean off his feet and onto his arse, long legs flailing wildly in the air.

Perhaps a better woman would have helped him. She would certainly have shown some concern for his wellbeing or offered him a hand. But not me. I was too busy leaning on the gate in fits of laughter, which I didn't even try to stifle, at all.

Chapter Ten

"Sorry about that, young man. Deidre's just eager for her breakfast." The lady rattled a tin bucket in her hand and the goat bleated excitedly.

"Who are you?" I asked, wiping the tears from my eyes and finally helping a disgruntled Teddy to his feet.

"I'm Agnes Timms. Who are you?"

"Hannah Havens," I replied. Facing her, a flush of fresh social awkwardness setting off warning sirens in my head, aware that she was probably a client at the veterinary practice.

Try not to be prickly, Hannah. Try to be nice.

I looked at Teddy for inspiration, but he was still sulkily cleaning goat excrement off his backside. So I tried a smile on for size and added rather lamely, "Nice to meet you."

"Nice to meet you too. Are you the new owners of The Rectory? Lovely to have a young couple living in it after all these years."

I started to stutter a reply about how we were most definitely *not* a couple, when Teddy broke out his most devastating grin, his previous terror now masked beneath a suave veneer, and he addressed Agnes directly. "I'm Ted Fraser. Are you one of our neighbours, Mrs Timms?"

Agnes nodded, and momentarily seemed at a loss for words, the sheer force of Teddy's charisma washing over her like the healing vibrations of a gong bath. Agnes stared dreamily up at him, while Deidre gently headbutted her leg, clattering the pail of goat food in her hands.

Teddy continued to smile back at her, then gently wrapped his arm around my shoulders and pulled me to his side. Upon which my mind exploded in a volcanic reaction to this tender contact between us, while my body simultaneously went into some sort of shock, melting against him like I was made of molasses. His voice rumbled through me when he spoke again.

"What a lovely goat you have, but may I ask why she's in my shed?"

"Oh, yes, sorry. My barn roof blew off in the winter storms and Deidre needed a sheltered spot for a few weeks, so I popped her in here, just until the place sold. I didn't know you'd moved in already." Agnes gave a rather flirty laugh, and looked back at Teddy from under her headscarf. "And please, call me Agnes."

"Ah, I see. Well, Agnes, it was a bit of a shock to discover her in here this morning, I must say. But no harm done." Teddy squeezed my shoulder and looked down at me almost lovingly. "Hannah's a vet and was just about to give her a check over."

Agnes smiled encouragingly and said, "Are you working with Giles?"

I nodded.

"How convenient."

"Yes."

Silence and awkward staring ensued.

"Your goat is blind," I said, desperately trying to think of something to say.

"I know."

"And ran through the gate, so it'll need to be fixed."

"Ok." Agnes gave me a slightly puzzled look.

"We should check she's not hurt."

"We should."

"She's quite elderly. Is she in good health?"

"I believe so," Agnes countered quietly.

"Has she been checked by—"

Teddy cut me off, using his arm around my shoulder to turn me slightly to face him. The action drew me even closer, causing my hip bone to bump against him and my breasts to be mashed against his torso. My brain was sending urgent messages to all extremities to execute an action plan to extricate myself from this grip, but my body would not comply. Instead, heat started to course through me because his lips brushed my hair and he whispered, "Be nice," before kissing me gently on the temple.

All hope was lost. With that smooth manoeuvre, my body was now stubbornly Velcroed to his. My brain a puddle of goo, sloshing about in my cranium. Where was my inner ice queen in my hour of need? It had probably melted or was hanging out on a beach somewhere with a margarita after just one of Teddy's scorching looks, dammit.

Agnes sighed and looked a bit moony-eyed as she watched us. I felt like I was about to pass out from the overt charm that Teddy was exuding, engulfed by his citrus smell and potent pheromones, which really should come with some kind of health warning. Even at school Teddy had been a hugely affectionate person with his friends. There'd always been manly hugs with the rugby team and handholding and kisses on the cheeks with girls. He'd never shied away from physical touch, and others had always readily initiated or reciprocated this with him. Teddy was tactile with other people, and comfortably so. I, generally, was not. And yet, right here, at this moment, my nervous system was alight with how absolutely perfect this felt.

"Right," I croaked, finally (reluctantly) pushing out of his embrace. I stepped towards the goat, gulping in some air to try and right the oxygen imbalance that was clearly addling my mind. "Perhaps we should sort this gate then."

Teddy looked amused, clearly picking up on my discomfort at the intimate moment that had just passed between us, while Agnes lured Deidre away from the broken end of the pen with the bucket.

"I think this calls for power tools," Teddy said as he picked up the bits of gate, inordinately excited to be contemplating using a battery-operated drill. "I'll be right back."

Left alone with Agnes, who was studying me intently while Deidre wolfed down the pellets in the bucket, another awkward silence began.

"We're not married," I blurted out after a beat.

Where did that come from?

"Ok."

"We're not even a couple."

There, disastrous mistake averted. Phew.

"If you say so, dear."

"We're not." Honestly, why would she even think that?

"There's no judgement from me if you're not married.

Marriage can be overrated anyway. Just keep on doing your own thing. Ignore what anyone else says. I always have."

"But—"

"Friends with benefits – that's what you young people do, isn't it? Sounds delightful to me."

"Yeah, we're not really friends either, with or without benefits," I muttered, horrified.

"Well, he's clearly totally besotted with you, so my advice is to just enjoy it, whatever you want to call it."

How could I explain this? *He's an old adversary from school who's trying to teach me how to be nice to people because I'm a grumpy cow and might lose my job*, didn't seem the right thing to say either. So I elected to keep quiet.

Turning her attention away from me, Agnes fondly watched her goat, rubbing the animal's ears while she ate. She seemed comfortable to remain silent. but my mind was now screeching with embarrassment, desperately trying to come up with something (not prickly) to say, something other than: *You're very old*, or *Have you had that goat checked by a veterinary professional?*, which were the only two thoughts pinging around in my head. Even I knew that neither of those was appropriate or friendly conversation starters.

Why is this so bloody hard?

Eventually, Teddy came back after what felt like four years of self-flagellating penitence in a Cistercian monastery, his cheery personality filling the thought vacuum I had created and making me sag with relief. He gave me a strange look – eyebrow cocked – and mouthed silently, "Are you ok?"

I nodded and eagerly jumped over the gate, spreading my arms wide and saying in a falsely bright tone, "How do you want me?"

Teddy choked slightly, before quickly regaining his composure and winking. "I want you everywhere, all the time. You know that, snuggle bun. But perhaps we should save those shenanigans for later, when we're *alone*."

Agnes cackled and slapped her thigh, her eyes glittering, and Teddy beamed mischievously at her and then back at me.

Meanwhile, all thoughts had shrivelled to raisins inside my head, and my skin had reddened so that I now resembled a giant illuminated cherry-tomato of embarrassment.

"You know what I meant, Ted."

"Oh, I definitely know what you meant," he replied. "But if you could just hold one end of the gate for now, that would be perfect."

Reluctantly I picked up the side of the gate that he had indicated and glared at him, but he just blew me a kiss as he grabbed the other end. I'd asked for this, I realised, when I wanted him to give me a masterclass in wooing; when I apparently enrolled in the fucking Fraser Foundation for Flirting.

Two can play this game of humiliation one-upmanship, Teddy Fraser. Let battle commence.

Just as he bent over the gate, drill in place, facing away from Agnes and Deidre (who still had her head buried in the bucket), I murmured nonchalantly, "Oooh! Watch your back there, Ted. I think the goat wants to say hello."

I've never before seen a man levitate in such a graceful, balletic way, while simultaneously launching a power drill across a barn and squealing like a stuck pig. It was a sight to behold, and I enjoyed the moment so much that I dropped my end of the gate and bent over double, wheezing with laughter.

Realising he was not about to be mauled to death by a goat,

Teddy retrieved the power tool from the ground and muttered, "What have I said about playing *nicely* with the other children, Hannah?"

"Oh, I'm sorry, snuggle bun. Did the thought of the cute, friendly blind goat frighten you?"

Teddy smirked and lifted up the gate again.

"Hold on to this and don't drop it again, honey bumpkins, ok?"

"You've got it, fuzzy flappy face."

Teddy chuckled and shook his head.

"I think maybe you should leave the endearments up to me, flowery bunny chops."

"Whatever you say, cheeky bum."

This one really made him laugh.

"Were you looking at my backside when you were meant to be holding the gate, Hannah? I mean, it's totally understandable and nothing to be embarrassed about. I do it all the time to you, my horny little cuddle muffin." Teddy picked up the broken wooden bars and began fixing them back together. "But try and keep your mind out of my pants, just for a few moments, and on the job at hand, all right, sugar dumpling?"

I blew out an exasperated breath. He was far too good at this, and I had nothing. Not a single witty retort left in my brain.

I glanced over at Agnes, who had been watching our exchange with growing amusement.

"Not a couple, huh? My backside," she said smugly.

When Teddy had mended the gate so that its new construction would stop an 800kg Hereford bull from getting through it, he gathered his tools together and I helped Agnes to top up Deidre's water and hay. I also gave her a brief check for injuries.

As we closed the door to the stable and headed back towards the house, Teddy turned to Agnes.

"Would you like a cup of tea? There's not much in the house yet to sit on, but I could probably rustle up a packing crate or two and some bourbon biscuits."

"Oh no, dear. I should be heading back, and I think there're other things that you two want to be getting on with." She shot a salacious look at us and patted Teddy's arm gently. "I'll be back to check on Deidre later, and I'll try to sort a corner of my garage to move her into temporarily."

"There's no need for that, Agnes. She can stay where she is for now, can't she, Hannah?"

I wasn't totally sure why he was asking me, but I nodded and gave Agnes a little thumbs up.

"Well, if you're sure? It would put my mind at ease. See you lovebirds later."

"Think nothing of it."

Teddy's eyes twinkled good-naturedly as he watched her depart through a hole in his hedge and disappear into what I assumed to be her own garden next door.

It suddenly struck me that maybe this wasn't an act. Maybe he genuinely liked people. He liked them enough to get to know them and to offer his services (and his shippen). He actually worried about hurting people's feelings, even if it meant his own life was trickier because of it.

"You're staring at me, Hannah."

"What? I am not," I huffed, annoyed that he'd caught me gawping at him. "Come on, Mr Fixit. You can make me a cup of tea if you're putting the kettle on, especially if there are bourbon biscuits on offer."

"Awww, you're so cute with your funny little pet names for me. It's almost as if you like me," he replied, reaching over and pinching my cheek.

"Don't get used to it. I'm only speaking like this to you when flirting class is in session. The usual names I have for you are not suitable for sensitive ears."

Chapter Eleven

"You shouldn't have let Agnes believe we're a couple, Ted," I said when we got into the house.

"Why?"

He was busy setting the kettle to boil on a small gas camping stove in his makeshift kitchen.

"Because she'll be upset when she finds out the truth about us."

"What is the truth about us, Hannah?"

Teddy was now leaning back against a wallpapering table that was doubling up as a workbench and kitchen counter. He had his arms folded and was watching me with careful amusement.

"Well, it's preposterous that anyone would even think we could be a couple, isn't it? We can't even justifiably call ourselves friends," I said, sitting awkwardly on an upturned packing crate. I pulled a hair bobble out of my pocket and scooped my long hair up into a messy bun. "I'm not at all sure *what* I'd call this bizarre teaching-me-to-be-nice arrangement we have."

Teddy had listened to all this with an intense expression, then he rubbed his hand over his jawline. The sound of his beard was rough against his fingers.

"Why is it preposterous? We've kissed once before and almost did it again the other night, or have you forgotten that?"

I had not forgotten that. I had relived it every time I'd closed my eyes since. Sometimes, I'd even let the fantasy carry on, pretending that I hadn't pulled away and imagining what might have happened. Where it could have led…

And it got pretty filthy sometimes, I'm not going to lie.

I snorted, trying to cover my embarrassment.

"Why did you kiss me, Ted, back in school?"

He contemplated me for a minute as the kettle bubbled noisily behind him.

"Because I wanted to. Because I wanted to know what it would be like."

Oh.

But I didn't have long to mull over this as he carried on. "We could have a relationship, couldn't we? And it could be really *nice*."

"Nice?"

"Mmm hmmm. Yep. I can totally teach you what's *nice*, Hannah." Teddy was watching me closely. His eyes had taken on a darkened quality and it seemed like his pupils were enlarged, the bright blue iris now just a narrow ring of light.

I think I was staring at him with my mouth open again, gawking to such an extent that he had an unobstructed view of my tonsils, because his lips quirked with wry amusement, and this slight movement kicked my brain back into action. I realised that this was his fundamental flirting technique being played out right in front of me. This was the whole focus of me being here: to make me like him; to make me fall for him. In order to teach me how to make people like me too.

He doesn't mean any of it. Remember that, Hannah. Get your mind back on the job in hand.

"Since you're quite obviously unable to talk to anyone *without* flirting, shamelessly, perhaps you should give me my first lesson in being nice to people?"

His shoulders sagged slightly but he went about pouring the tea, and reaching up to a high cupboard for the biscuits, his T-shirt riding up and revealing the taut musculature of his stomach.

"You won't learn anything if I tell you what to do. We need to get you out in the wild so we can start practising on real people – and not just me, because I already like you."

"What do you suggest?" I asked. My voice sounded a little hoarse and I knew it was because my mouth was as dry as the desert after the brief, tantalising view of his body. This hopeless thirsting for him was annoying. Why did he have to be so attractive? And why the bloody hell did he have to say he liked me? And he'd wanted to kiss me? That really wasn't helping at all.

"My parents are hosting a charity garden party next week. All the local businesses pitch in, and it's a very grand affair – perfect for networking and being seen."

"I haven't been invited." And good God, I really didn't want to network, and I definitely didn't want to be seen. It sounded like hell on earth, quite frankly.

"You can come as my plus one."

"Your date?"

"If you like."

"No."

"Why not?"

"I don't want your family to think we're an item, Ted."

Plus, I really would be quite happy if I never saw any of them again after the shitshow in the pub the other night.

"I'll tell them we're just friends."

"No."

"Giles will be there. It's your chance to show him how personable you can be."

How was he so persuasive? How did he manage to coerce me into these situations? Why was my brain freaking out while my body was already willing me into a dress and high heels? Maybe, with a few ground rules, I could be his platonic plus one at this event.

"No touching."

Teddy laughed and held up his hands in front of him. "All right. No touching."

"That includes no attempts at handholding or unexpected cuddles."

"As long as you're sure you can keep your hands off me, I think I can resist the urge to unexpectedly cuddle you."

His expression was mischievous as he blew on his steaming mug of tea and watched me.

"Ok."

It was a begrudging agreement because I couldn't afford to lose my job. At least, that's what I told myself.

I dunked my bourbon biscuit sloshily into my tea.

"Excellent."

Chapter Twelve

"First things first. As my DIY skivvy, and not my friend, or heaven forbid, *girlfriend*, you need to put on some old clothes before we get started."

Teddy was busy rummaging in a large box.

"And since I couldn't possibly bear the barrage of disdain you would direct at me if you ruined your own things, especially those expensive-looking and very tight trousers"— he perused my jodhpurs appreciatively for a moment, until he caught my glare—"you can wear some of mine." He threw a large black T-shirt and a pair of jogging bottoms at me. "Put these on. I'll turn my back."

"There's no way these will fit me, Ted."

I eyed the huge jogging bottoms with fear.

"You can cinch them in at the waist or something. Get creative, Hannah."

The T-shirt had been neatly folded and smelled of washing powder and that citrusy scent that I subconsciously associated with Teddy. I shook it out and started to laugh, at first giggle-snorting and then hiccoughing loudly.

"Why do you have a *Dirty Dancing* T-shirt?" This was so at odds with his uber cool, ladies' man image that I couldn't comprehend it. "Did Henry get it for you as a joke?"

"No, he did not." He folded his arms and fixed his shrewd gaze on me, looking cross.

"Oh."

"It's a good film. Maybe you shouldn't have that one." He walked over and snatched it back, quickly finding a plain white one in the box and throwing it over.

"Ok. If you say so." I continued to chuckle as I took off my boots, before stopping at my belt buckle when he hadn't yet turned around. Twirling my index finger in a circle, I gave him a hard stare until he begrudgingly spun to face the window, while I stripped out of my jodhpurs and polo shirt and down to my underwear.

"I knew you'd take off your clothes for me at some point."

"Funny. Keep your eyes forward, Fraser." The T-shirt swamped me, but the jogging bottoms must have belonged to an actual giant. "This isn't going to work."

He faced me again, a strange light in his eyes, his expression serious and broody for a split second, before his usual boyish expression appeared. "You're a strange little hobbit, aren't you?"

"I'm five foot five and a half. So, above average, thank you very much."

"That is a curiously specific yet still vertically unimpressive answer," he replied, laughing.

I went to put my hands on my hips in a matronly way, and the jogging bottoms began to slide down my legs. I quickly grabbed them, bunching the excess material protectively around my middle.

"There's a tie cord in them somewhere. Just tighten them up?" Teddy suggested.

Pulling the white string as tight as I could, wriggling and puffing from the exertion, with angry, exaggerated movements, I persisted for a few moments under his wry gaze. And yet they were still miles too big, leaving a void of space between my body and the waistband. "Now what?"

Teddy sighed as he came over to me, taking the string from my fingers and pulling tighter, his knuckles grazing the skin of my stomach as he worked. He practically lifted me off the floor as he yanked the waist as small as it would go, knocking me off balance, so that I fell forwards, hand braced on his chest.

Glancing at this point of contact, the place where my palm was conveniently nestled over a rather impressively firm pectoral muscle, Teddy tutted. "I thought we agreed no touching?"

I was flustered. Who wouldn't be? I was fairly sure that even Emmeline Pankhurst would have copped a bit of a feel at this point. He was annoyingly and unbelievably toned.

Stepping back to roll the jogging bottoms up so I could find my feet, I put my boots back on and tied a 90s-style knot in the hem of the T-shirt so that it no longer fell to my knees. "Ta da. Haute couture, DIY style."

Teddy smiled a soft, genuine smile until the T-shirt slipped off my shoulder, revealing my bra strap, and he swallowed.

"Let's get to it. You're going to learn how to mix plaster today, Dr Havens."

Good grief.

He wasn't going to start with something easy then.

"I thought I was here to make tea?"

"Tea break's over."

With a resigned humph, I followed him out of the kitchen and up the grandiose curved wooden staircase. Shafts of sunlight reached like fingers through the bannisters, highlighting the dust motes that danced in the disturbed air around us, a miniature universe of twinkling stars swirling in space. Crossing the expansive landing, we entered one of the empty bedrooms where bags of plaster and buckets of water were already lying in wait.

"Lucky me, getting you to undress *and* come up to my bedroom. This is proving to be quite a day."

Teddy was tracking my movements with an amused expression, leaning against the doorframe as I wandered around, boots clumping loudly on the bare floorboards.

"Have you dialled the wooing up to advanced levels?"

"No, we're still just covering the basics."

"God help me."

Teddy grinned his best mischievous grin, flashing teeth and dimples as if he didn't have a care in the world. And yet my insides were spinning, shifting me off my usual centre of gravity, propelling me towards inevitable doom, and into a whole series of fantasies about his mouth. I had to bloody well stop this.

"Well, maybe we need to focus on fundamentals in plastering and not flirting," I said with a frown, pausing by the open window where I had a good view of the surgery, my flat peeking out over The Rectory's walled garden. The glorious, delicate scent of the dog roses that climbed the honey-coloured stone of the house and wound around the sill gently wafted under my nose, and I inhaled deeply.

"Right, let's get to it." Teddy was busy lifting sacks of plaster, his T-shirt pulling tight over his arms as he manhandled everything into the middle of the room. "It's a one-to-one ratio of plaster to water, ok?"

I nodded. How hard could this be?

Pulling out a power drill he inserted a long metal rod with a twirly end into the chuck, tightening a nut and giving it an exploratory whizz so that it spun around at an alarming speed. Satisfied, he turned it off and placed it next to a large black bucket. He began gathering various trowels and boards around him, before handing over some goggles and staring at me expectantly.

"Aren't you going to mix the first batch?" I asked, putting on the goggles.

"No. Off you go."

This felt like a practical skills assessment, the sort I'd been subjected to many a time at vet school. Feeling my prickles begin to resurface, my face contorted into its usual grimace of incredulity that seemed to be a regular feature in the presence of Teddy Fraser. I opened the plaster sack.

"You're so cute when you scowl, you know."

The teasing lilt to his voice was unmistakeable and the crease between my eyebrows deepened further.

Using the measuring jug, I angrily scooped the orangey dust into the black bucket, using another jug to slop equal amounts of water onto it. With trepidation, fingers grasping the heavy drill, I had to use both hands to aim the end of the mixing bit into the bucket. The on switch was an innocuous-looking grey button, but when I slid it along the barrel, the drill erupted like an angry Jack Russell terrier, shaking me violently until I let go with a yelp.

The next ten seconds occurred in slow motion. And it was a monumental horror show. Trust me.

The drill continued to vibrate at maximum speed. The bucket of plaster that encased it shuddered and shook across the floor as if taking part in some sort of primal dance. Both Teddy and I lurched forwards as the bucket began to tip. I was closer, and I managed to grab the drill again, but this didn't really help. No, I just joined in the shaky dance-a-thon, desperately trying to switch it off as the bucket teetered and I fell backwards onto my arse, hoisting the spiralling drill aloft and splattering semi-mixed, watery plaster everywhere. Most notably pebble-dashing the entirety of Teddy's face and chest with pinky-orange water, and globules of partially dissolved plaster.

Wiping his forearm over his goggles, he stalked towards me, glowering under the rapidly drying face pack he was wearing, and grabbed the still vibrating drill to turn it off.

I was trying desperately hard not to laugh. "Sorry."

"Are you?"

"Yes. I didn't expect the drill to vibrate so much. I'm used to using little ones for inserting pins and screws into animal bones." I kept my hand over my mouth, trying to manually force the giggles back down my throat.

"You see, I'm not sure I believe you. At. All." He discarded his goggles and I could see that his gaze had become dark, tanned skin forming an eye mask around his features, so that he looked as though he was some kind of cartoonish racoon villain.

A snort bubbled into my nose, which I tried to cover with a cough.

"Oh."

Leisurely, Teddy bent over, holding out a hand as if to help me up, but when I reached to take it, he deftly moved to the side, grabbing a handful of sloppy plaster mix from the bottom of the bucket and dumping it on my head. He smeared it across my cheek and then stood back up and out of reach.

"Hey!"

In defiance, I reached into the bucket, sliding my fingers into the silky slop and lobbing a generous amount of it towards him, which landed with a satisfyingly wet thud in the centre of his chest.

He looked at the mess sliding down his clothes, then he smiled back up at me menacingly.

"You're going to lose this one. You do know this, don't you, Havens?"

I suddenly felt nervous. But my ever-helpful brain decided that bravado was the best course of action as I took off my goggles to see him better.

"Maybe you'll be the one to regret it, Fraser."

Yeah, why not poke the bear, Hannah? Good one.

He nodded thoughtfully. "That's how you want to play it?"

I was still sitting on the floor, the plaster bucket closer to me than to him, when he crouched down to look me in the eye. Quick as a flash, I grabbed the bucket and threw the entire contents towards him, hooting with laughter as the remaining plaster mix coated his groin and thighs. Teddy gasped and fell backwards as his ripped jeans absorbed the cool mixture, which had the consistency of a lumpy milkshake. From the surprised and slightly disgusted look on his face, I assumed it was soaking through to his underwear.

Goal!

His returning glare was stony. Frowny. Lips a bit pouty.

Without hesitation, I scrambled to my feet, sprinting out of the bedroom and across the landing. Self-preservation was kicking in and adrenaline began to bound wildly as I heard him make chase. Before I had got far, an arm wrapped around my waist, and I was lifted high into the air and thrown over a very well-muscled shoulder.

"Put me down!" I yelled, screaming with hysterical laughter.

"No. We need to wash this plaster off you before it irritates your skin."

I wriggled and wriggled, unceremoniously hanging upside down, but unable to escape his death grip on my thighs.

"You know, you could have been a fireman if you'd wanted to! You don't have to re-enact these fantasies with me."

"This is just one of many fantasies that I would like to re-enact with you," he muttered.

We left the house, going back out into the bright sunshine. I was banging about like a sack of potatoes, while he was walking languidly as if I weighed little more than an empty handbag. Reaching down as far as I could, I smacked his backside hard enough that my palm stung. But he just laughed and smacked me back, softly, on my airborne derrière.

"Easy, tiger. There's plenty of time for that sort of thing after we've got you all clean."

Before I could come up with a sufficiently indignant or cutting rebuke, I was transferred into a bridal hold, and simultaneously dangled over a very overgrown and decidedly sludgy-looking pond.

"You wouldn't dare," I hissed.

"Wouldn't I?" He grunted as I squirmed furiously in his arms, loudly shouting for help, but his expression was patient and amused. Dangerous. "I'm doing this for your own good, Hannah."

"If I'm going in, so are you!" I declared mutinously.

He chuckled and raised an eyebrow, and as he went to launch me into the pond, I thrust one hand into his left armpit and began to tickle. His upper body twisted violently in surprise, causing him to lose his balance and trip on a broken paving stone, so that we both toppled forward. At the last minute, Teddy contorted his body and as we hit the water, he took the full brunt of the impact, me straddling his waist as we both became almost fully submerged in two feet and twenty-plus years of stagnant water, rotting leaves, and pond scum.

Breaking the surface mere milliseconds after me, Teddy gasped.

"Fuck, that's cold and it stinks like foetid arse!"

Tugging my waterlogged jogging bottoms back up to my hips, I stalked out of the pond, hauling myself onto the patio area. I was preparing to give him a piece of my mind, which became inexplicably empty the minute I looked at him.

The filthy water ran down his body as he stood, T-shirt clinging to him like a second skin. It was practically transparent, the planes and angles of his torso all highlighted for my viewing pleasure. But it was the moment when he reached up and ran both his hands over his hair, biceps flexing, pushing the damp curls and pondweed from his forehead, that my mouth ceased to produce any saliva. I felt like the living embodiment of Miss Elizabeth Bennet standing on the pristine lawns at Pemberley, and shamelessly ogling a delicious and dripping Mr Darcy. And while historical romance films were not really my thing, even I'd had inappropriate thoughts about Colin Firth in a wet shirt.

I finally dragged my greedy little eyes back up to his face only to catch him staring back at me, cheeks lightly tinged with pink. Following his gaze, I looked down to see that my T-shirt was also now almost entirely see-through, giving him an unobstructed view of the decidedly unsexy turquoise sports bra I had on. Teddy swallowed, suddenly appearing desperate to look anywhere other than at me.

"I think perhaps we should get changed," he said gruffly, opening and closing his fists as if dealing with some sort of inner turmoil, a dark intensity etched on his features.

"Good idea," I agreed, and fled back to the kitchen to retrieve my own clothes. And any shreds of dignity I may once have had.

Chapter Thirteen

Hot, clean water from the shower was definitely preferable to slimy pondwater for washing plaster out of my hair. The smell of decay steadily swirled away down the drain, along with some rather dubious-looking pond-based detritus. But every time I closed my eyes, a video reel of Teddy looped behind my lids, meticulously focussing on the visual splendour of the emerging-from-the-water scene. Or him leaning against a door frame with a mischievous smile. Or him almost kissing me in the car. Furiously scrubbing my fingers over my scalp, I tried to recall him falling on his arse as he was butted by a blind goat, but my brain simply turned it into a cute and adorable moment, his grumpy, slightly fearful expression now endearing and not at all annoying.

Gah! What's happening to me?

I needed a healthy dose of reality to reset my Ted-ometer back to "infuriatingly irritating" and away from "eminently likeable". I needed to stop this stupid crush in its tracks.

Swiftly wrapping my hair in a towel turban and pulling on

clothes, I headed to the kitchen for a consolatory cup of tea, affectionately scratching Lady Fraser on the chin as I passed by, empty mug in hand, when my door buzzer rang.

"You could have just come straight up," I said as I swung the front door open, but instead of Teddy, who I was expecting any moment for his own ablutions in my bathroom, I was greeted with a wide pair of hazel eyes, floppy sandy hair, and a smug expression.

Shit.

"Jonathan! What are you doing here?"

"Nice to see you too, Hannah. May I come in?"

No you bloody well may not! I screamed inside my head. But my body was already moving aside and beckoning him in.

Damn you, polite English sensibilities.

Jonathan stepped over the threshold and appraised the small confines of my flat in a single glance with a curious expression. Lady Fraser let out a low growl from behind me and slunk away, belly low to the floor, eventually disappearing into my bedroom.

"So how are you? Seems like you're, ah, doing well for yourself?"

The undertone was there. His obvious sense of superiority fuelled by his perceived lack of my success.

Fists bunching the soft denim of my shorts, I took a steadying breath.

Don't bow down to his fuckwittery, Hannah. Come on.

"What do you want?"

"I just thought I'd pop in and see you. It's been a while."

He smiled, sickeningly sweetly, and I scowled in return.

"You know, I've always thought you'd be much prettier if you smiled more."

Murder is wrong, isn't it? Even following that kind of smarmy comment.

"What. Do. You. Want," I repeated, enunciating each word.

"A cup of tea would be very nice. Then perhaps we could have a little chat."

"I don't think we have anything to chat about."

"How about we start with how much I've missed you?"

I must have been staring open-mouthed because Jonathan broke into a wide smile and walked over, taking the mug from my limp fingers.

"I'll make the tea, shall I?"

Just having him here made it feel like my flat was sullied and dirty. He made the new life I had carved out for myself seem worthless, just another domain under his control. He busied himself in the tiny kitchen, finding teabags and another mug, humming softly, in a very pleased-with-himself way as the kettle boiled noisily. I had the irrational urge to spray everything he was touching with bleach.

"How did you find me?"

"I asked Georgina in the office if she had a forwarding address for you." He raised his eyebrows. "You're not as elusive as you thought. Fairly predictable, actually, heading home to your parents. I thought you might need someone to look after you when we broke up. Turns out I was right."

I growled. Actually growled, like a feral animal. The answering smirk was almost unbearable. He knew he was getting under my skin. He knew the buttons to press in order to really rile me up. I couldn't even see an inkling of the charm and sophistication that had drawn me to him in the beginning.

"Come now, darling, we were so good together. I messed up, and I'm sorry."

"Sorry I found out, you mean," I muttered.

"No, I know it was a mistake – the worst of my life – and I'm here to try and make things right."

"Right?"

"To convince you to give me another chance."

In the periphery of my consciousness I was aware of the sound of footsteps bounding up the stairs, then a deep voice shouted through the door, "I really hope you're naked in there, Hannah, because I'm coming in."

Teddy appeared in the doorway, larger than life, in his dirty work clothes, like a white knight in plaster-soiled armour, charging up the tower to save me from the evil clutches of the wicked wizard. Relief at him being here engulfed me and I beamed at him, so utterly grateful for his presence in this moment.

Teddy's returning smile was radiant. "Loving the pink towel turban. It's a good look, although I'm sad you didn't wait for me before you showered. I was really hoping we could have shared one – you know, just to save water, obviously."

His comedy eyebrow waggle was halted mid-rise, as he clocked Jonathan in the kitchen area, two steaming mugs in his hands.

The change in the two men was tangible. Teddy grew taller, his posture stiffening. He seemed, all of a sudden, more rugged and confident, while Jonathan's response was to increase the levels of smugness to epic proportions, self-assurance coming off him in waves.

"I didn't realise you had workmen coming in, Hannah." Jonathan said, moving closer as he handed me a cup of tea, which I promptly put down on the table and then stepped away, bumping against the armchair as I desperately sought personal space.

Teddy's eyes narrowed and he glanced between us, trying to work out what was going on.

In a cool, calm voice, he said, "Hi, I'm Ted Fraser. I live next door."

I was mute.

Jonathan took Teddy's outstretched hand and shook it belligerently, clearly feeling this was beneath him. "Hello. Since Hannah's forgotten her manners, I'd better introduce myself," he said with a tut. "I'm Professor Jonathan Pierce." He paused, but when Teddy gave no indication that he was either impressed or awed at this declaration, Jonathan continued, "I'm Hannah's significant other."

Teddy's eyebrows shot into his hairline and he turned to me with a quizzical expression.

"You are my *ex*-boyfriend, Jonathan," I answered in irritation.

"I'm here to take her back with me to Bristol." Jonathan addressed Teddy directly, ignoring me, so utterly confident of himself, so completely sure that he had the winning hand here. It was the most infuriating kind of infuriating, the kind of fucking irritation that made my brain buzz with annoyance.

"Oh, that's right, because hell has actually frozen over?" I pulled the soggy towel from my head, crumpling it forcefully in my hands and allowing my damp hair to fall free and untamed, the swirling golden-red strands tumbling across my face.

"I think you should leave." Teddy said, laying a proprietary arm around my shoulders for the second time that day. The warmth of his body was oddly comforting and calming, and I felt some of the tension dissipate from my body.

"And *I* think Hannah needs to listen to me and stop wasting her time in this dead-end place."

Teddy and Jonathan glared over the top of me. It was like two rams sizing each other up before they started butting heads.

"Not that anyone seems to care what I think," I muttered, wondering how it had come to be that two men were making all the decisions about my life, in my home, without even considering my input. Crossing my arms, fingers biting into the flesh of my biceps, I stepped away from Teddy and directed a furious stare towards Jonathan, my anger back with a vengeance.

"It so happens that *I* also think you should leave, because there is not a single thing that you could possibly say to make me want to return with you."

"You must know that your talents are being wasted here in this pitiful, backwater practice?"

"I like it here. The change of scenery is doing me good." I paused, picking at the frayed edge of my denim shorts, busy fingers working out the tension I was feeling. "How's Daisy, by the way?"

"I've told you, it was a mistake, and I finished things with her straight away," he said petulantly.

Teddy reached out and brushed his fingers over the back of my hand, and Jonathan's gaze zoomed in on the contact before he spoke again.

"I can see that you're obviously partaking in some sort of relationship with this man, and I understand you're probably doing this as a kind of rebound."

"For fuck's sake, Jonathan!"

He was unbelievable.

He held up a hand. "But, I want you back. I'll even let you move in with me if that's what it takes."

Something rumbled in Teddy's chest, something furious. It was an apex predator type of noise, and Jonathan blanched, his arrogance dissolving instantaneously. I briefly laced my fingers through Teddy's, squeezing and silently asking him to step down; to let me fight this battle.

"Let's get something straight here: nothing, NOTHING, will convince me to go back to you. Ever. And I'd rather eat my own eyeballs marinaded in bovine spongiform encephalopathy prions than have to have unsatisfactory sex with you ever again. So you can take your co-habitation offer and stick it up your arse. Sideways."

Teddy stifled a snigger, but Jonathan was not finished yet.

"But I love you." He thrust this into the air theatrically, as if delivering a Shakespearean monologue.

Did he honestly think I would swoon and fall into his arms, helpless with love and desire?

Yeah, no.

"The feeling is not mutual," I replied in a flat, dead tone.

All the bluster and confidence seemed to deflate out of him, shrinking down before my eyes. He suddenly looked very tired. Beaten. A surge of pity erupted in my chest.

"I need you, Hannah."

"What?"

"I need you. I can't go back without you. Please." Desperation had turned his voice high-pitched, whiny.

"Why?"

There had to be a reason that he had resorted to begging.

Had he really realised that he couldn't live without me? Had it taken me leaving for him to decide I was the love of his life? Surely not.

Jonathan glanced at Teddy again, and then back to me.

"I've realised how much I miss you, and how stupid I was. Losing you is the worst thing that has ever happened to me – I want you to know that."

Gathering his cup from the table where he'd put it, his movements suddenly less sure, he rinsed it in the sink, before heading towards the door.

"I really do love you, Hannah. Please just give it some thought."

And with that he slipped through the door, closing it quietly behind him and leaving a vacuum of weird silence and confusion in his wake.

I slumped into a chair while Teddy checked the stairwell to make sure he'd left, locking the bottom door and returning to my flat a little cautiously.

"Are you ok?"

"Yeah."

"He's a monumental dickhead, isn't he?"

"Yes." I was tired. The confrontation and the piled-on emotions had battered me. Jonathan's declaration had hit me like a cricket bat to the head. "Help yourself to a shower."

"Thanks." Teddy knelt down in front of me. "Easy for me to say, but don't let him get to you. Do the right thing for you, whatever that might be. Your happiness is important, Hannah."

His expression was sincere, eyes clear and bright. There was no hint of mocking me, no flinching away in disgust.

"Why are you being so nice to me, Ted?"

"I like you. Why wouldn't I be nice to you?"

"You didn't like me in school, and you definitely weren't nice to me then. What's changed?"

I was in self-destruct mode now, confused and unsure, poking at a wound and allowing my feelings to fester into something even more unpleasant. Pushing and challenging, coating myself in spikes to ensure I didn't get hurt again.

"I've always liked you. But I don't think you liked me very much when we were teenagers. I'm hoping that might be changing?" His voice was hopeful, vulnerable.

"Why? Because you're playing this flirting game with me? I suppose you've never had a woman that it doesn't work on," I said sourly.

"It's not a game, Hannah. I'm genuinely trying to get to know you again, to show you that I'm not the hopeless idiot you seem to think I am."

"Why?"

Teddy shook his head in exasperation. "Because I *really* like you, hard as you seem to find it to believe."

Realisation dawned. His flirting had a wider purpose…

Oh God, this is really bad.

"You actually do want to sleep with me?"

"Well, the thought has crossed my mind a few times, yes, but that's not all I want."

Of course. I had wounded his Casanova's pride by not falling into his arms in a gooey mess of fluttering eyelashes, by not leaping into bed with him just because he flashed me a smile or two. Despite the temptation he presented, despite the fact that he was quite possibly the most attractive man I'd ever seen, and despite the memory of the rugby club snog that lived rent-free in my head, there was no way I was doing this. No way I was going there. Because I knew once he'd scratched that particular itch, I would be dropped and he'd move on to his next conquest. Challenge conquered. Ego (and other things) stroked and satisfied. But I would be left feeling used, discarded like a piece of litter once more. Wrecked for anyone else ever again.

"I'm going out. Feel free to have a shower. Pull the front door closed behind you when you leave." Getting to my feet, I retrieved my car keys from the pot in the kitchen and grabbed my riding boots and jodhpurs, knowing that more time with Pluto was what I needed.

"What? Wait! Hannah! Where are you going?"

"I think I've probably learnt all I need from your flirting masterclass, and I think you're now fully aware of my lack of DIY prowess. So whatever this is"—I gestured between us—"can absolutely stop now."

"Please, wait! Just give me a chance?"

He ran his hands through his hair, and a few wet leaves dropped to the carpet, but I already had the door handle in my fingers and was twisting it forcefully in my haste to get away.

Racing down the stairs, all I heard was him shout after me, "Shit! Why am I so bad at this with you?"

Chapter Fourteen

The slow creep of dawn had turned the Cotswolds countryside into a misty wonderland of spiderwebs glistening with dew, the warmth of the sun leaching into the day, and the promise of a heatwave ahead. Another late-night call-out had left me exhausted, and I sat alone in the car park, head leaning gently against my steering wheel with my eyes closed as I relished the quiet of this time of day.

I hadn't seen Teddy for a few days, and had purposefully ignored his calls and texts, believing it would be better not to see him, even though there was a strange, empty feeling inside me now. Emptiness that had, I think, been there for a very long time, but had recently been filled to the brim with flirty banter and daft antics, a warm sort of friendship, and more laughter than I can ever remember having had before. But now I'd been left with an architect-shaped hole in my chest which I was refusing to dwell on, and I swallowed away the desire to call him or see him; or watch him squeal and run away from a goat, or fall on his backside covered in plaster. No, I was not going to let my guard down with the world's biggest flirt, because falling for him was not on the agenda and would likely end up being a catastrophic pain in my arse. And in my heart.

Reluctantly, I got out of the car, forcing myself to face the day. Yearning for some toast and a strong cup of tea to fortify myself for the undoubtedly busy clinics that lay ahead, in order to try and be civil, doing my best to read other people and respond accordingly. Despite Ted's preliminary training, the spiky hedgehog was definitely back. Perhaps it had even morphed into a poison-tipped puffer fish of prickliness. Even Giles hadn't been brave enough to pick me up on my snappiness, and clients were, wisely, choosing not to complain. Not to my face anyway. There were a couple of worryingly titled emails in my inbox, which I hadn't yet opened. Perhaps returning to academia was the right thing to do? Perhaps Jonathan's declaration was the open door I needed. I could slip into the anonymity of research once again and remove myself from too much "peopling". I could hide behind a lab coat and goggles... Could I give *him* another chance? I shuddered at the prospect, but the opportunity to be successful, to be respected, to get back to being the me I always thought I'd be was dangling like a carrot in front of my nose.

Locking the car door behind me, a glimmer of movement across the car park caught my eye.

"Agnes?"

Barefoot and clad only in a long white cotton nightgown, our elderly neighbour was bending over and examining the underneath of the hedge. She was muttering something I couldn't quite catch from this distance, and her movements were jerky and agitated.

"Agnes, are you ok?"

But she didn't seem to hear me. She only tugged at her loose grey curls with one hand and bunched her nightdress in the white-knuckled fist of the other.

"What are you looking for?"

As I got closer, she finally noticed me, the startled twitch of her body making her stumble forwards, but the stare that she returned was blank, glassy, and devoid of any recognition.

Slowly I reached my hand out towards her.

"Agnes, are you sure you're ok? It's me, Hannah, from the vet's."

She watched my hand creep towards her, fascinated and horrified all at once, and as my fingers brushed the crêpey skin on the back of her hand, she slapped me away, her palm stinging against my wrist.

"You're not Hannah. She has dark brown hair like me." Her expression was mulish as she looked into my face. "I don't know who you are, but you're not my sister."

"No, I'm not your sister, Agnes. I'm one of the vets. What are you doing out here at this time of the morning?"

She shook her head, confusion flitting over her features.

"I'm looking for Edward. He said he'd be back soon. He went to get me strawberries, but I haven't seen him since yesterday."

"Do you mean Ted?"

Agnes knitted her brows and folded her arms. "He doesn't like being called Ted."

"Oh, ok."

"He said he'd be back. He said he wouldn't leave me alone if anything happened to Frank." A tremor was shuddering through her body, and I couldn't tell if it was the slight chill of the morning air or anxiety that was making her tremble. "But he hasn't come back. Where can he be, Hannah?"

"I don't know."

Slowly, so as not to spook her, I removed my jacket and inched forwards, draping it over her thin shoulders. She finally smiled at me.

"I love him, you know?"

"You do?"

"Yes, with all my heart."

"Edward?"

I tried to manoeuvre her across the car park, back towards the lane, but she dug her heels into the gravel, yanking away from my touch.

"No! Frank! Why would I love Edward? He's far too young." Agnes tutted in disgust.

"Ok, I think maybe I should take you home."

"I'm not leaving until I've found Edward!" she screeched at me, and I backed away, hands held up in defeat. I was out of my depth here, not really understanding what was going on. I needed help. And there was only one person I could turn to. Annoyingly.

"I could call him for you?" But Agnes had returned to ferreting around in the hedge, softly calling out into the undergrowth and completely ignoring me.

Reaching for my phone, I tentatively swiped Teddy's number, keeping my fingers crossed that he'd answer. And he did, on the third ring, his voice breathless, groggy, and panicked.

"Hannah? What's wrong? Are you ok?"

"Yes, I'm fine. I've found Agnes wandering about in the surgery car park."

"Oh." He yawned loudly.

"I need your help. She's a bit confused. Can you come?"

"Confused? Just take her home. It's 5.30am."

"I know that, but she won't come with me. She's looking for a guy named Edward. I wondered if she meant you?"

"What? I doubt it."

"I'm not getting anywhere with her and she might listen to you. Please?"

"I don't know. I was asleep. You woke me up." A pause. "Plus, I got the distinct feeling that you didn't want to see me, Hannah."

His words hung in the air for a minute. A little bit of hurt suspended between us. He was, quite rightly, not going to make this easy for me.

"I'm sorry. I've been busy."

This was true, but it wasn't the real reason for ghosting him these last few days. I couldn't let him know just how much he'd got under my skin though. How desperate I was to try and break the cycle of wanting him against my better judgement. I tried a different approach in response to the incoherent grumble in my ear.

"Listen, grumpy chops, I wasn't going to call it in so soon, but after the great devil sheep rescue, you do owe me a favour…" There was a long sigh down the line, but I could almost hear him smiling, and I couldn't help it as my lips quirked in response. "Please, Ted, I'm struggling here and I really need your help. Don't make me beg."

"I'd like to make you beg."

A flush crept over my skin, a flock of butterflies danced in my stomach, and sweat broke out on my palms. All because of that one comment.

Rein it in, Hannah, for fuck's sake.

My hand tightened on the phone as another tension-filled pause commenced, an instant in time where I wasn't sure which way this would go, but he finally said, "I'll just put some clothes on and be right there."

About three minutes later, Teddy appeared in a pair of flip-flops, grey jogging bottoms, and a black fitted T-shirt. His hair was mussed and sticking up, he had a slight crease in the skin of his cheek on which he'd obviously been lying just a few moments ago. My heart stuttered and stopped. He had absolutely no bloody right to do this to me. No right, at all, to look like some sort of sleepy bearded Greek god. And definitely no right whatsoever to be staring at me like that. Like he might just devour me whole.

Agnes looked up as Teddy approached her.

"There you are, you monkey! Where have you been?"

"Asleep, in bed, the whole time. Why don't we take you home?" The low, calm tone of his voice sent goose pimples flitting across my skin.

Agnes looked a bit melty and nodded, then inclined her head in my direction.

"You'll have to excuse my sister. She's only gone and dyed her hair. Silly sausage, isn't she?"

"A very silly sausage indeed," Teddy agreed, eyebrow arched as he glanced over.

"Although it suits her, doesn't it? Makes her look pretty, don't you think?" Agnes was gazing at me thoughtfully and I blushed under her scrutiny. I wished my hair was down so I could shelter behind it and hide my face from any further inspection, lest they start to notice and comment on my many imperfections.

"Oh yes, she's very pretty. Really quite beautiful, in fact." Teddy's voice was raspy and had a toe-curlingly seductive quality to it. It was official – I was done for. I swayed towards him, but as quickly as the moment came it was gone, and he turned back towards Agnes. "She can help us get you home and tucked back into bed, can't she?"

Agnes tutted at me. "I wish you two would get married already. He needs someone to take care of him. And I'd like an excuse to buy a new hat."

Teddy laughed, threading Agnes's arm into the crook of his elbow. "Come along now. If I married Hannah, how would I be able to look after you? She's very demanding!"

"Tell me about it!"

They chuckled good-naturedly and Teddy led her just a few hundred metres down the country lane past The Old Rectory. We arrived at her small thatched cottage, set back from the road behind a beautiful garden alive with the humming of insects and the scent of honeysuckle.

The faded and peeling blue front door stood open and there was a winding dog rose trained around the frame that was swaying in the breeze, thorns hooking my T-shirt as I brushed past and into the gloomy interior. Where I promptly barrelled straight into Teddy's stationary form, crushing my nose painfully into the firm muscles between his shoulder blades. He reached backwards to steady me, clutching at my hand and squeezing my digits tightly.

"Shit, Hannah. Look at this place," he whispered.

Agnes continued on ahead, winding her way down the corridor, artfully avoiding the heaps of belongings that covered nearly all the available floorspace, while we stared incredulously about us. The house was packed to the rafters with stuff. Every available nook and cranny was crammed with knick-knacks, every shelf and cupboard overflowing with odds and ends, while sheets of paper and envelopes littered the floor like autumn leaves. Every tread of the stairs was piled precariously with things, and as the floorboards creaked beneath our feet, a tinkling of crockery came from teetering skyscrapers of boxes all around.

Teddy met my eye, and I shook my head in disbelief.

"What should we do?"

"What can we do? It's her choice to live this way." I shrugged, feeling helpless.

"But she's obviously struggling to cope," he said.

Before I could answer, Agnes called from somewhere deep inside the house, its Aladdin's cave interior muffling her voice.

"Come on, you two. Let's have a cup of tea."

We found her in the kitchen, and she gestured to a small cleared area at the 1980s-style yellow Formica table. She was busy shuffling crockery to make space on the work surface and an ancient kettle began to whistle noisily on an old gas hob. I hesitantly took a seat on the end of a bench, pushing a carrier bag full of brand-new washing up sponges to the side to make room, while Teddy leant against the countertop, his head almost touching the low, sagging ceiling.

"Now, why are you here, at this time in the morning? I'm sure you have much better things to be doing than stopping by to see this batty old woman?"

The usual clarity and shrewd intelligence was back in her eyes, and there was no hint of the dazed and confused person we had encountered in the car park.

"We just wanted to check on our favourite neighbour, that's

all," Teddy said kindly, reaching into the fridge and passing her the milk.

"Well, aren't you just a sweetheart? You should hold on to him, Hannah."

"That's what I keep telling her, Agnes, but I'm not sure she agrees."

"What a silly sausage!"

"Very." He levelled an unbearably smug smirk at me.

"Who's Frank?" I asked quietly, and she froze momentarily.

"He was my husband, but he was killed in action when he was in the army."

"Oh, I'm so sorry to hear that, Agnes."

"It was a very long time ago, when there were a lot of IRA bombings in the 70s. He was in the wrong place at the wrong time." She handed out the tea and then reached up to a shelf and pulled out a faded photograph of a dapper young man in a military uniform from behind a dusty teapot, his smile lopsided and mischievous. "He was very handsome, just like this one." She leant over and patted Teddy's cheek, who grinned in reply.

"And Edward, who was he?"

Agnes's wrinkled face flushed, her brow creasing.

"Gosh, I haven't thought about him for a long time. He was Frank's much younger brother, and a very gallant young man. He came round to call on me when Frank died and made sure that I was ok. He was a good boy…" Her voice trailed off and her eyes misted over.

I sipped my tea and the oppressively crowded house loomed inwards. Agnes was momentarily lost to long-forgotten memories, while Teddy and I glanced at each other.

"Do you have many visitors, Agnes?" he asked, breaking

the quiet. His deep voice was rich and warming after the pensive silence that had engulfed us.

"Oh no, dear, just me and my goats. No one much bothers with me nowadays."

"Oh." Teddy looked visibly pained.

"Anyway, nothing to be maudlin about. I've had a good life, and now I have some lovely new neighbours!" She smiled broadly at us.

"Too right," Teddy murmured, looking at me again.

Agnes had no obvious recollection of the episode in the surgery car park, and she seemed to be happy gazing at us over the rim of her teacup once again.

"I should get going, I'm afraid. I was called out to a tricky foaling last night and I've got a clinic starting at eight."

I stood, stretching my aching limbs, my fingertips brushing the cracked and stained ceiling above, before moving to the sink to rinse my teacup, where Teddy joined me, offering to dry up, our shoulders bumping in the cramped space.

"I have to head in to the office this morning too," Teddy added, turning back to Agnes. "But pop in and see me when you feed Deidre later?"

"Oh yes, that would be nice. I could bake a cake?"

"I have a Victoria sponge with your name on it," Teddy said, touching her arm gently.

"If you're sure?" Agnes's face was eager, her eyes wide with the promise of cake and company. "When do you finish, Hannah? I'll come over then?"

"Oh, er…" My head whipped around wildly, looking to Teddy to help me get out of this, to tell her we weren't together. That I needn't be included in this social neighbourly gathering.

But he was just nodding his agreement. "We can wait for you to finish your evening clinic. When's your last appointment?"

"Six," I said weakly.

"I'll rustle up some dinner for six-thirty." Teddy was beaming triumphantly. "I hope you like salad?"

"Yes, delicious. I can bring some cherry tomatoes from my greenhouse," Agnes said, and I nodded mutely, unsure how I had been coerced into spending time with Teddy against my better judgement. Again.

Yet inside me, a kernel of warmth bloomed, bright and hot. And horrifyingly hopeful.

Chapter Fifteen

After finishing a rather uncomfortable clinic composed largely of panting dogs and red-faced owners, I finally closed down my computer and wiped the examining table over, relieved to be putting my white coat back on its hook. My last patient had been a grumpy and rather bitey ferret, and with bleeding fingers I was now raiding the first aid kit for plasters and antiseptic wipes.

Betsy bustled past, humming the theme from *Jaws* as she went into the dispensary.

"Very funny," I grumbled.

"Doing anything tonight?" she asked, coming back out with a large sack of dog food in her arms.

"I'm having dinner with Teddy."

The dog food slid from her grip and landed on the floor with a thud.

"Teddy Fraser?"

"Yes."

"The same Teddy Fraser who you hated at school?"

"Yes."

"*The* Teddy Fraser you've been moaning about ever since he brought that cat in here the other day?"

"Yes."

"*The* Teddy Fraser who looks at you like he wants to cover you in whipped cream and eat you for dessert?"

"What?"

"The Teddy Fras—"

"Er, thanks, Betsy, I think we've worked out who he is," I said hastily, cutting her off in case she chose to provide any more of her insights in to how Teddy was or was not looking at me.

She sucked in a long breath over her teeth and put her hands on her hips.

"Oooh, I hope you know what you're doing, girl."

"I'm not doing anything other than eating dinner with him."

It was twenty past six and my phone dinged from my back pocket.

Ted: Just checking we're still on for dinner? Agnes is here and we're hungry!

Hannah: Just hanging up my white coat. Be there in five.

Ted: Excellent. Looking forward to it.

Ted: By the way, I like your white coat. You're like a sexy scientist in it.

I rolled my eyes but couldn't help the pleased feeling that was swirling in my chest. His unshakeable need to flirt with me was somehow helping to rebuild my self-confidence, one tiny brick at a time.

"From that look, I'm guessing that's the man himself?" Betsy was studying me intently. I nodded. "Now I'm no expert in the male sex – I've been with Emily getting on for ten years now, and the last time I snogged a man, I was very, very drunk, and it was awful…" She pulled a face, which made me smile. "But I actually think, under all that blustering and swaggering and macho posturing he does, he's actually pretty legit."

"You do?"

"I do. But, Hannah, do you even like him?"

I thought about this and elected to keep the blossoming extent of my crush to myself. Betsy didn't need to know what an idiot I was becoming over him. "We've met Agnes, an old lady who lives in the cottage next to The Rectory, and we're having dinner with her. It's not a date – don't worry."

It's not a date. Obviously.

And I would keep telling myself this over and over, this evening and every day henceforth.

"Mrs Timms? Oh she's lovely, but can be a bit odd." Betsy had picked up the dog food again.

"She seems to be struggling on her own. Do you know her well?"

"Not very. Giles deals with her goaty issues, but I know she's pretty much a recluse."

"I found her in the car park this morning when I came back from a call-out. She was very confused and disoriented."

"Talk to Giles. He might know if she has family or not." Betsy gave me a sympathetic smile then hiked her rucksack onto her shoulder and shifted the dog food onto her hip as she headed for the door. "Showing concern for others is definitely a non-prickly thing, just so you know, practically normal, non-sociopathic behaviour."

"Noted."

"Right, while you might not be having a date tonight, Emily is taking me out for tapas in Cheltenham, so I should be going and making myself beautiful for her. See you tomorrow."

"Have a lovely time," I called out to her retreating back, while I grabbed my keys and did a quick change into shorts and a T-shirt, ready for my not-date with Teddy and Agnes.

Outside, the air was smothering. It felt like it weighed something, wrapping searing fingers into my clothes and hair, bearing down on my skin like a thick duvet with not a breath of wind to ease the discomfort. In the distance, huge, dark clouds roiled across the sky as I pushed open the rickety gates of The Old Rectory and made my way up the garden path.

The front door was ajar.

"Hello?"

Agnes's tinkling laughter filtered through from the back of the house, and I followed the sound, my own face breaking into a grin at the deep rumble of Teddy's returning chuckle. The kitchen was still a bit of a mess, the wallpapering bench in use but with the addition of a huge scrubbed pine table, which was already laid for dinner. There was crusty bread and a rainbow-coloured salad along with a glorious Victoria sponge as the centrepiece.

Teddy had his back to me, and I was given a moment to admire his broad shoulders that tapered to a narrow waist, the navy chino shorts that hugged his backside, feet in flip-flops on the flagstone floors. Even from this angle he made my heart lurch.

I could feel my resistance crumbling and I almost backed out of the room and fled. But then Agnes saw me and her softening expression as our gaze met caused Teddy to turn around. A smile lit up his face.

"There you are," he said softly. He walked over and planted a gentle kiss on my cheek, his fingers faintly caressing the back of my hand. "I hope you're hungry?"

I nodded. And from that one brief touch, I was also about to pass out, it seemed.

The meal was delicious and conversation flowed easily between us. Teddy and I gently teased each other, quickly falling into the flirty banter that seemed to come so naturally, while Agnes told a whole raft of funny and poignant stories, mostly about her time as a journalist on Fleet Street in the 1980s. Her life had been a whirlwind of colour and controversy and she had lived it to the full. She'd retired to the Cotswolds twenty years ago, bought the cottage, and got some goats to keep her company, enjoying a life of peace and solitude. But her words were tinged with regret, like there was something or someone missing, and it seemed to me that there was a chink of hollow emptiness in her smile.

Teddy told Agnes about our time at school together, and she delighted in his tales of mischief on the rugby team and his awe at my dedication to my studies. His self-deprecation was funny and heart-warming as he simultaneously shone a light on my own achievements. As the evening drew in, darkness began to shadow the garden outside and a faint rumble of thunder rattled the windows.

"Perhaps I should walk you home, Agnes. It sounds like it might rain soon," Teddy said.

"Yes, you're right." Agnes sighed. "It's been years since I've had such a lovely evening. Thank you both." She stood and Teddy helped her into her jacket, which had a large hand-knitted poppy drooping from the lapel. "I'm so happy you've moved in here. It's rare to see two people who are so obviously made for each other. That's a treasure that you should hold on to with both hands."

I couldn't look at Teddy. I didn't want to see the derision that would be on his face at such sentimentality when we both knew he was actually only after one thing with me. One thing that would probably be bloody amazing, but would be over and done with and not destined to last a lifetime.

"I'll just be a minute while I make sure that Agnes gets home safely, ok?"

"Ok." I took a sip of water. "Lovely to see you, Agnes."

And I actually meant it. This was definite growth for me – being civil, interested, and polite to another human being. Maybe Betsy was right and I was close to becoming a fully functioning member of society after all.

"You too, dear."

When they left, their forms were highlighted, ghost-like, by the lightning that forked in the distance, a rumble of thunder following closely after. I scooped up the dinner things, washing them in the makeshift sink under the window, while the first huge splats of rain battered the pane. Another bright flash of lightning lit up the garden, so close that the crash of thunder was almost instantaneous. It illuminated a human shape creeping past the window and my usual rationality fled. My brain dreamt up all sorts of heinous serial killers or kidnappers intent on such abhorrent bodily harm that I screamed, dropping the wooden salad bowl that I was drying, and it clattered loudly on the stone floor.

"Hannah! Christ! It's just me," Teddy said, stepping in through the French doors and closing them against the tempest that was starting to rage outside. While I clutched my heaving chest like an over-the-top pantomime dame, he shook the rain from his hair and smirked. "And you say I'm the dramatic one."

The cool air and earthy, petrichor smell had accompanied him inside as the crashing thunder got louder and the windowpanes rattled in protest. More lightning streaked in forks across the inky sky, making the house lights dim momentarily.

"I should go."

"Why don't you wait out the storm here. Have another glass of wine. It would be silly to get soaked running home in this." Teddy's tone was low and persuasive.

"I'm not sure that's such a good idea." Leaning back against the table, I avoided his gaze, my heart thumping in my chest at being alone with him. Staying would definitely be a bad idea.

He sighed and ran his hands over his face.

"About what I said last week, Hannah—"

"It's ok," I cut him off, not wanting to have this conversation. I was worried I might break down and launch myself at him in a desperate bid for affection, giving in to the rampant desire that he seemed to provoke in me. It would have to be kept purely physical, just a fling, of course, in it for a good time and nothing more.

Could I ignore the fact that it would just be meaningless sex? For him at any rate.

I sighed.

Probably not.

Stand firm, Hannah. You can do this.

"I want to apologise," Teddy said.

Ah, right. This is the part where he tells me he didn't mean it. He was just joking. Just practising his flirting technique. No big deal. No need to jump to conclusions.

Part of me was relieved but also more than a little disappointed. But then, what did I really expect? That someone who looked like Teddy, who could have anyone he wanted, would admit his undying love for a freckly-faced geek like me?

"Honestly, it's fine. Don't worry about it," I said to the floor, not daring to look up at him.

"I'm sorry for upsetting you." He paused, then carried on in a low tone. "But I'm not sorry for what I said. I meant it, whether you believe it or not."

"Which bit of it?"

I finally allowed myself to peek at his face.

"Bloody hell, Hannah! All of it! I fancy the pants off you. I always have. You're the most intriguing and infuriating person I've ever met."

He ran his hands over his face, frustration tightening the angle of his shoulders.

"Right."

Is this a compliment?

I couldn't be sure.

"And, while I absolutely would love to whisk you up the

stairs and into my bed so I can do unspeakable things to you, I think I can manage not to ravage you while we wait out the storm."

Is he blushing?

It was hard to see in the dim light of the kitchen. He gave me a small, shy smile.

"Please stay a little longer. I'll be a perfect gentleman. Scout's honour."

"I-I-I..." The stuttering had started again. Words weren't really forming. My brain was functioning about as well as the number four reactor at Chernobyl.

"I had hoped that my wooing might have made you hate me a little less?" He raised an eyebrow enquiringly.

Taking a deep breath and giving myself a mental shake, I managed to say, my voice a quavering whisper, "I don't hate you, Teddy."

"So where are we then, on your sliding scale of liking me?"

"Well, I didn't bring my emasculators tonight." I said with a small smile.

He huffed out a laugh, when suddenly an almighty crash reverberated around us. Thunder boomed and a bright light flashed, the crack so loud and so close it felt as though it had hit the centre of the house. All the lights went out, and another fork of lightning painted jagged, watery shadows on the walls.

"I should check the fuses," Teddy said, and I heard him stumbling around near me. Blinded and then plunged into darkness, my other senses kicked into overdrive and I could smell his citrus fresh scent as if it had been concentrated and bottled and sprayed straight up my nose. The warmth of his body prickled my skin as he passed by.

I was just bathing indulgently in these sensations when there was a fairly loud thump, followed by, "Oww. Shit."

"Are you ok?"

"I just walked into a low door frame," Teddy replied weakly.

"What have you hit?"

"My head," he whispered. "I feel a bit funny, Hannah."

Arms outstretched zombie-like, I felt my way forwards, grasping at the air, until my hands collided with the wall of solid muscle that was Teddy. I may or may not have copped a good feel of his firmly-ridged abdomen beneath his T-shirt on the pretence of trying to work out where he was.

"Is that you?" I whispered, seriously impressed yet again at how toned he was.

"Who else would it be?" he answered with a sigh. "You know, if you wanted to touch me up, you only need say. I'd be a very willing participant."

Right, Hannah, engage brain.

I quickly dropped my hands to my sides.

"Shush. Where does it hurt?"

"My forehead. I think I need to sit down." A chair nearby was scraped back along the flagstone floor and I heard him sit heavily. "There's a torch in a box under the sink."

"Right."

Lightning briefly lit up the kitchen again, while I rummaged around until I found and turned on the torch.

Returning to Teddy and standing between his legs, I gently ran my fingertips over his forehead, sweeping his hair back and finding a small lump appearing above his eyebrow.

"Oof! You've whacked it pretty hard," I exclaimed, and he winced, hissing out a breath as I prodded it. "Sorry."

"It's ok," he replied, cautiously cracking open his eyes and looking up into my face. "When I have a black eye tomorrow, I'll just tell everyone you did it."

I smiled down at him, using the pad of my thumb to gently caress the lump.

"Where are the fuses? I can check them for you."

"Under the back stairs," he replied, his hand brushing against mine where it rested lightly on his forehead.

Flustered by this brief touch, I pulled away and went in search of the fuse box, but even after flicking everything off and on again, there was still no electric, and I returned to the kitchen.

"We should probably go and check on Agnes," Teddy said. "Her house will go up like a tinderbox if she starts lighting candles in there."

"I'll go. You can wait here, Mr Bump."

"No, you definitely won't be doing that on your own. I'm fine."

He stood a little shakily and reached out a hand, gripping my shoulder.

"Teddy, don't bloody well collapse. You're too big for me, and if you go down I'll never get you up again."

He sniggered – a horny teenage-boy snigger. "I'm flattered that you think I'm too big for you, but I reckon you'd definitely manage me."

The dirty connotations were too obvious to be ignored. "Who's got their mind in the gutter now?"

"I let the *going down on you* and *getting me up again* comments slide. So I'd say my mind is spick and span, actually," he said, seemingly steadier on his feet, but he left his hand where it was on my shoulder.

"Of course it is. Come on, Mary Poppins. Let's go and find Agnes."

Chapter Sixteen

Outside, the storm was starting to recede. Its crashing and flashing was now further away, unleashing its wrath on the treeline in the distance, the rain now a steady downpour.

I hadn't brought a coat with me, and when I stepped into the garden, I turned my face up to the sky and allowed the cool water droplets to splash onto my skin, absorbing the freshening quality that the storm had brought to the air.

"Here, have this."

Teddy draped his jacket around my shoulders and pulled the hood over my head so that it flopped across my face, drowning me and partially obscuring my view. I felt like a kid wearing my dad's coat – the hem reached almost to my knees and my hands were hidden in enormously long sleeves as we splashed down the road, which was now lost beneath a river of rain water.

I knocked on Agnes's door. "It's Hannah and Teddy. We've come to check that you're ok."

The flickering of candlelight could be seen through the windows and Teddy's face was pinched and drawn, creases lining his forehead in consternation.

Panicked, he called loudly, "Agnes?"

The door creaked open and she looked bemused to see us on her doorstep.

"Hello, again. What are you doing here?"

"Just checking on you, with the electricity out."

"I'm ok."

Teddy glanced at the ancient-looking candle holder in her hand. The flame danced in the breeze and wax dribbled down the side, drawing his gaze to the piles of newspaper by the door. "Are you sure? We're worried about you on your own with no electricity."

He looked at me, urging me to agree.

"Yes, we are." I nodded, keeping time with Teddy's enthusiastic head-bobbing.

"Ah, I'll be fine. I've got the stove to make myself a cup of tea in the morning, and I have plenty of candles to see me through the night."

Teddy's expression was now thoroughly panic-stricken.

"The surgery has a back-up generator so there will be electricity in the flat," I said, suddenly remembering this fact.

"It does?" both Teddy and Agnes said at once.

"Yes. So, um, we could all go there?"

"Yes!" Teddy exclaimed. "Come on, Agnes. Then you'll be safe until we can contact the electricity company in the morning."

"I'll be fine."

"Please, I won't sleep for worrying about you, and you wouldn't want to be the cause of my lost beauty sleep and deep wrinkles, would you?" he said teasingly, making her smile.

"Oh, you are a worrywart, aren't you? All right. Let me grab a few bits."

Ten minutes later, we were all in the surgery flat, the back-up generator rumbling quietly away in the shed outside. Cups of tea in hand, Agnes yawned widely.

"You can have the bedroom, Agnes. Let me show you." Pushing the door open, we found Lady Fraser sleeping on the bed, and she gave a little chirrup as we entered.

"Oh, Aphrodite! There you are!" Agnes rushed over to the cat, mashing her in a warm embrace. "What scrapes have you got yourself into this time?"

"She's your cat?" I asked.

"Yes! I've been worried sick!"

"Teddy found her with an abscess. It's pretty much all healed now."

"You two are angels, you know that?"

Lady Fraser – Aphrodite, it seemed – was purring ferociously, head-bumping the old lady and dribbling slightly, delighted to be reacquainted with Agnes.

"It was no problem, at all." Teddy was smiling softly. "She's a very brilliant cat."

Closing the bedroom door and leaving Agnes to get ready for bed, we turned back to the living area and had to face the elephant in the room: I only had one bed in my flat, and Agnes was in it. Other than the bathroom, and the kitchen-living area we were standing in, there were no other rooms in my very small abode.

"Where the hell are we going to sleep?"

Teddy looked at me in confusion and rubbed his hand up the back of his neck.

"Don't you have another bedroom?"

I shook my head. "Just the one."

I hadn't really thought this through, had I? I'd lured him here with the promise of electricity and that had forced us into close proximity for the night. Yes, that old chestnut. It was such a cliché – a truly avoidable and unnecessary situation, right?

"Right." He paused. "I could go home?"

Yes, this is exactly what he should do. He should go back to his own house. It would avoid all awkwardness and weirdness between us. He wouldn't get any ideas and I wouldn't unintentionally (absolutely intentionally) reciprocate them. But why wasn't I agreeing with him? Why was my mouth stubbornly remaining shut?

The storm seemed to have returned and was really raging now. A huge gust of wind suddenly battered the building, making the roof tiles rattle above our heads.

"I'm sure we can figure something out."

What am I saying?

My brain was clearly malfunctioning in a spectacular and horrible way.

"If you're sure?"

No, I'm not sure. I'm bonkers. Obviously.

I eyed the small armchairs and wondered if we could contort ourselves into one each and sleep there. But there wasn't very much padding in the seats and if I had to be honest, they smelled a bit like wet dog. Even standing next to them, Teddy made them look as though they were straight out of Lilliput.

Ferreting about in the airing cupboard, I found some extra

pillows and blankets. "We can use these to fashion something on the floor, but it might not be very comfy."

We set about moving the furniture to the edge of the small room, creating as much floor space as possible, laying down the cushions and blankets into two makeshift beds, that were, unavoidably, quite close together. We both stared at the nest we'd made, not looking at each other. It seemed too intimate, too dangerous. And far too far away from being a purely platonic situation.

There were a few moments of silence and an awkward game of eyeball tennis during which we quickly averted our gazes whenever they met, before Teddy cleared his throat and murmured quietly, "Should we just go to bed then?"

"Right. Ok. Righto," I replied before darting away to the bathroom to change into a pair of pyjamas. When I returned to the living room, Teddy was dressed only in his boxers and was in the process of climbing under the covers. He wriggled about to try and get comfortable on the floor-bed under the window.

"Are you sure you're ok down there?" I asked, getting into the other bed, the soft hue of the table lamp casting long shadows on his face.

"Yep, very comfortable, thanks," he said, smiling over at me.

"How's your head?"

"Better."

"Ok, goodnight," I whispered, turning off the light and rolling onto my side to face away from him.

"Goodnight, Hannah."

I lay still for a few minutes, but my mind would not switch off. I was acutely aware of Teddy's scent as it tortuously pervaded my nostrils, and even the sound of him breathing was loud in my ears. I shifted about a bit, trying to get comfy, but eventually I turned back over. My eyes had adjusted to the dark enough that I could pick out his profile just a foot or so away.

"Teddy?"

"Yes?"

"Are you asleep?"

"Clearly not. Why?"

"Oh. I can't get to sleep."

"I'm fairly aware of that fact, but what would you like me to do?"

"Stop breathing."

"That's a bit harsh."

"Well. Stop breathing so loudly. All I can focus on is your loud man-breathing."

Teddy gave a derisive snort. "I'm not doing 'man-breathing'. I'm breathing normally."

"Normal for a walrus with sinusitis," I retorted.

"Fine. I'll try to breathe quietly, like a teeny tiny mouse, if that helps. But if I die of asphyxiation in my sleep, then it's completely your fault."

"I'd really appreciate your rodent-breathing efforts, thanks."

We were silent for a while, and I noticed with amusement that he was indeed trying really hard to breathe inordinately quietly. I closed my eyes, finally starting to relax, until I felt myself drifting towards blissful nothingness, concentrating on my own inhalation and exhalation to settle my mind further.

"Hannah?"

My eyes flew open.

Dammit.

"What is it, Teddy?" I asked with a sigh.

"What happened with Jonathan?"

I remained still for a moment, unsure what to say. I could tell him to mind his own beeswax. Or I could gloss over the horrible truth of the relationship and try to preserve a little dignity. Or I could tell him the whole, ugly story.

And I honestly didn't know which I was going to choose before I opened my mouth.

"He cheated on me with his PhD student."

"Wow. What an arsehole."

"Yes. But it was all my fault, apparently."

"How did you work that one out, Hannah?" Teddy shifted on the floor, his voice getting louder as he turned towards me.

"I didn't need to work it out. He told me as much to my face."

"What an arsehole," he said once more. His voice was indignant – outraged on my behalf.

"Again, yes."

"You're not going to go back to him, are you?"

"I don't know." That was the honest answer because I really didn't know.

"I don't think you should."

"Noted."

The following moments of silence made me believe that the conversation was over. I closed my eyes, staring unflinchingly at the dark insides of my eyelids and fighting down the nausea that still erupted in me whenever I relived the afternoon of that horrible discovery. The feelings of rejection and disgust still lived so close to the surface, even now, so many months later. Yet, how could it be that the lure of my old life was still so strong?

"Is that why you're so reluctant to believe anyone could possibly like you?" Teddy whispered.

"What?"

"Because of what he did … how he blamed you? It wasn't your fault."

I looked up at the ceiling, the faint shapes of the living room furniture just visible in the gloom. The oppressive darkness sat heavily on my chest. "I'm reluctant to believe that charismatic, flirtatious men have the ability to remain faithful so they're best kept at arm's length."

"I see." Teddy sighed. "And you've put me in that category?"

"Firmly."

There were a few moments where we didn't speak, while I tried to squash the shallow tremble of unease that bubbled in my stomach, mesmerised by the loud beating of my heart in my ears as I waited for his response.

"You're wrong, you know," Teddy said eventually.

"About all flirty men being promiscuous?"

"About me." His tone had softened, and there was a quiet, sad edge to his voice.

I didn't know what to say, so I stayed silent, hoping we could move along from this.

"Goodnight, Hannah."

"Goodnight, Teddy."

"Morning, lovebirds!"

Agnes's voice cut through my sleep, waking me to groggy consciousness. The dream of frolicking in a Valencian orange grove disappeared from my mind's eye and I became acutely aware of a heavy weight across my thighs.

Cracking open my eyelids, I found myself tucked firmly against a bare and expansive muscled chest, a smattering of hairs tickling my nose. Long arms were wrapped around me and one leg was thrown over my hips.

Shit.

I made to wriggle away, but Teddy held me tighter, pulling me to him and mumbling incoherently into my hair.

"Teddy, wake up," I hissed, pushing on his torso, but to no avail.

His bear hug still gripped me securely, his breath fluttered strands of my hair over my face. And, while there were certain parts of my anatomy that were doing a celebratory jig at this predicament (especially when considering the *very* firm appendage pressed against my stomach), my mind was screaming extrication protocols left, right, and centre in a desperate bid to save me from further intense mortification. Or from doing something I would most definitely regret. Like nuzzling in closer, or gently biting the skin over his collar bone.

There was only one thing for it. Worming a little space between us and fighting off the tingly dead-arm feeling that was making my brain think my hand was now huge, I reached up, poking tickling fingers along his ribcage and up the underside of his arm, gently stroking and edging ever closer to his armpit, until he jerked away with a strangled, sleepy cry.

"Oh my God, Hannah! Tickling is not a nice way to wake someone up!" he moaned, rolling away from me and smacking his head against the leg of the armchair. "Oww! Shit!"

Having achieved my freedom, I scooched back to my side

of the communal floor-bed that we had shared, letting out a relieved breath and hastily pulling my unruly hair into a bun. I seriously don't know what happens when I'm asleep because my hair ends up so big and crazy, as if it's attended a hirsute rock and roll party all on its own. And it was particularly wild this morning.

Teddy glanced over, rubbing at his temple with long fingers. "Sleep well?"

I nodded. I really had. I'd not woken once in the night, despite my nocturnal wandering and illicit snuggling. "You?"

"Yep. Really well. Even though you talk in your sleep and hog all the covers."

"I do not talk in my sleep."

"Oh Teddy, please let me press myself against your manly body!" he teased, laughing as I threw a pillow at his smug, delighted face. "I knew you wouldn't be able to resist cuddling me at some point."

"Tea?" Agnes called from the kitchen, stopping me from leaping over and smothering him with another pillow.

Teddy yawned and stretched, the muscles of his shoulders and arms flexing in a way that made my mouth actually water, as if I were contemplating a fillet steak in Béarnaise sauce, ready to be eaten. A smouldering gaze met mine – he knew exactly what he was doing. Yet again, my resolve to keep my distance shrivelled a tiny bit more. I was a monumental perv and needed to avert my eyes.

Agnes pottered into the living area with a warm smile on her face and placed two mugs of steaming hot tea on the small coffee table. "Thanks for putting me up last night, but I need to go home and check on my goats."

Teddy smiled and reached for his T-shirt, pulling it over his head.

"I should get going too. I've got some work to do this morning and I want to ring the electricity company again to see where we are with getting the supply back up."

I watched his easy gracefulness as he pulled his jeans on and took a mouthful of tea, placing an arm around Agnes. "Shall I walk you back?"

She nodded gratefully.

"Thanks. Would you be a dear and bring Aphrodite too?"

Teddy looked momentarily confused until the diminutive cat chirruped and rubbed against his ankles. "Yes of course. Aphrodite."

They bustled around, collecting their belongings, while I sat on the floor and watched.

"You haven't forgotten that you're helping me with the kitchen renovations later, right?" Teddy said, holding the door while Agnes gave me a little wave and disappeared down the stairs.

"I am?"

I'd really hoped he'd forgotten about our agreement. No such luck.

"See you at six? You might even have fun. You never know..."

He picked up Aphrodite before giving me a wink and closing the door behind him, leaving me alone, and in a right bloody panic.

Chapter Seventeen

The electricity came back on around lunchtime and Teddy gleefully texted to let me know we were definitely still on to move some kitchen furniture around. So, like the brain-dead people pleaser that I seemed to have become, I headed to his house after work, wearing old clothes and a determined expression. But when I got there, Teddy was no where to be found and all the doors to the house were locked.

Wandering around the back of The Old Rectory, I called out, hoping I might find him in the garden or in the goat shed, but to no avail. After feeding Deidre some dandelions and giving her a quick scratch behind her ears, I pottered back, heading for the French doors into the kitchen. Peering inside, nose pressed against the cool glass, I called his name again, but there was still no sign.

"Where the hell are you?" I muttered, feeling sure he had to be here as his Land Rover was in the drive and his text message had definitely said to come over for six. Sitting on the low stone wall of the ramshackle patio, I pulled out my phone and called his number, hearing the ringing of his phone coming from somewhere deep inside the house. But it went to voicemail.

About to give up and go home, I heard the very faint call of my name.

"Teddy?" I shouted back.

There was another desperate cry, but louder this time, as I followed the sound down a narrow path between the high wall of the surgery car park and around the side of the house.

"Hannah! Down here!"

In the overgrown border of the garden was a smallish opening in the wall of the house at ground level that dropped away into darkness.

"Teddy?"

His face appeared at the bottom of the hole. "I'm so glad you're here." He paused and scratched his head, his shadowed face a little sheepish. "I may have got myself into a slightly tricky predicament in the name of the Goddess of Love."

A loud meow echoed from the hole.

Teddy looked up at me from the dark pit he was in and seemed in two minds whether to fess up about what was going on.

"So…" I prompted, "what's she done?"

"She fell down the coal chute here, and without really thinking I scrambled in to get her, and now we're both stuck in the cellar."

Teddy disappeared from view and the next moment, Aphrodite's patchwork tortoiseshell face was being thrust up towards me. Leaning down to take her from Teddy's outstretched hands, I placed her on the path, where she gave a little shake and trotted off down the garden without a backward glance.

"Are you coming out now then?"

"Yeah, about that." Teddy's embarrassment seemed to have magnified. "You see, I accidentally locked myself out of the house, so I opened the coal chute to see if I could get in that way when Aphrodite jumped in. I thought I could get out through the cellar door into the main house but it's jammed, so I can't open it from this side."

"So you're stuck?"

"Yes."

"Can you not just climb back out the way you went in?"

"No, I've tried and it's not happening. There are no hand holes or ledges, so I can't get any purchase. I'm definitely stuck."

"Rescuing you is becoming a habit, Ted." Incoherent grumbling came back at me from the darkness. "How did you even fit down there in the first place?"

"It was pretty tight."

We both contemplated the situation at hand from our varying viewpoints while the stifling silence and mustiness of the coal cellar wafted up to me from the bottom of the chute.

"Shall I call Henry?"

"No!" he shouted, sounding almost desperate.

"So what do you propose to do, Ted?"

"I have a plan."

I was distinctly aware that I would not like this plan. Call it a gut feeling, if you like, but somehow I knew it was going to involve a significant amount of effort and discomfort on my part.

"And that is?"

"You need to come down the chute and join me in the cellar."

"No."

Teddy carried on as if he hadn't heard me. "I took up some floorboards in the dining room to fix a leaky radiator pipe yesterday and I've found the hole from down here. It's just big enough between the joists that I think you could squeeze through."

"It's still a no. Has no one got a spare key?"

"No, they don't."

"That's a mistake you should rectify."

"Yes, thank you for that pearl of wisdom, Dr Havens. I'll be sure to do that once I'm out of this fucking cellar." I could hear him moving about below me and then his face came back into view. "Right. This is how it will work: I'll lift you up so you can climb through the gap in the floorboards and that will get you into the house. Then you go to the cellar door, un-jam it, and let me out." He paused theatrically. "Ta da! I'm a genius."

"All the actual no's, Ted." There wasn't a single part of this plan I liked – mostly because I'm really quite claustrophobic and the thought of being in the tight confines of the coal chute was making my palms sweat already.

"You kind of have to, Hannah, or else I'll wither away to a stinking corpse in here and then come and haunt you for eternity."

"That's a plan I can get on board with."

"Please?" He paused. "There's a homemade lasagne in the Aga that I'm willing to share."

"You can't buy me with food." I mean, he probably could, actually, because I could already feel my resolve slipping, and he seemed to have picked up on the fact that I'm always really hungry.

"I have Viennetta too, and it's the mint one."

Dammit.

"All right. Fine."

Looking at the point of entry to the cellar, I contemplated how I was going to manage this. Head first? Or feet first? My heart was already thumping along in abject terror at immersing myself into the dark, bottomless hole. My throat closed at the thought of being stuck in there forever, the walls closing in like a vice. And my brain began to fog up with panic.

"Feet in first, Hannah, and I'll catch you at this end because there's a bit of a drop."

Manoeuvring into position, my legs dangling into the hole, I faltered as dread wrapped around me like a cold, wet blanket.

"Ready?" came the voice from the depths, like a merman calling me to my briny death in Davey Jones's locker.

"Of course I'm not bloody ready," I said before taking a lungful of air and hurling myself into the shadowy hole that had already swallowed my feet.

At this point I should make it clear that I expected to slide gracefully down this tunnel of doom and land light as a feather in Teddy's outstretched arms, a picture of elegance and femininity.

It did not, however, happen like this. Not even close.

Primarily this was because the chute was quite a lot smaller than I had anticipated, so that when most of me was inside, I ground to a halt, arms wedged by my sides.

"You've got to keep moving," Teddy called out helpfully.

"No shit, Sherlock! How did you even fit in here?" I muttered in reply, engaging in a worm-esque full-body wriggle in an attempt to propel me further into the cellar. I barely moved, and suddenly an overwhelming fear of imminent death swamped me. An alarming inevitability that I was going to be entombed in this tunnel forever.

I lay there hyperventilating for a moment, until hands grasped my ankles and Teddy began to pull. My clothes caught on a rough patch of concrete as I bumped down the remainder of the chute, and I heard a faint ripping sound that accompanied my frantic breathing and occasional squeaks of surprise. And when I finally emerged out of the hole, landing in a heap at Teddy's feet on the cellar floor, I was acutely aware of a cool breeze wafting about my skin in the region of my derrière.

"Shit. I think I've ripped my jeans."

"Where?"

Hand outstretched, Teddy helped me up and I got my phone out of my pocket, switching on the torch and twisting around to view the carnage, but couldn't quite see what had happened to the back of my jeans.

Teddy craned his neck to get a good view of my spotlighted arse, which was now illuminated like the actual moon by my phone light.

"Oooh, you really have as well."

"How bad is it?" Still unable to see my own bum sufficiently, I moved my phone to better light up the area.

"Let's put it this way, I no longer have to imagine what you look like in pink knickers, Hannah."

"Shit," I said again, exploring with increasing dismay the gaping hole where the pocket of my jeans once resided, fingers brushing against the obviously highly visible cotton of my pants. How fucking marvellous. "Right, well, that's these jeans in the bin when I get home then. Should we try and get out of here?" When Teddy didn't reply, I shone the torch light into his slightly vacant face. "Earth to Edward?"

"Oh, yeah, sorry, where were we?" Teddy's voice sounded like he'd just returned from somewhere very far away indeed.

"Getting out of this cellar, with another of your cunningly cunning plans?"

"Right." He gave himself a little shake and guided me through the damp-smelling cellar towards a chink of light at the other end of the room.

I'm going to have to lift you through that gap in the joists," he said, pointing to a small square above our heads where the missing floorboards revealed the enticing light of the dining room. "It might be a squeeze."

Excellent. Contorting my body into another small gap was exactly what I wanted to do right now. Reaching up as far as I could, my fingertips only brushed the very bottom of the wooden joists, and I had to accept that there was no way I'd be able to haul myself up there without his help.

"Fine. Hold your hands together and I'll use them as a step."

Teddy looked dubious.

"I thought I'd just pick you up and push you through the hole."

Memories of being in Teddy's arms the last time he "just picked me up" flashed through my mind, and the annoying fluttering butterflies of desire started their little dance again. Touching really did need to be kept to a minimum. "I don't think that'll be necessary."

With a sigh he bent down and laced his fingers together underneath my right boot.

"On the count of three, I'll boost you up, ok?"

"Ok."

"One, two, three!" And with an almighty shove, he propelled me airborne and towards the hole above my head.

Grasping the rough wooden joists, I used all my strength to try and clamber through the hole with Teddy grunting below at my incessant wriggling. As I got my head and shoulders through, I attempted to lift myself up and onto the dining room floor, but I just wasn't strong enough.

"Can you go any higher?" Teddy called out.

"No. Boost me again?"

"I can, but it would be better if I pushed you from higher up your body."

"Like where?"

"There is a delectable-looking arse in my face. How about there?"

"In your face?" I replied in horror.

"I'm not complaining, but I reckon this would be over quicker if I pushed you from there."

"Of course it would," I muttered.

"We doing it then?"

"There's really nowhere else?"

"There are plenty of places I can think to put my hands, but right now I think this would be the most effective launchpad to get you through that hole."

"Fine." I tensed in anticipation as he repositioned his large hands to snugly cup my backside, the warmth of his skin against mine where the jeans had ripped sending a ripple of heat through my whole body.

"You have a spectacular bum, Hannah."

"Just bloody push it, will you?"

"Push it real good?" He sang, then chuckled at his own hilarity and 1980s Salt-N-Pepa reference, and I begrudgingly began to smile again. That tiny kernel of self-confidence that had been squashed before grew a little brighter for just a minute because of Teddy, because of his merciless flirting, before he steadily and skilfully shoved my entire body through the gap.

With more of my torso now out of the hole, I was able to drag myself up and onto the dining room floor, where I lay for a minute amidst the shafts of sunlight and the comforting, bookish smell of the house.

"I'll see you at the cellar door in the back passage, Hannah. It's the one next to the old servants' staircase."

"The back passage?"

"Honestly, get your mind out of the gutter. It's what I call the corridor off the kitchen that leads to the utility room."

"Right." Unlike me at this point, he was able to think some non-arse-related things then.

Got it. Good.

Getting to my feet, I went through the house, marvelling as always at the glorious parquet floors and oak panelling that had been witness to at least a century of history. I inhaled deeply the glorious atmosphere that imbued every inch of the building, making it feel like a living, breathing thing and not just a house. In the kitchen, an old half-glazed door stood slightly ajar to the side of a huge pine dresser and, pushing it open, I entered a corridor of rooms joined together in a chain that skirted the back of the house. Next to a narrow spiral stone staircase stood another door with paint pots, sacks of plaster mix, and used tools wedged against it, and a hook and latch barring it from being opened from the other side. Lifting the items and stacking them carefully at the foot of the stairs, I cleared a path to the wooden door and unlatched the rickety metal catch, tugging the handle but it wouldn't budge.

"Ted, are you there? The door's clear now, but you'll need to give it a shove from your side."

"Righto," came the muffled reply. With a grunt and the telltale screech of wood against stone, the door slowly opened towards me and Teddy emerged from the gloom with a wry smile. "What do you think of my back passage then?"

"Better than expected," I replied and couldn't help the bubbly little snort of laughter that erupted from my nose.

After we'd moved some new cabinets for the kitchen into the house from the garage, and I'd held various pieces of worktop and screws while Teddy worked, we eventually sat down for dinner, tired and distinctly grubby. I had to admit that Teddy was a rather excellent cook as I stuffed my own bodyweight of lasagne into my mouth, barely taking time to breathe between bites.

"I think you might have to roll me home," I sighed, patting my belly and leaning back in my chair.

"Bribery with food is my top-tier flirting technique."

I undid the button on my jeans to relieve some of the pressure on my bulging abdomen. "It's working."

Teddy smirked. "I can see that. Are you going to remove those tattered jeans entirely?"

"Shush. Let me sink into this food coma in peace, you heathen."

Teddy scooped the remainder of the lasagne into a spare bowl and covered it with tin foil, placing it on the counter near the fridge to cool. "I'll drop this into Agnes tomorrow for her to reheat. I forgot to say that I saw her this morning and I'm a bit worried about her."

"Why?"

"Well, after that incident in the car park the other day, and the state of her house, don't you think we should contact someone about helping her?"

"I spoke with Giles about her and I'm not sure she wants any help, Teddy." I was uncomfortable thinking about this. She was struggling, undoubtedly, but in her lucid moments she was as capable as anyone I'd ever met. I felt her independence at my very core and saw her unshakeable tenacity as something to which I could only aspire to on my very best days.

"Not social services, but family?"

"Perhaps, if you can find anyone. Do you think she'd be upset if we went behind her back though?"

Teddy looked doubtful for a moment. "I don't know. I'm just not sure I can sit back and do nothing."

"Well, why don't you talk to her about her family. Perhaps her husband's brother is still alive? See where you get to with it."

Teddy nodded and took another sip of wine, seemingly placated that I was on board with his do-gooding. "You haven't forgotten that it's the garden party tomorrow, have you? We need to leave by 8pm."

"Yes, right, of course."

I'd completely forgotten about this. I'd blanked out the horror of the scenario from my mind in a vain attempt at hoping this obligation would go away. No such luck.

"You might even have fun. You never know."

The withering look that appeared unbidden on my face must have been a sight to behold because Teddy roared with laughter. He stood up and pulled me reluctantly to my feet.

"Come on. I'll walk you back to yours so we can both get clean in your shower."

Chapter Eighteen

"Betsy? I need your help."

"Hey, girl. What's up?" Her reply to my panicked phone call was calm, her voice a smooth, welcoming shot of tranquillity to my fraught nerves.

"Are you going to the Business Community garden party tonight?"

"Oh, yeah, I am! Giles asked me as Jenny didn't want to go. He said you were going with someone else. Are you?"

"I'm meant to be, but I'm having second thoughts and serious wardrobe issues." I glanced at all of my clothes that were strewn across my bed, haphazardly spread like I'd been burgled and the villain had left in disgust at my severe lack of anything even remotely fashionable to steal. In fact, he'd probably just nipped out to Marks & Spencer to get me a decent set of underwear and a pair of trousers that weren't jeans. "I need your help."

"I'll be right over." The phone went dead and the heavy weight of hopelessness started to lift just a little.

She arrived precisely twenty-three minutes later and grilled me as to my invite. When she found out Teddy had asked me, her eyes went round, like teacups, their dark, soulful depths widening in surprise and pleasure.

"Then we need to go shopping and get you something to knock his socks off."

"That won't be necessary," I spluttered, thinking that I really didn't need to give Teddy any hint of an idea that I'd dressed up for his benefit. He'd be unbearable, and I really didn't want to give him any idea of the astronomical levels of attraction I seemed to be developing for him.

"Nonsense. I saw this stunning green dress in the vintage shop that would look so beautiful on you."

And that was that. No brokering a deal, or telling me that the slightly wrinkled and moth-eaten dress I'd worn for my graduation ball ten years ago would be ok. Nope, I was whisked into town so that my hair could be cut and my eyebrows shaped, courtesy of Betsy's friend Melinda. Then, the most beautiful emerald-green silk halter-neck dress was carefully wrapped in tissue and placed reverentially into a posh paper bag, along with a pair of silver strappy sandals. My purse left significantly lighter.

It was getting close to 7pm when Betsy finally left, having worked her magic with some make-up which made my eyes look huge and doe-like and my skin fresh and dewy with a hint of colour to my cheeks and lips. I stared and stared at myself in the full-length mirror, not fully able to process the reflection that gazed back at me. Not beautiful, no, but striking perhaps? The angular points of my face had been softened and my freckles were no longer the aspect that drew my eye, even though they were as prominent as ever.

I jumped when the door buzzer rang and, taking a deep, fortifying breath, I opened the door… To James Freaking Bond.

My mouth fell open, in a manner that was not at all ladylike. Teddy was in a tuxedo and bow tie, his hair tidy and styled, the gently curling lengths tamed and flattened; his beard trimmed and neat, and he was smelling completely and utterly delicious. He looked like an A-list movie star.

Damn him.

When I dragged my gaze back to his face (desperately trying to distract myself from my musings about his other impressive attributes that filled out his suit), an expression I couldn't quite place was flitting over his features. He let out a long breath, sounding almost like he was blowing a raspberry, then ran his hand through his hair, dishevelling it in a delightful, roguish way.

"You look amazing, Hannah," he said softly. "Stunningly, unequivocally beautiful."

I flushed and let my hair fall over my face.

"It's just the dress, and make-up – Betsy helped me and she's a wonder at it." I paused and then huffed a sad little laugh. "Mutton dressed as lamb, right?"

Teddy frowned, the crease between his eyebrows deep and severe. "No, don't do that. Don't put yourself down."

His tone startled me. The rough timbre of his voice was unexpected, shaking through me with its sincerity and gravity.

"You're beautiful – why don't you believe it?" he said.

Taking a step towards me, he went to reach for my hand, before thinking better of it and running his fingers through his hair again.

"We should go," I said, deflecting the unease that we were both obviously now feeling, that frisson of tension that seemed to erupt when the jokes subsided, an undercurrent that perhaps there was something else going on, something deeper or more serious between us than mere flirting. But I pushed those thoughts away, still unable to thank him for the compliment, unable to take it at face value or see it as anything more than a throwaway comment that he didn't really mean.

"Right."

Teddy stepped back again, holding the door with one hand and I squeezed past him and down the steps, letting him pull it closed behind us.

Outside in the surgery car park, in the space next to my estate car, was a very slinky red Jaguar whose indicators flashed as Teddy pressed the key fob.

"That's a very silly car," I said, unable to help a derisive snort from escaping.

"Funny – Clara said exactly the same thing the first time too, apparently," Teddy muttered, opening the passenger door for me. Then, in response to the quizzical eyebrow tilt I levelled at him, he continued, "This is Henry's car. I thought I'd take you to the party in style rather than in my battered old Land Rover."

In the process of contorting my body into the car, the split in my dress opened up to mid-thigh, flashing more leg than I was strictly comfortable showing. Catching Teddy's rakish grin, I tutted and wagged a finger.

"Oi! You're meant to be being a gentleman!"

"Sorry, but that was an unexpected and delightful view from this perspective." He laughed and closed the door jogging around the front of the car and sliding into the driver's side.

"I think I'd prefer the Land Rover," I said, scowling and folding my arms over my chest as he buckled his seatbelt.

"Whereas I'm liking this car rather a lot now."

The smirk was unmistakeable, a twinkling mischievousness that turned my thought processes to slush so that they slopped around in my head, and made me entirely forget my peevishness. Which was pretty bloody annoying, actually.

We pulled in to the grand circular drive of the Fraser family home just as the sun was starting to get low in the sky. Glittering fairy lights adorned the paths around the garden and the golden house was lit up with the last throws of sunlight, marred only by long shadows cast by the tall trees in the grounds. Beautifully dressed people were gathering in groups, chatting casually. One woman in a stunning red dress tossed her hair coquettishly, touching the arm of an older man who was transfixed. The sound of laughter and music drifted into the car, the noises of a party, and all the connotations that brought with it. And I froze.

"I can't do this, Teddy," I whispered from my seat, the icy claws of apprehension holding me prisoner. The desire to hide and never be seen was overwhelmingly present in my brain.

Turning to face me, Teddy reached over and laid his warm hand over my militantly clenched fist, gently rubbing his thumb over my knuckles.

"Yes, you can."

"I really can't."

Teddy leant in closely, moving his hand to gently cup my

face. His gaze darted to my lips for the briefest of moments, before meeting my wide-eyed, startled stare.

"I'm right here, and will be by your side all night, ok?"

"Will you do all the talking?"

He chuckled. "No. Remember your flirtation training – the words will come from inside you, Hannah-san."

"Did you just badly quote the *Karate Kid* movie? What are you, Mr Miyagi now?"

Teddy grinned. "Yes, and later we'll be waxing Henry's car and catching flies with chopsticks. I hope you're ready."

The tension seemed to be dissolving from my shoulders as a reluctant smile spread like golden syrup, coupled with a strange sensation of relief and something else, like a fire blooming in my chest. As I looked into Teddy's eyes, their blue depths warm and kind, his fingers lightly brushed my cheek again, before he dropped his hand back into his lap.

"Should we do this then?"

I nodded, an almost imperceptible twitch of my head, all the while giving myself a mental slap. Peopling shouldn't be this hard. I'd delivered lectures on limb biomechanics in racehorses to an auditorium full of students, and presented my PhD thesis on degenerative joint disease to two of the world-leading experts in the field, for fuck's sake. I could do small talk with local business people and not freak the hell out. But even this mental shakedown couldn't avoid the real issue: I had no science or research to hide behind and I wasn't here to deliver information or offer advice in a professional capacity. I was here to get to know people, to be nice, and to let people get to know me, all the while reining in the perpetual need to be defensive or deflective, to turn attention away from me as a person, and to prevent any actual real scrutiny. I had nothing here, no protective shield.

Apart from Teddy. Teddy and his glowing, iridescent personality and infinite charm, which I sincerely hoped would blind all onlookers and leave me unseen. It was the only hope I had of getting through this evening unscathed.

With a final encouraging look and squeeze of my hand, Teddy got out and opened my door, helping me to emerge from the car in a much more elegant fashion than how I'd got into it. Walking towards the party, heads turned to stare at us – well, at Teddy; they turned to stare at Teddy, let's be honest, and I felt myself begin to shrink, letting him absorb the attention, while I lurked sheepishly in his shadow. Playing my role as a funny little troll creature in make-up and a green dress, hiding behind his back.

But Teddy wasn't having any of it. He tugged me forwards, placing my hand in the crook of his elbow, and began heading for a group of people. My heart thundered in my ears, loud and crashing, in a crescendo of panic. This was really happening. Socialising was a go.

As we neared the group, one of the men turned to look at us and to my utter relief I came face to face with Henry, who smiled warmly and nodded at Teddy.

"I hope my car's still in one piece, dickhead?" He turned to me then and said, "Hey, Hannah. Nice to see you again."

I was now faced with quite a large number of people, all staring at me curiously. Recognising Clara, who gave me a big grin and a funny little wave, I made a beeline for her, the warmth she generated radiating outwards and drawing me in. There was a lot of inter-Fraser hugging, as I noticed Dan and

Tom Fraser, Henry and Teddy's other brothers, also in the group, as well as an Asian couple, and a tall, dark-haired chap who stood slightly to one side and looked as uncomfortable as I felt.

"Hi! I love your dress! You look amazing!" Clara leant in and whispered, "These bloody Frasers and their relentless hugging compulsion! I'll introduce you to everyone else and you might just escape being mauled to death."

With a grateful smile, I stepped back and she began talking again. "You all know Ted, and this is Hannah Havens, one of the local vets here and Ted and Henry's friend from school." Tilting her head towards the other Fraser brothers, she carried on, "I think you remember Dan and Tom?" I nodded and gave them a wave and they raised their glasses in reply. "This is Simmy Anand and her husband, Bhavin, and this is Oscar Moretti." She gestured at the glamorous Asian woman and the tall, strained-looking man. "I work with these two at Pharmavoltis."

"Hi."

"I'll get us a drink," Teddy said, casually wandering off into the crowd to intercept a waiter, leaving me standing next to Oscar Moretti. I quickly started to realise that if I was a prickly hedgehog, then he was most definitely a bristling, indignant porcupine. Clutching his wine glass menacingly, he glanced at me and then away, his straightened spine and rigid shoulders unnaturally still and tense. Even the molecules of air around us seemed to be avoiding him. I briefly wondered if we'd been separated at birth – except he was very tall and Italian-looking and I was of average height and decidedly Nordic. But otherwise, twins. Obviously.

With this apparent similarity bolstering my confidence, I

said the first thing that came into my head. "You're not really enjoying being here, are you?"

He turned so quickly that I'm pretty sure he gave himself whiplash.

"What makes you say that?"

"The look on your face."

Where the hell is my brain-to-mouth filter?

Teddy was going to kill me, but I was distinctly aware of Clara chuckling quietly next to me.

Oscar narrowed his eyes. "You don't look so happy yourself now that your boyfriend's gone."

"He's not my boyfriend."

"No?" Oscar Moretti seemed to be losing interest in the conversation.

Well, this is going spectacularly badly...

But Clara gave me an encouraging and sympathetic smile and a little elbow bump, seemingly urging me to carry on with this feeble attempt at socialising with a stranger. And he was strange, even if I did recognise a sort of kindred spirit in him. She whispered, not actually that quietly, in my ear, "Please talk to him. We don't let him out of the laboratory much and it shows."

Turning back to the object of my experiment, my gaze flitting over the designer stubble and impossibly dark brown eyes, I decided that honesty was the best option here. Truth or bust.

What's the worst that could happen?

He'd already judged me to be a social pariah. Or an idiot.

I can only go up in his estimation, right? And does it really matter what he thinks of me anyway?

Right. Shit. Ok, here goes.

"No, he's not my boyfriend. He's teaching me how to be nice to other people, in an attempt to stop me being perceived as prickly."

Without missing a beat he replied, "It's not working."

I snorted with laughter and watched as the ghostly hint of a smile twitched over his lips.

"My lessons have only just started – this is my first test."

"It shows."

"I'm trying to make people like me."

Oscar took a sip of his wine. "If I tell you I like you, will you stop talking to me?"

"Yes, I promise." I hesitantly went to shake his hand, which he clasped firmly but briefly. "And might I suggest that you enrol in Ted's people-skills masterclass? It might help you with your facial expression. And your conversational ability. I'm sure he'd take you on – he loves a challenge."

At this Oscar laughed – actually laughed – his features lighting up and changing to something almost angelic, warm, and open.

"Fine, Hannah. I find you to be a faintly likeable human being."

"Thank you. Do you want me to put a word in for you with Ted??"

Teddy was coming back towards us with two glasses, smiling and chatting with people as he went.

"I suppose it couldn't hurt, actually…" Oscar murmured, a hint of something troubling flashing behind his eyes before a mask of cold indifference shuttered down over his face again.

"Should we mingle, Hannah?" Teddy asked, handing me a glass of Pimm's complete with bobbing fruit and a straw.

My returning look of horror must have been like the white

mask from the *Scream* films because our little group collectively gave me a sympathetic nod, and Clara reached out to touch my arm.

But it was Oscar who spoke. "I have to say, despite your very unusual and direct approach, you are not at all prickly, and we most definitely shouldn't keep your unique and amusing conversational skills to ourselves."

He took a sip of wine and Clara and Henry stared at him agog. He merely shrugged, hiding a small smile behind his glass.

Chapter Nineteen

"Making friends?" Teddy enquired as we crunched down a gravel path lit with candles in glass jars and strings of fairy lights above our heads.

"Oscar has the same affliction as I do."

"In what way?"

Teddy touched his hand to the small of my back and ushered me through an archway in a privet hedge and out onto a large lawned area, where people were milling around and a string quartet was playing.

"He doesn't like people or socialising. I was instinctively drawn to him."

"Were you?" His voice had become a bit gravelly.

"Yes, and turns out that making conversation by insulting someone can actually work – who knew?"

"You insulted him?" Teddy spluttered, starting to laugh.

"Sort of. I suggested that his face and conversational ability needed some work, and that maybe you could help him."

Teddy stopped, now snorting with laughter. "You really said that? To someone you've never met before?"

"Yes, I really said that."

An answering smile tugged at my cheeks, burning, itching to break into a huge grin.

"Well, let's see if we can hone your abilities on someone a little more 'normal' than Oscar Moretti, shall we?"

On the other side of the hedge were Giles and Betsy, sipping prosecco and chatting with Mrs Wainscott and her very large husband – the disgruntled owners of Bridgit, the snappy dachshund.

Excellent.

"Oh look. There's Giles, and Betsy. We should start there, right?" Teddy said, steering me towards the little group. The expression on my boss's face was a marvellous picture of horror, and he subtly began shaking his head. But Teddy was like a steam roller and ploughed on towards them, smiling and dragging me along with him. "This will be an easy first conversation."

"Well, actually, Ted, not really—"

"Oh, don't be defeatist. This'll be fine."

"But—"

"Hannah!" Betsy exclaimed, and the Wainscotts looked up, obliterating any hope of avoiding this splendid car crash of an encounter.

"Hannah, Ted, so nice to see you," Giles said in a strangled voice.

"And you." Teddy turned and beamed at Mrs Wainscott, who, I think, may have actually swooned a bit when he shook her hand. *Interesting.* When he grasped Mr Wainscott's meaty paw, he carried on. "I'm Ted Fraser. I live next door to Giles and Hannah's surgery."

"Fraser? Jim Fraser's son?"

"Yes. You know Hannah Havens, do you?"

Teddy ushered me forwards, forcing me from my attempt to hide behind his back and pretend I was anywhere else but here, the fiery pits of hell being entirely preferable right now.

"Yes, we do." Mrs Wainscott narrowed her eyes and glanced at Giles, who was trying, and failing, not to look like a caged rabbit about to be dropped into a stew.

A slightly awkward silence ensued, and Teddy lightly brushed my fingers with his.

Oh shit. It's my turn to speak isn't it?

I felt my mouth begin to open, and hoped to hell that whatever was about to come out wasn't going to be the final nail in the coffin of my dwindling clinical career.

Clearing my throat, I said, "How is Bridgit, Mrs Wainscott?"

"Fine, thank you for asking." Her tone was terse and Mr Wainscott had puffed himself up slightly next to her.

"Is Bridgit your patient?" Teddy asked mildly, innocently opening that can of wriggly, acrid worms.

"Yes. Mr and Mrs Wainscott have a rather beautifully bred dachshund. Her father was a Crufts champion," I replied cautiously.

Giles, Betsy, and Mr and Mrs Wainscott all gaped at me.

Oh, balls, what've I done now?

"I have no idea about dog breeding," Teddy said, "but even I've heard of Crufts. You must be very proud of her?"

Mrs Wainscott nodded.

"We're working very hard to keep her as healthy as possible, aren't we, Mrs Wainscott?" Betsy said quietly.

The old lady turned towards me, a flash of regret and acknowledgement flaring in her warm brown eyes. "Yes."

"She truly is a lovely dog, a real credit to you."

I was being sincere – we'd had our run-ins but she wasn't the first and would not be the last dog to try and take a chunk out of my hand on the consulting table. I hoped she could hear this in my voice. "It's a pleasure to see you both in my consulting room."

"Thank you, Hannah. That means the world to me." Mrs Wainscott gave a little sniff, and tentatively touched my arm. "She's been to see the stud dog, so I'll be in next week for her pregnancy check. I'll be sure to ask Jenny to book us in with you."

The smile that lit up my face was genuine and was quickly returned.

"That's very exciting. I look forward to seeing you both."

Giles blew out a long breath and everyone turned to look at him in surprise. He raised his glass in a toast and everyone returned the gesture in complete confusion. "To Bridgit and her puppies."

"To Bridgit and her puppies," we all replied in unison.

"I hope you don't mind, but there are a few other people I'd like Hannah to meet," Teddy said, gently cupping my elbow as my sign to leave. "Excuse us, won't you?"

There was a lot of nodding, and a few murmurs of "lovely couple" that I didn't quite catch as I was manoeuvred away from the group.

"Was that your complaining client?" Teddy murmured out of the side of his mouth as we walked away.

"Yes, one of them."

"You did great."

"It could have gone either way. Giles nearly passed out from the tension," I joked, and Teddy laughed.

"He should have a little more faith in you."

We began to circle the lawned area, Teddy introducing me to various people, all charm and civility when talking to businessmen and women, some of whom were clients at our practice. And do you know what? With each new person I talked to, it became easier. My face began to relax and my brain no longer freaked out as much, each conversation relying less and less on Teddy to prompt me or support me. People smiled and laughed at my intentional jokes, no one recoiled in horror, and no one threatened to write my boss a strongly worded email of complaint. And not one person compared me to a spiny-coated small mammal – at least, not to my face. Could it be that I was actually getting good at this?

No, surely not.

Once we'd completed a full circuit of the party, we ended up in a darkened corner close to where the band was playing.

"Will you dance with me?"

"Ah, Teddy, I'm really not very good at that shit."

"Just follow me. I'll help you."

"Advanced flirting technique?"

"Postgraduate level. Only for the most gifted of students."

Teddy smiled and took my hand.

The sun had fully gone down now and a bright moon hung in the sky, a giant silvery bauble lighting the night, casting monochrome shadows across the grass and dappling my feet as I gazed self-consciously down at them. Teddy stepped in closer, tilting his head below mine to force me to meet his gaze.

"Come on. You can do it."

"Ok," I whispered.

This was a really bad idea and I knew it, but I didn't seem able to stop myself moving towards him. The warmth of his body radiated through his tux, drawing me in like an industrial-strength magnet. As he gathered me to him, a slight pressure on my waist, his other fingers curling around mine, I knew, with total clarity, that I was absolutely bloody well done for.

"Everything ok?" he murmured into my ear, ruffling strands of my hair, so that they tickled my neck and goose pimples rose in a line on my skin.

"Mmm hmmm."

I was barely coherent. All my senses were assaulted at once, overloaded with all the input he was throwing in my direction, but my feet seemed to just magically follow Teddy's as he slow-danced me steadily in circles on the grass. I was eminently grateful that at least I had some motor function remaining, because I seemed to be experiencing significant wiring issues in the rest of my brain.

We started off with our bodies barely touching, but slowly the gap between us closed until my dress brushed the front of his jacket, and I could feel his cheek close to my hair, his breathing light and regular. With my nose this close to the crook of his neck, his scent was at its most intoxicating, citrus and spice, coupled with fresh male skin and pheromones. I wasn't sure what the ingredients were, but it was as if he'd bottled sexual attraction and liberally sprayed it on himself.

The feel of his body under my hand suddenly seemed intrusively intimate and my mind was unable to think of anything but the hard, broad muscles of his shoulder and chest beneath his clothes. I couldn't escape the occasional bump of our hips, but it was the firm hold he now had on my body that was elevating my blood pressure to cardiac instability levels.

"You did really well with the peopling, you know," Teddy murmured, breaking the spell and allowing me to breathe again, banishing the impending girly faint that was threatening to engulf me.

"I managed not to insult or offend any of Chipping-on-the-Water's key business owners, so Giles will definitely see that as a win."

He huffed a laugh, causing warm air to tickle across my neck and send an electric shock down my spine. Leaning away from me he looked into my eyes.

"I think you've learnt all I am able to teach you, Hannah-san."

"Is this the end of our student–teacher relationship then, Mr Miyagi."

Teddy smiled and stared at my lips. "I really hope so."

"You do? Was I that bad a student?"

"You were pretty awful."

"Thanks! Don't spare my feelings, will you?"

Teddy shifted slightly, both hands dropping to my waist, so that I instinctively reached up around his neck. Our bodies were now aligned and close, inescapably face to face.

"I spend an inordinate amount of time trying to work out your feelings, Hannah."

"You do?"

"I do. It's like a full-time scientific study for me."

"And what conclusions have you drawn?"

A flash of uncertainty crossed his face, but then the usual charm and swagger returned and his gaze darkened.

"I think I will only know your true feelings by retracing our steps back to my eighteenth birthday party. Perhaps we should revisit that particularly profound moment in my life and see how it plays out a second time?"

"Can I give you some advice? Don't call me a porn star – it won't go well."

With a soft laugh, he edged in closer. "Oh no, I'd never say something like that. Hot librarian perhaps?"

Our noses were almost touching and it felt like the world around us had faded to black; as if we were the only ones here dancing in this dark corner of a moonlit garden.

"I think hot librarian is better, but still not ideal."

"No?"

I could practically taste him, we were that close together – the faint aroma of Pimm's, the long-anticipated feel of his mouth just millimetres from mine. His unique flavour, one that had been seared onto my memory, was now just a hair's breadth away. Tantalisingly close.

"No," I confirmed

"Mmmmm." The sound rumbled over my skin, my lips parting involuntarily. "How about the ravishing vet?"

"Now you're talking…"

His grip on my body tightened and I was lost. I knew that at this moment he could do exactly what he wanted and I would be entirely complicit. I let out a little sigh, a strange gusty sound that made his pupils widen.

"Teddy?"

The voice was like a bucket of ice-cold water on my libido, and I instinctively jumped back, ripping out of Teddy's grasp and turning away, the familiar feelings of acute embarrassment and self-loathing spiking within me.

"What are you doing loitering in this dark corner?" came the voice again.

"Hello, Mandy."

It couldn't have been anyone else really, could it? Teddy reached out and tried to take my hand, but I shrank away, doing my best to meld into the hedge behind us and disappear.

"Oh, I didn't realise you had company. Is that Hannah Havens?"

My name was said with a mixture of surprise and revulsion, like she had just discovered a slug in her mouth.

"Hi," I said quietly.

"Yes, Hannah and I came together. How are you? Having a nice time?" Teddy's voice was smooth and charming, but standing this close to him I could sense a very faint undercurrent of tension in his posture.

But Mandy was oblivious. She batted her eyelashes and her ample cleavage threatened to spill out of a very low-cut dress as she stepped closer.

"I'm good, but disappointed that you haven't called me yet."

"Sorry, I've been very busy – you know how it is."

"I'll always make time for you," she replied in a seductive tone that was really not necessary.

"Good to know."

I remained rooted to the spot, feeling the uncomfortably familiar feeling of being a third wheel – not just a gooseberry but an entire gooseberry bush. I wondered when he was going to tell her to bog off, but he didn't. He just smiled broadly at her and she seemed to melt into a pile of pink chiffon-coated gloop in front of him.

"I'm just going to find the loo," I said, from my position in the bush, theatrically rolling my eyes.

"Ok, just wait. I'll—"

"Sounds like a great idea, Hannah," Mandy answered, cutting Teddy off and not even bothering to glance in my direction.

"Catch you later, Ted."

Bitterness laced every word. Hurt creeping back in that he would let this happen all over again; that *I* had let this happen all over again. Why hadn't I learnt anything from his previous form? Of course he'd always bow down to the cool gang, and most definitely avoid any real association with Nerdy McNerdface, here.

"Hannah, wait—"

"I'll be fine. I'm sure I can find my own way. I'm a big girl."

And with that I stomped off, allowing these old school chums to get reacquainted.

Because, once again, I was the humiliated teenager, the odd one out, leaving in a huff. A spooky re-enactment of Teddy's eighteenth birthday party, just as he'd asked for.

Chapter Twenty

Seething. That's a good word, isn't it? When your skin feels like it'll crawl completely off your body, the intense dislike and humiliation causing a physical reaction in your outermost layer, while simultaneously wondering if your blood might really be boiling you alive on the inside. Yes, well, that's exactly the level I was at. Mostly at Mandy, but also at myself and more than a tiny bit at Teddy. But in reality I had no right to feel like this. He was just being his usual affable self, so why did it make me so mad? Why hadn't he told her to get lost? Why had he picked her? Again.

Washing my hands in the basin of the posh trailer of portable toilets, I glanced in the mirror. Prickly pufferfish mode was engaged. A spiky sticking plaster of stroppiness to cover the intense embarrassment and disappointment I was feeling, accompanied by the horror of being transported right back to being eighteen and knowing that Mandy's awfulness went unseen by everyone but me. Still.

I knew that despite the make-up and the fancy clothes, I

was still as unattractive as I'd always been. And my heart crumbled away inside me like dust as the mocking voice in my head berated me for ever considering myself to be anything other than a freckly-faced geek. My expression was drawn into a deep scowl, so that even I shied away from the fearsome-looking woman in the mirror and scrubbed my lipstick away with a tissue.

But do you know the worst thing? The main thought that was running through my head? And it was a truly disastrous one. But there it was, spinning like a top in my brain. The only thing I didn't feel able to let go of was that the last time she'd barged in on us, at least I'd managed to get a snog first.

See? Ridiculous, right? It would be better not to think like that. It should be a relief that we hadn't actually kissed this time, that there was nothing to miss and nothing to lament or apologise for. Nothing to fuel the fire inside me further. I should be grateful that Mandy had turned up when she did, right? She saved me from my hormones because no good could come of fanning the flames of this absurd crush.

After drying my hands, I teetered down the little metal steps of the trailer and out onto the gravelled courtyard, deciding to try to find Henry and Clara, via the bar, when I was instantly engulfed in pungent perfume, long talon-like nails gripping my wrist and tugging me backwards.

"Hey! I want to talk to you."

"I have nothing to say to you, Mandy."

"Why do you have to be such a bitch? You haven't changed, have you?"

I faced her. She was a little taller than me, especially in the skyscraper heels she had on, but I was not going to be intimidated by her.

"Oh I definitely have changed, believe me. There's no way I'm going to tolerate any of your bullshit tonight, that's for sure."

"Not a change for the better then." Mandy pouted and narrowed her eyes at me. "I understand that you were jealous of me back in school, but I have a real chance with Teddy again now, so I'd appreciate it if you could back the hell off."

Peeling her fingers off my wrist I stepped away.

"He's all yours Mandy. I don't want him."

Lies, it was all lies.

But I couldn't let this slide without trying to keep hold of some of my dignity. Not when I'd nearly snogged his face off twice in the last few weeks.

"Is that what you think? You think *you* get to decide?" she sneered. "Someone like *you* doesn't get to choose someone like *him*. You should be grateful he pities you enough to even bother talking to you."

"Is that right?"

"Yes."

"In which case, why do you need me to back off? I'm no threat to you."

Mandy lurched at me, wagging her finger in my face.

"Because, you spotty-faced freak, he feels some sort of obligation to be nice to you and has done since we were teenagers. God knows, I don't understand it, but it means that whenever you're around he's unable to go out and actually have some fun with someone who's in his league … visually, if you get what I mean."

"I'm reading you loud and clear."

Ah, another blow to my fragile confidence. My ever-present brain gremlin nodded sagely.

Yes, settle yourself back in for the long haul of self-loathing, my old friend.

"You're holding him back and you should just fuck off and let him be happy."

"If that's what you think, it must be true," Betsy stepped out from around the side of the toilet trailer, an expression of pure fury on her face.

"Oh look. Your butch little sidekick come to dry your snivelling tears. You two are made for each other."

Her expression was smug, self-satisfied, and eminently slappable. But I didn't. I resisted, instead schooling my features into my best withering look and preparing to extricate myself before all my self-worth shrivelled away to nothing.

Contemptuously, Mandy checked her nails and carried on, "Maybe you should have been going after girls all along, Hannah."

"I don't understand your problem, I really don't. We're not at school anymore, and swanning about as the school bully is pathetic when you're a teenager but downright fucking tragic when you're in your thirties," Betsy said, standing beside me in a show of solidarity, like she always had, picking me up each time I got knocked down like this by Mandy or anyone else.

"Bully? What are you talking about? Who the hell did I bully?" Mandy was petulant now.

"Hannah and Betsy by the look of things." Teddy appeared from the shadows, his face like thunder, and Mandy visibly blanched, wobbling in her heels as she backed away.

"Teddy, I—"

"Do you know what? Hannah always said you were a

mean girl, and I didn't know what she meant, but now I've seen your true colours for myself."

"But—"

Again he cut her off, this time with a wave of his hand. He turned to me. "I'm sorry I didn't ever see any of this for myself before. Is this what she's always been like with you?"

"Finally, he fucking sees it!" Betsy exclaimed, throwing her hands in the air in exasperation. "Seriously, Teddy, you've got the wherewithal of a fruit fly sometimes."

Teddy huffed a sad little laugh.

"I am so sorry I never saw this before." Grasping both my hands, he said, "Hannah, you are more beautiful on the outside and on the inside than anyone else I've ever met."

Mandy snorted, but he didn't even look at her.

"Should we get out of here?"

When I didn't respond, he gently squeezed my fingers.

"Come on. We can find somewhere quiet and away from everyone."

"Betsy, you want to come too?" I didn't want to abandon my wingwoman after she'd saved me so heroically.

"Ah, no, girl. I'm heading home to my wife and a mug of hot chocolate." Wrapping me in a hug, she whispered in my ear, "You've got this. You are so wonderful and beautiful that even this idiot sees it"—she gestured to Teddy, who grinned—"but if all else fails, then there's always Jamie Dornan. He's pretty enough that even I could be turned."

"You're not going to leave, are you?" Mandy whined, desperation infusing every word. "I was hoping we could all catch up again, like a school reunion. That would be fun, wouldn't it? Hannah knows I was joking, right, Hannah?"

"I don't think so, Mandy."

"Please, Teddy?"

But he had turned away from her and was leading me by the hand towards the side of a large stone building and through an unlit area of the garden.

Pausing, I looked back at Mandy. Her face was mutinous and I said, "Do you know what would be a fun reunion? You trying not to be a total and utter cow every time we run into each other."

Her expression told me everything I needed to know. "Oh, do fuck off."

"That's quite enough from you," Betsy said, ushering Mandy as far away as possible from me.

———————

Teddy led the way through a tall gate and into an apple orchard, lit only by the moon and the sprinkling of stars that pierced the night sky.

"Where are we going, Ted?"

"My dad built a treehouse in here when we were kids. It was our favourite place."

"I'm not sure I can climb a tree in this outfit," I said, stumbling as my strappy heels dug into the soft grass.

In a sweeping gesture that made me squeak, Teddy turned and picked me up, grinning.

"It's a great dress, Hannah."

"You don't need to carry me! I can walk," I said petulantly.

But Teddy did not relent, taking me to a large tree that towered over a broken-down stone wall at the far side of the orchard, and as we neared I saw a long rope ladder reaching to the ground.

"But I like carrying you."

"You'd better not be planning to drop me in a pond again."

He laughed. "Where'd you get the idea I'd do something like that?"

"You have form, my friend."

Gently, Teddy placed me back on the ground at the foot of the ladder. "I'll go first and check it's safe, then follow me up?"

"In these shoes?"

Bending down, he crouched at my feet, gently wrapping a warm hand around my ankle and unbuckled the strap, easing my foot out of one sandal and then the other. He held them reverentially in one hand and drew me towards the tree.

"That should be easier."

He scaled the ladder with effortless grace. At the top, he turned on the platform and gestured for me to come up too. The trailing lengths of my dress were going to be a hinderance, so I tucked the excess material into the waistband of my knickers and tentatively gripped a rung of the ladder and began my ascent, questioning my sanity with every step. Eventually, I grasped Teddy's outstretched hand at the top and he helped me over the edge.

From the treehouse platform, we had an unobstructed view of the garden party in full swing, its golden light bathing us and casting tree branch shadows all around. I turned in a circle, taking in the monochrome Cotswolds countryside that stretched out to meet the twinkling streetlights of Chipping-on-the-Water in the distance. It was magical.

Teddy had taken off his jacket and was untying his bow tie, pulling the ends free from the collar and undoing the top button. I watched, entranced, as he sat on a rickety wooden swing, gesturing me to join him on the other one.

"It's perfectly safe. My dad's a very good architect," he said with amusement at my indecision.

"Are you a very good architect too?" I asked, perching on the little wooden seat, my bare toes pushing against the treehouse boards to swing gently, the silk of my dress sliding over my thighs as the hem pooled on the floor.

"I don't know."

The sudden humility and echo of self-doubt in his voice hit me in my heart. I hadn't expected that. I'd expected an arrogant and confident response.

"Oh."

Teddy laughed softly. "Did you expect me to brag about how great I am?"

"Well, yes."

Blowing out a long sigh, Teddy looked away into the distance. "It's all an act, Hannah."

"An act?"

"Yeah. I don't have a clue what the hell I'm doing most of the time. I'm just bullshitting my way through life."

I let that sink in, keeping quiet, the faint music from the party and the soft creak of the swings the only sounds.

"You're the only one who's ever called me out, Hannah." Teddy glanced at me. "You see through all my crap. You always have."

"But you're doing great, right?"

"I'm not so sure."

"What impossible ideal are you holding yourself up to here, Teddy?"

"My father? Henry?" There was a bitter note to his tone.

"Have you and Henry fallen out?"

Teddy put his head in his hands and sighed. I watched, entranced, as he flexed his fingers in his hair.

"No."

"So, what is it?"

"What's what?"

"I'm definitely calling you out on your bullshit now, Teddy. I understand why you'd look up to your father and his achievements, but you're just as successful as Henry, so what's going on between you two?"

"I'm nowhere near as perfect as Henry. No one on this fucking planet is."

"Teddy, what the hell?" His outburst was a shock.

"Sorry, ignore me. I hate parties; that's why I always try to escape to a quiet place."

He was shattering every illusion I had about him.

"You hate parties? Who are you and what have you done with Teddy Fraser?"

The returning laugh was sad.

"Don't tell anyone, but Teddy Fraser is a fraud. He likes pottering about in his old house. He likes log fires, watching 1980s romcoms, and collecting old books. And, bizarrely he's recently developed an affinity for goats."

"No way?" I laughed. "Not goats. Surely not!"

"See, a complete and utter fraud."

I got off the swing and knelt down in front of him, placing my hands on his knees and looking up to his raw and broken expression. The vulnerability made my heart lurch.

"Ted, what is this? What's going on?"

"God, you're beautiful when you're on your knees in front of me." The smirk was real but carried a little less conviction than normal.

I snorted and smacked his thigh. This was a mistake because his eyes darkened, and in my braless state I couldn't hide my body's reaction to him.

"Teddy, tell me what's going on. We're friends, aren't we?"

"Friends," he repeated.

"Yes. So tell me."

His hand covered mine where it lay on his leg, his thumb brushing my skin.

"Our whole lives we've been compared: who's brighter, who's funnier, who's better looking. And Henry's always won. Always. It's like watching the best version of yourself being played out in front of you, and you never match up, not once."

"That's not true. Henry's great but you're different people."

"Do you know what my parents used to say to me when I was a child, all the time?" I shook my head. "Why can't you be more like your brother? Just do what your brother does. And they didn't mean Tom or Dan."

"Teddy, I—"

"It's ok, Hannah. I've always been the black sheep of the family. They never had such high expectations of me, so I never let them down. If you're going to be labelled, best to live up to it, right? That's why I decided that I'd be the bad twin, so I could excel at something. I could finally be better than Henry at something."

My heart broke for him at that moment, the vulnerable little boy laying his soul bare. That feeling of inadequacy and self-doubt resonated so strongly with me that tears sprang up in the corners of my eyes.

"Oh Teddy, you're not *bad*."

"I can be."

His eyes glinted in the moonlight, fixating on my mouth as I gulped at the dark promise in his words.

"But you can also be generous and kind."

"Hmph."

"How you are with Agnes, with me, those aren't the actions of a bad person, Teddy."

"I really want to be bad with you though, Hannah."

"You're only saying this to get a reaction from me, to try and make me mad at you. I won't fall for it."

"I'm saying it because it's true. I want to kiss you so fucking badly. And I really want to make you scream my name in this treehouse."

Standing quickly, I backed away from him, desperate to put some distance between us before I ripped off his clothes and jumped on top of him like a rodeo rider. "We both know you don't mean that."

"I don't?" Teddy had stood up as well and was stalking towards me.

"No, you don't. Stop trying to be the bad boy, Teddy. Just be *you*. Just be the person you really are inside."

"This *is* me."

"You're only saying that because I'm here and available. We both know that having sex with me is just you scratching an itch."

Teddy stopped in his tracks, like I'd just slapped him, his expression unsure, and then a deep sadness darkened his face.

"You're right. I should take you home."

The mechanical way he stooped to pick up his jacket and bow tie, the tight slant of his shoulders, and the closed-off expression pierced me straight through the ribcage, spearing my heart with empathy and acknowledgement.

This man was truly broken inside. Why had I not seen it before?

Chapter Twenty-One

My phone was ringing and it was after midnight and I wasn't on call.

What the hell?

I'd had a busy few days since the garden party and had been really looking forward to an early night and a bit of downtime. Teddy and I had shared a few text messages since the party but hadn't seen each other, which was probably for the best. I'd had no time to obsess about what had happened and definitely no time to replay the dance, the almost-kiss, or the treehouse conversation. It wasn't on an incessant loop in my brain. Honestly.

Knocking my phone off the bedside table and onto the floor, I slithered from the bed and retrieved it from the rug, answering groggily.

"Yes?"

"Hannah, come quickly! It's Deidre. She's dying." Teddy sounded panicked.

"What?"

"She's dying! Hannah, come quickly!"

I took a moment and shook my head, hoping this would clear everything up and confirm that I was just having a dream.

"Hannah, are you there? I'll come over there and drag your arse out of bed if you don't come quickly."

"When you say dying, what is she doing?"

"She's lying down and groaning, and there's some panting and puffing." The sound of Deidre bleating mournfully in the background filtered through.

"Fine. Let me grab some bits and pieces and I'll be there shortly. Stop panicking – it won't help her."

"Is she going to be ok?"

"I'll do everything I can for her."

I hung up the phone and pulled on jeans and a jumper over my pyjamas, then nipped to my car to load some essential items into a case before jogging round to Teddy's.

Opening the door to his shed, I found him crouched over the prostrate goat, who was lying on her side and straining. He held a torch over her and was gently stroking her neck and whispering soothing words. As if he sensed my presence, he looked up and saw me, and the deep creases in his forehead relaxed.

"Thank Christ you're here. She's getting worse."

Hopping over the gate, I assessed the scene – the churned-up straw, the heavy breathing, and the heaving flanks of the goat.

"Teddy, this is serious."

All the colour drained from his face.

"What's wrong with her?"

"Prepare yourself. I need to tell you something important that will change your life." I paused for dramatic effect. "You're going to be a daddy."

"W-w-what?"

Teddy's eyes turned huge.

"A goat daddy. Deidre's not dying; she's in labour."

"Oh. Very funny, Hannah." Loosing a shaky breath, he looked back where his hand was still smoothing the white coat on Deidre's neck. "What should I do? Do you need hot water and towels? A midwife?"

I chuckled. "Some warm water and a towel would be great, but I reckon we can leave the midwife out of it."

Teddy rushed away to get the water – little did he know it was just so I could wash my hands later – and I began to examine my patient more closely. The amniotic sack had burst and I quickly found a couple of little goat limbs and noses, jostling to get out into the world. With a little bit of manipulation, I worked out which limbs belonged to which snout and soon had the first little soggy bundle delivered. Clearing her little pink nose and giving her a rub with some clean straw to stimulate her breathing, I placed her under Deidre's nose, and she immediately started licking and snuffling the new arrival, her delighted bleats matched only by the happy little sounds coming from her new baby.

Teddy arrived with about four bath towels under his arm and two huge buckets of steaming water. "Thank God I got the hot water working. Is this ok? Wow."

He placed everything on the ground and crept over to where Deidre was busy with goat kid number one, and he watched in awe as the two animals softly snuffled at each other. Meanwhile, baby goat number two slipped out, again healthy and kicking, shaking his head and bleating loudly within minutes of landing in the straw. Quickly I placed him next to his slightly smaller sister, and Deidre delightedly started to fuss this one too.

"Twins?" Teddy whispered.

"Yes. Deidre's done brilliantly."

Checking for injuries and finding none at all, I stood up and helped myself to the warm water, washing off the inevitable slime and blood that accompanied all births. Then I sourced some more clean straw for fresh bedding for the new family, before sitting back and watching the miracle of life unfolding before me. This was the part that never ceased to be amazing, the magic and perfection of these tiny new beings who were already flexing their limbs, testing them and trying to stand. The love and dedication that Deidre showed as her instincts kicked in was beautiful and astounding, It was these special moments in my job that got me in the feels, every single time.

"Do we need to do anything else?" Teddy whispered.

"No, I think Deidre has it under control. I'll pop back in the morning and check that she's delivered all the afterbirth, but I think she's done this before so we should just give them some space and let them get to know each other."

"Do we need to wake Agnes up and tell her?"

"No. It's pretty late so I think she'll be ok to see them in the morning too."

"Ok." He hesitated before stepping back, unable to look away from the goats. "It's amazing, isn't it?"

"Yes, even after all the births I've seen, it never gets less incredible."

Teddy turned to look at me, a soft light in his eyes.

"Thanks for coming and helping."

"You're welcome. And you didn't even pass out at the blood. I'm impressed."

"Well, I elected to stay away from the business end and let Deidre maintain some modesty."

I laughed. "I reckon she appreciated your gentlemanly behaviour."

Teddy smiled shyly and ducked his head, rubbing the back of his neck distractedly.

"Do you want a drink? I could really do with a drink."

"A drink sounds great. Come on." I picked up all the towels, handing him a few, and closed the shed door as we wandered slowly back towards the lights of The Rectory kitchen.

Inside, I slipped off my boots while Teddy got some glasses and poured a couple of fingers of whisky into each one. Whisky wasn't my favourite, so in a practised move from my university days, I downed the lot in one and tried not to gag.

Teddy coughed and stared at me.

"That was a ten-year-old single malt, Hannah."

"I don't like whisky," I replied, my voice rough and not unlike a sixty-a-day smoker.

"Oh. Right." Teddy quickly finished his whisky too. "How about champagne, or is that too excessive?"

"For the celebration of new life? Definitely not." I had a mid-week day off scheduled for tomorrow, so I absolutely was in the mood for a bit of champers. "That would be lovely."

Teddy grinned and found some rather expensive-looking flutes then popped the cork from the bottle with a flourish.

"To new life," he said, clinking his glass against mine. "And to Hannah, the ravishing vet, who saved me from yet another caprine emergency."

"To Ted, the most attentive goat-father I've ever met."

"I'm the goat-father? Just call me Ted Corleone," he said in a poor imitation of Marlon Brando that made me laugh and snort a bit of champagne out of my nose, the bubbles burning my nostrils so that my eyes watered.

Grabbing the bottle and still chuckling, he ushered me into the sitting room, which was in the process of being renovated. A few candles were flickering in the fireplace and one small sofa was pulled up near the hearth. A couple of books were open on the floor and a pair of reading glasses lay neatly on top.

"Romantic evening for one?" I quipped, tilting my head towards the flickering flames and low lamplight that made the large room feel cosy.

"Something like that."

Teddy sat down next to me, his proximity inevitable in the small seat, his solid thigh brushing mine. Quickly, I gulped more champagne as tingly warmth spread over my skin, but luckily Teddy seemed oblivious as he stared into his glass. I wriggled uncomfortably, trying to get some space, but just ended up rubbing my leg even more obviously against his. I knew it was dangerous to be alone and close to Teddy – I'd already struggled to keep my head in similar predicaments, and here I was leg- humping him and getting myself all hot and bothered again.

"You drank that one quickly. Are you ok?" Teddy asked, hesitantly filling my glass again.

"It's lovely!" Taking another large swig, I felt any resolve that I had garnered since the party fully scarper. I was alone. Alone with a raging libido and a walking, talking sex god sitting perilously close to me. My inhibitions giggled gleefully as they too made a hasty exit.

Shit.

Teddy smiled as he took a sip of champagne. "Seriously, are you all right? You're looking at me a little strangely, Hannah."

"Baby goats!" I practically shouted at him, making him jump and spill a bit of champagne on his jeans. "They're cute, right?"

"Erm, yep," he replied, dabbing at his wet crotch before giving up with a sigh and looking a little fearfully in my direction. "Very cute. Maybe even cuter when not covered in birth slime and blood. I'll reserve my judgement until they're all clean and fluffy tomorrow."

"Ha ha ha!" That was a weird noise. My attempt at laughing sounded particularly grating and false.

Have another sip of champagne you weirdo.

But my glass was empty again, and Teddy looked a little alarmed when I shook my flute under his nose. Leaning forwards, over his legs, my torso pressed against his thighs, I reached for the champagne bottle and topped myself up. Swinging back past his shocked face as I sat upright again, and using my hand on his knee to push myself up, I accidentally gave it a little squeeze. Accidentally. Yes. Absolutely by accident.

I was staring at him. I knew I was, but I didn't seem to be able to help it. He was delicious, wasn't he? I mean, really almost edible. With a face like that and such a firmly muscled body, why had I resisted this long? I considered moving my hand higher up his thigh, the chance of further squeezing opportunities filling my brain. I attempted a seductive smile in his direction.

Teddy chuckled. "Are you drunk already?"

"Nope. High on life, my friend, high on life."

"Who are you and what have you done with my prickly hedgehog of a friend?"

"Ah yes, friendssssssssssssss. We need to chat about that." I took another gulp of champagne and leant forwards.

"We do?"

"We do." I nodded firmly, gesturing with my glass and sloshing more champagne on him. "Ooh sorry."

I went to dab at the liquid on his blue-checked shirt and my fingers ended up caressing the smattering of hairs that were peeking over the V-shape of his open collar, unintentionally flicking open another button, and resting on the warm skin underneath.

Ooh this is rather nice. Very nice, in fact.

"Hannah..." Teddy said, his voice a little growly as it reverberated through his chest and electrified my fingertips. Reluctantly, I dragged my gaze from this point of contact and up to his face. His eyes were dark pools, his lips parted.

I wanted to kiss him so badly. Just as he'd said the other night, *really fucking badly.*

Placing my empty champagne flute on the ground, I turned back to face my quarry, my hand still nestled snugly inside his shirt. In one swift move, I swung my leg over so I was straddling his lap and looking down into his face, which he angled backwards, resting his head on the back of the sofa.

Slowly, I undid another button of his shirt before his free

hand, the one not holding a champagne flute, gently grabbed mine.

"Hannah, what are you doing?"

"I'm seducing you. Badly, it would seem."

"You don't need to seduce me. I'm not having sex with you when you're drunk."

I pouted and leant down, my lips brushing the shell of his ear.

"What if I were offering you wild, uninhibited, do-anything-you-want-to-me sex right now on this sofa?"

Teddy moaned against my neck. It was a restless, wanton noise, a mix of need and frustration, a kind of animalistic sound that had me humming in response. After a moment during which his body had gone completely still, barely breathing, he whispered hoarsely, "I think this is just the champagne and cute baby goats talking. You don't mean it and would hate me in the morning."

"Are you turning me down, Edward Fraser?"

I sat up and pulled my hair out of its ponytail, letting the long strands fall around my shoulders and then wriggled seductively in his lap, feeling his body respond.

"Fuck, you're really making this difficult for me."

"Hard, some might say?" I replied and sniggered.

God, I'm really funny, aren't I?

He raised an eyebrow. "Indeed."

"One kiss, then? Just one and then I'll leave you alone. And I won't hate you in the morning."

Teddy laughed. "You won't?"

"I won't, I promise," I said, saluting.

I could do meaningless kissing with this man. I could just

enjoy my own physical reaction to him, couldn't I? No catching feelings. He smiled and my stomach flipped over.

Shit. Who am I kidding.

"All right, Havens. One kiss. And it'd better be your best porn star one or I won't be happy."

I licked my lips and he traced the edge of my jawline with his fingers before gently cupping the back of my head. I leant down again, and on a soft exhale with all the breathiness I could muster, I said, "Yes, sir."

"Mmmmm, I never thought you'd say that to me."

"Do you like it?"

"Oh yes, I fucking love it."

My lips hovered over his, expecting him to come to me, but he didn't. He remained exactly where he was, watching, waiting, letting me take control of this moment. So I did. I absolutely did. I went in for the kiss, brushing my lips tentatively against his, revelling in the sudden warmth and taste of him – the scratch of his beard against my skin and the huff of his breath mingling with mine. When he responded, eagerly, a blast of nostalgia and familiarity hit me in the chest with the full force of a hurricane, and I was a ship lost at sea, hopelessly bobbing in the tempest of my own feelings.

Hungrily, I pressed into him more firmly, sucking his bottom lip into my mouth and letting out a little gasp as his fingers tightened their hold in my hair. His mouth opened, urging me on. And I took that invitation wholeheartedly, allowing my tongue to explore against his, my mind starting to shatter with the growing intensity of the kiss as he pushed back at me.

A groan rumbled in his throat. Breaking away, I kissed his jaw, his neck and then back up to his lips, frantically touching his face, his shoulders, his chest, a sudden urgency coursing through me. But then he was changing the angle, pivoting until I began to slide underneath him. The champagne flute was magically gone as both of his hands were now covering my body, large and warm and desperate as he tugged at my clothes revealing more skin to the heat of his touch. He was showering me with attention, his solid weight caging me in – and I absolutely bloody loved it.

Every part of me was alive to the feel of him, every press of his lips, every stroke of his fingers a bolt of lightning, fuelling my desire and encouraging me to be reckless. I pulled at his shirt to open it, revealing an expanse of warm skin, and like an eager explorer my fingertips followed the dips and ridges of his chest and abdomen, heading south to the waistband of his jeans.

"Mmmmm, this is so *nice*, Teddy," I murmured, instinctively arching up towards him.

"Shit, we need to stop. *I* need to stop," Teddy rasped, breathless, his voice thick with lust and emotion as he attempted to pull away from me.

But I didn't want to stop. I didn't want to be sensible. I wanted to feel. I wanted to be wanted. I wanted to pretend I was desirable just for a few more moments. Reaching up to his face, I traced the line of his mouth.

"Please, Teddy. I need this."

He looked torn, distraught. "I don't want to do anything rash, anything that you'll regret."

"I won't," I promised, so hazy with passion that my words seemed to come out slurred, slow and deliberate.

But Teddy was already getting up off the sofa, releasing his hold on me as he tried to readjust his jeans and button up his shirt with shaky hands.

"It's just meaningless fun between friends, right?" I said, sitting up.

My head was swimming but I desperately wanted to reassure him that I'd manage my own expectations; that he could rely on me not to fall for him. I knew, though, with absolute clarity, that I was too far gone already, but he didn't need to know this. I could pop this into a little box and squirrel it away in the corner of my mind, in the dark and dusty place I kept reserved for all self-destructive thoughts.

"Meaningless?"

"Of course, Teddy. Don't worry – I'm not going to fall in love with you."

My laugh was bright but unconvincing to my own ears. I could feel my heart thudding along like a galloping horse, and I had to grasp the seat cushion to stop myself swaying.

"Right. Of course you won't." Rubbing his hands over his face, Teddy sat back down on the arm of the sofa, careful to remain out of touching distance. "That's a relief."

Trying not to let him see how much his indifference stung, I crawled across the sofa towards him.

"Can we do some more snogging now?"

Reaching over, he cupped my chin gently. He leant down, his lips hovering over mine, just out of reach.

"But we agreed just one, Hannah."

"But that wasn't my best porn star kiss, Teddy." I pouted and pushed forward, trying to catch his mouth with mine.

Teddy moved back just a fraction, denying me.

"It wasn't?"

"No."

"Damn."

He swallowed and rubbed a thumb over my lips, the rough pad catching on the aching and sensitive flesh there.

I could still taste him, feel him, hear his groan, and I wanted more. Wobbling slightly, I batted my eyelashes – hopefully coquettishly and not just as though I had something irritating my corneas.

"Shall we have another go, so I can show you?"

Teddy laughed a little sadly.

"I would absolutely love to have another go, but not now. Not until you've sobered up." He paused, gazing into my eyes and pushing my hair behind my ear. "And not until you realise that when *we* kiss, Hannah, it's never, ever, meaningless."

He stood up and I fell forwards on the sofa into a jelly-like heap of uncertainty and chaos. A major internal malfunction was occurring. Something was happening inside my brain that I was wholly incapable of processing just now. The room began to spin and I remained motionless while Teddy tidied up around me. The faint sounds of him washing up came from the kitchen as my consciousness started to seep away, suddenly inexorably tired and groggy.

The feel of his arms around me as he lifted me gently from the sofa couldn't even encourage me to open my eyes, but I did snuggle into his warmth, pressing my nose into his neck and inhaling deeply.

"You smell delicious, like spicy oranges and pheromones."

Teddy laughed. "To bed, my inebriated little hedgehog of a friend."

"At last, Teddy the sex god has shown up and is taking me to his bed!"

I giggled, feeling my body bounce against him as he carried me upstairs.

"You really are drunk, and on so little alcohol too. Impressive."

He placed me down gently on my back, and I was immediately enveloped in fresh-smelling sheets. I burrowed down into the soft warmth of the bed and felt myself relax.

"Get some sleep, you gorgeous little weirdo," he continued, placing a gentle lingering kiss on my forehead and turning out the lights.

Chapter Twenty-Two

The thickened, befuddled mess of waking up was worse this morning, compounded by the taste of what could only be the remnants of a dead ferret in my mouth and a hyperactive woodpecker trying to bore a hole into my brain. Through my eyeballs. Stomach churning, I groaned and turned onto my back, an intense feeling of doom seeping into my body as awareness started to really take hold and some sketchy goat memories lit up in a hazy movie reel behind my eyes.

The sheets surrounding me were unfamiliar and I tentatively explored the bed, searching for any other limbs or the hint of having spent the night with another person. But other than my warm little cocoon, the rest of the bed was cool and unruffled. Bravely lifting the covers from over my head, I squinted into the brightly lit expanse of Teddy's bedroom, but there was no sign of anyone. The large house was surprisingly quiet, only the chatter of sparrows outside the window filtering through the fug of my hangover. Haphazardly thrown over the chair by the wardrobe were the clothes that Teddy had been wearing yesterday, the bedroom door was ajar, and the curtains were open.

I held my breath and listened, and it was with some mixed emotions that I deduced I was entirely alone. The instant relief of not having to face Teddy began to dissipate and the sleezy, slimy crawl of mortifying humiliation slithered over my body. He'd run away, and who could blame him? My mind was now replaying the Miss Whiplash seduction trainwreck I'd instigated on the couch, and it was a cringe-inducing horror show. Groaning again, I buried myself back under the covers. How could I have been so stupid and reckless? Thank God Teddy had some sort of moral code about not sleeping with drunken women who hurled themselves at him. Although, to be fair, he'd probably had a lot of practice at deflecting unwanted attention from wanton hussies in his lifetime.

Wallowing in self-pity and regret, I didn't notice the shadowy presence at first, a dark shape creeping across the window as I sank deeper into the murky recesses of my own mind. But a chirrup and a crash finally shook me back to reality in time to see the fuzzy mottled shape of Aphrodite launching herself from the sill towards the bedside table. In an explosion of claws, paws, and fur, she skidded across the polished wood, sending everything in her path flying including a precariously placed full glass of orange juice, which teetered and spun in her wake before finally spilling its contents over everything.

"Shit! Aph—"

But I was cut off as she landed on me, sliding over my mouth so that I briefly choked on her belly fluff, before landing in a heap on the pillow. With a happy little feline noise, she began purring and bumping her head against mine in delight.

Shaking her off, I surveyed the carnage she had created. Orange juice was seeping into the well-thumbed pages of a thriller novel, dripping off the table and onto the newly sanded floorboards by the bed. Luckily the bedside lamp had avoided the spillage, but a foil blister packet of paracetamol was swimming about in the orange lake, and a spiral notepad was the final juice-related victim.

"Christ!"

Leaping up from the bed was a bad idea. My brain swished about sloppily, like a cork bobbing in a sea of residual alcohol, making the room spin and my head thump, but the pressing need to tidy up drove me downstairs and into the kitchen to gather cleaning equipment.

Once I'd mopped up the juice and cleaned the table and floor, I placed the thriller novel into the bin bag of crime-scene evidence and decided to buy him a replacement copy, then reached for the pad. While it too was soaked right through, having taken the brunt of the flood, there was the beginnings of a note on the first page, but I could only make out my name and "sorry about" before the handwriting disappeared, the blue ink running in swirling patterns that rendered it entirely indecipherable.

Sitting on the edge of the bed and staring at the soggy paper, I wondered what else he had written. Was he apologising for not sleeping with me? Was he apologising for something else? Something I didn't remember? Had we actually done anything he needed to apologise for? I remained fully clothed so it was unlikely. I racked my brain, but nothing other than the couch snog and being carried upstairs came to me. Perhaps he was apologising for leaving this morning? That seemed unlikely – rakes infamously snuck out and left women in their bed, didn't they? So that would be nothing new to him. Perhaps he was saying sorry for inviting me in. Perhaps he regretted having me in his home at all.

If I was being honest, it was quite clear that I had made a total fool of myself with Teddy last night, and he'd realised that he needed to distance himself from me and that it was a mistake to carry on with this friendship in whatever form it had taken. And who could really blame him?

Sensible me – the one who could rationally control her emotions and who could dispassionately deliver bad news to devastated people when they lost their beloved companions – she knew this was for the best. She knew it should never have got this far. Yeah, she was already squirrelling away the stinging hurt and shame, putting it in a box to deal with later (never). But the quiet, squidgy marshmallow part of me, the part that had been bruised before, the part that yearned to be loved and accepted, well, that part imploded, releasing a surge of feelings that I was struggling to place, struck by a painful and suffocating blow to my already fragile heart.

Aphrodite quietly slunk onto my lap, rubbing her head against my hand and tentatively kneading my denim-clad leg. When a solitary tear slid down my cheek, I dashed it away crossly.

"This is no bloody good, is it?"

Stroking the thick fur of the cat, her purr now rumbling like a diesel engine, I felt my inner equilibrium start to stabilise. Slowly, piece by piece, I began to resurrect the armour I usually wore around myself, stiffening my spine and coating myself in prickles. Getting ready to face the world again.

"Let's take you back to Agnes, shall we?" I said, lifting Aphrodite off my knee and standing up.

Outside, the air was still and already warming with the new morning sunshine, a reminder of the imminent arrival of the summer solstice. In the garden, I made a beeline for the hole in the hedge into Agnes's overgrown and ramshackle property, catching sight of her in a dressing gown watering some tomato plants on her kitchen windowsill and singing softly to herself.

"Good morning, Agnes. I've brought Aphrodite back for you."

I was greeted by a slightly blank look, devoid of recognition for the briefest of moments, before the light returned to her eyes, and she smiled warmly. "Hannah, so lovely to see you. Thanks for returning the little rascal. I hope she hasn't been causing trouble?"

I elected not to tell her about the orange juice tsunami incident, just shaking my head with a smile and placing her on the ground by my feet. "No, she's been her usual angelic self."

The cat padded off through the kitchen door, tail waving in the air like a flag, and I turned back to look at Agnes, who was trying to lift the watering can higher to reach some hanging baskets whose inhabitants looked very dead indeed.

"Here, let me help you with that," I offered, and she gratefully handed the watering can to me. "Oh, by the way, Deidre had twins last night."

"She did? Oh, that's a bit earlier than I'd thought. Everything ok?"

"Yes, she did great. You have a beautiful new nanny and a strong billy. I was just going to do a little check on them. Do you want to come along?"

Agnes nodded, then said wistfully, "The magic of new life

still surprises me every time. Did you and Teddy see it happen?"

My heart lurched at his name, but I smiled and led her back through the hole in the hedge and towards the shippen.

"Yes. Teddy was very worried about her. I think he might have a few new grey hairs from the experience!"

She laughed. "He's a sensitive soul, isn't he?"

I nodded, not really trusting myself to speak.

Inside the shippen, Deidre was busily eating hay, while the two kids were up and nursing. When Agnes called her, shaking a bucket with pellets, she bleated excitedly and trotted towards us.

"She looks good and both babies seem fine," she said, softly stroking Deidre while I examined the trio, happy to see nothing out of the ordinary.

"Yes, I think she's passed the afterbirth cleanly, and these two seem good and strong," I replied, adding some more straw to the area and topping up the water and hay in her pen.

"Thank you for caring about them, Hannah."

The kind, gentle tone of her voice had tears pricking behind my eyes, and I turned away from her to sniff discreetly. This was so unlike me – I never cried, not even after everything with Jonathan; not even following the personal and professional devastation of leaving my research position behind. In all the putrid vileness of the last few months, not a single tear had escaped my eyes. No, I prided myself on being the mistress of the frosty veneer, ensuring I was protected by a thick covering of ice so no one could peek inside and catch even a hint of the vulnerability hidden deep down. Yet recently, this all seemed to be changing.

My voice was surprisingly gruff when I finally spoke. "You're welcome."

"I saw Teddy leaving very early this morning. Is everything ok?"

"Yes, fine." Tight-lipped, I climbed over the gate to get out of the pen. "I should get going, unless you need anything else?"

"No, I think they should stay here for a few more days before I put them out in the paddock. Do you think that will be ok?"

"Good idea."

We left Deidre eating peacefully, the two kids sleeping quietly in the fresh straw, and closed the shed door behind us.

"I'm glad they've come along now. Actually, Giles asked if I might bring some goats to the country fayre on Saturday. The little ones should be ok to do that, don't you think? Deidre goes every year – she loves the attention from all the children."

"I'm sure that will be fine."

"Will I see you there?"

"Um, sure," I said.

Parting ways in the garden, Agnes gave me a cheery wave and disappeared back through the hedge, while I headed to the surgery car park. A new worry weighed on my shoulders: the Chipping-on-the-Water Country Fayre and Scarecrow Festival. Yes, indeed, a bizarre local tradition that I'd attended as a child – one which I'd blanked out of my mind for many years and which I had totally forgotten that I'd agreed to attend. Actually, *agreed* wasn't quite accurate; Giles had strong-armed me into judging one of the classes in the dog show. Which, quite frankly, sounded like a very special kind of torture reserved for a disciple of Satan himself. *Excellent.*

Chapter Twenty-Three

S aturday came around rather more quickly than I would have liked. Our small town was awash with bunting and stalls and the large green in the town centre was set up with marquees and white-roped rings for various show classes and displays. The shopkeepers had dressed up in bright colours and ridiculous hats, and absurd and increasingly elaborate scarecrows graced every garden. The excitement of the annual country fayre turned the locals into nutcases. Clearly.

Teddy had sporadically texted me in the last few days, just brief "How are you?" messages, which, at first, I had responded to politely and concisely, but his own answers had been sketchy, inconsistent, and definitely not keen, so I gradually stopped replying. Repairing my bruised ego was easier without his physical presence nearby, so I was grateful that he seemed to have disappeared. It left me to try my hardest to get back to normal, almost able to squash the uncomfortable feelings, to swallow them away, pretend they'd never messed me up at all – and that I'd not acted like an uncontrollable dog in heat in his presence. Because, frankly it was absolutely mortifying.

Turning thoughts away from Teddy, my social anxiety spiked as I accompanied Giles to the fayre committee tent, where a lot of tweed-clad local bigwigs were busy peopling and organising, loudly and importantly. Palms clammy and my feet suddenly leaden, I began to slow down, dropping back from Giles's side. He turned to me with a puzzled expression.

Then I heard it: the unmistakeable laugh, the false and overtly brash sound that was indelibly etched on my mind, the sort of laugh reserved for those he secretly despised but whom he was intent on smarming up to.

"Are you ok?" Giles asked, twisting his whole body to face me.

"I, um…" My voice dropped off as Jonathan appeared from the tent, his arm linked in my mother's. Her usually tight, drawn features were open and smiling delightedly up at him. She was almost swooning, which was pretty sickening to observe.

"What's wrong?"

Giles came back to where I had ground to a halt, my boots taking root in the ground and rendering me immobile.

"Nothing." But my wide-eyed stare was fooling no one.

"Hannah? Seriously, what is it?"

He turned to follow my gaze.

"What's he doing here?"

Giles looked uncomfortable for a moment. "Professor Pierce? Well, he contacted me recently about including us in a trial he's setting up in first-opinion practices, and I said we'd be delighted. It's a great opportunity for the practice and I was going to talk to you about leading it from our side. I thought you'd like to dip your toe back into some research again?"

"What?"

My head was swimming. Jonathan had absolutely zero interest in first-opinion practice. He'd always sneered at the daily routine, suggesting that vaccinations and dealing with overweight animals and distraught owners was beneath him. He'd focussed on the most interesting and challenging cases in the referral practice at the vet school, cherry-picking the ones that would give him the most glory or allow him to test a new cutting-edge treatment. I could smell his bullshit a mile away. What the actual hell was he doing now?

At that moment, Jonathan saw us, and a slow, arrogant smile spread over his face. Without breaking eye contact with me, he leant down and whispered something to my mother, making her giggle and flick her long hair flirtatiously and then they started to walk towards us.

"Giles, what is he doing here, today, right now?" I hissed, wretched loathing almost swallowing me whole as they neared.

"He called the other day to talk through the trial and said he'd pop down this weekend to show me some of the data so far. When I told him about the fayre he offered to judge."

"Which bit?"

"The dog show." Giles winced as he said it, shrivelling under my ferocious glare.

Of course he did.

"Right, well, you don't need me then, do you?" I turned abruptly and stalked off back the way I'd come, head down, muttering curses and demonic incantations under my breath in a bid to expel the fiery rage building inside. Running away from him, and not facing up to another shitstorm of emotion and regret definitely seemed like the best course of action at this point.

"Hannah, wait!" Jonathan's voice spurred me on and I almost broke into a trot, desperate to be anywhere else. To escape. To hide away. But he too had clearly quickened his pace in a bid to catch up with me. He took hold of my hand, sending ripples of revulsion under my skin at his touch.

"Don't run away from me, you silly thing," Jonathan said with a laugh, as though he were reprimanding an errant child.

Bastard.

Wrenching my hand free, I spun to face him, honey-badger mode locked and loaded.

"Either you leave, or I will."

"Now why would I do that? I'm the head judge of the dog show," he replied, not even bothering to hide his disdain.

"Fine, then I'm most definitely leaving."

I turned around again, heading for the exit, but he stepped in front of me and blocked my path.

"You can't leave. You're my trusty wingman, just like the good old days." This time the slippery and persuasive lilt to his voice was back, one that I knew so well. It immediately put me on high alert. "I thought I was clear. I need you. I love you, and I'll do anything to get you back."

Staring into his face, I was slapped again with the odd realisation that I had once had feelings for this man, but that seemed so alien and obnoxious now – nausea-inducing, in fact. I racked my brains, trying to summon up any compassion or empathy towards him, but all I felt was cold and frozen, and unable to bear another moment in his presence.

"You and your needs can take a long walk off a short pier into alligator-infested waters."

"That's not very nice, Hannah." Jonathan's attention flicked over my head to the crowd of people undoubtedly gathering around us. "I thought you might have had enough time to come to your senses by now."

"No. But then, you absolutely do not deserve my niceties. You gave up any right to me being *nice* to you when you cheated on me with your PhD student, or have you had enough time to forget I know about that?"

"I've apologised for my indiscretions. Come on, we're both grown-ups. We should be able to get past it," Jonathan said quietly, likely hoping that our audience wouldn't hear this bit.

"Get past it?" I repeated, incredulously.

"Yes, you need to get over what happened. You need to accept my apology so we can get back to normal. You know deep down that we're good together." He went to grab my hand again but I balked, stepping out of reach. "Your mother says you've never been happier than when we were together, and that I'm just what you need."

If he thought my mother's opinion was the way to talk me round, it just showed how little he knew or cared about me.

"I think you'll find that my mother, rather like you, is so wrapped up in herself and what she can get from other people that she wouldn't have a clue if I was happy or not. In fact, she'd likely not have the wherewithal to piss on me if I was on fire."

"Hannah!"

My mother's screech was ear-splitting. Part of me was actually glad she'd heard that. I really needed the whole world to just bugger off right about now. I was an erupting, self-righteous volcano of putrid indignation and self-destruction. A mountain of mutinous spikes. And should most definitely be left well alone.

Giles sidled up to us and the obnoxious retort that was poised on the tip of my tongue evaporated into thin air as Jonathan put his arm around his shoulders in a matey fashion, casting a sly look in my direction.

Giles stared at him like he was a rock star, then turned to me. "Everything ok?"

"Yes. I think we just took Hannah by surprise. She really doesn't like not knowing what's going on, even when we're all working together in her best interests, right?"

Giles glanced at me and flushed. "Sorry, I should have told you, but I thought you'd be happy to share the judging with Professor Pierce."

"Jonathan, please," he replied warmly, making Giles blush a little more. They were dickheads, the pair of them, and I absolutely did not need to be witness to this revolting bromance. A strange, disgusted little noise escaped my lips, a huffy grunt of displeasure now out in the open, so that my feelings on this sickening display of mutual appreciation were now available for external analysis.

Jonathan narrowed his eyes, obviously sensing my desire to flee, or to maim him.

"Come on, Hannah. Don't let me and Giles down."

Glancing around at the small circle of people watching intently, my mother giving me a slitty-eyed and pouty-lipped stare, undoubtedly lobbing mental daggers in my direction, I was suddenly faced with the impossible situation of letting my true feelings show or being the bigger person here. I knew I needed to demonstrate that I wasn't just a prickly and petulant hedgehog, that I could be the professional veterinary surgeon Giles needed me to be. And it was an almost excruciatingly difficult decision.

"Fine, I will judge one class, and Professor Pierce can do the rest," I said finally, satisfaction blooming as Jonathan's face fell. "I'll do the class for the dog the judge would most like to take home."

Knowing this was the first class to be judged, meaning I could leave promptly and escape to somewhere where other people weren't. I gave myself a mental pat on the back for my clear and rational decision.

"No, no! I thought we'd judge together?"

Jonathan was panicking. He'd be stuck here all day looking at endless dogs and talking to besotted owners about all their health niggles. Hell on earth for him.

Perfect.

"As an eminent professor of veterinary medicine at one of the most prestigious vet schools in the country, your credentials are far superior to mine, and let's not forget your numerous television appearances. A famous vet judging the dog show? The contestants will be over the moon to talk to you. I'd only get in the way of your moment of glory, right?"

"W-w-w-what? No!"

"I'll go and grab a coffee and get ready for my class then. It's kicking off in a few minutes – isn't that right, Giles?" He nodded while Jonathan just stared at me furiously. "Good."

Taking a deep breath, and with a final smile and nod to the now not insignificant audience that had gathered, I made my way over to the coffee stand and joined the back of the small queue, my boiling insides finally calming down.

"Well that was exceedingly rude, and no way to talk about the woman who gave birth to you."

My mother sidled up to me with a superficially ethereal and yet eerily demonic, calm.

"I'm sorry." I sighed rubbing my hands over my eyes. "I probably shouldn't have said the thing about you piss—"

"Yes, thank you, Hannah," she said abruptly, cutting me off and pinching the bridge of her nose in obvious despair. "Neither was it a good way to treat a man who's obviously only trying to do what's right for you."

"Right for me?"

"He clearly cares about you and your career and is a hugely successful person."

"And why should that matter? I'm successful too."

My mother gave me a once-over with an appraising eye. "He told me he's kept your place in his laboratory open for you. He wants you to return with him."

"He told you that?"

He wanted me back in the department? The thought of my academic career being dangled like a carrot before me was oddly exciting and unsettling.

"Yes, he did. He was enormously complimentary of your potential and your ability. He feels you're wasting your talents here, and frankly so do I."

"I'm not going back."

My voice carried a weight of conviction I wasn't sure I was really feeling.

"Why wouldn't you want to return to Bristol? Why wouldn't you want to make something of yourself rather than just settling for this unfulfilled existence?"

Undisguised, easy criticism laced every word, her tone clearly stating that this was a rhetorical question.

"He's said he'll take you back and let you move in with him as well. Surely it's worth considering?"

As I ordered an iced coffee at the counter, I let my mind drift. Undeniably, the pull of research was still there, tugging at my heart. It was an inescapable itch, a yearning to contribute to the bigger picture, to do something worthy. I wanted to continue to expand my knowledge, to ask questions, to be involved in the absolute cutting edge of veterinary medicine. I wanted to be proud of my achievements.

"Dr Havens?"

A quiet voice dragged me back from the brink of my inner turmoil, and I came face to face with Amelia Harris, a teenage girl whose horse, Sparkie, I'd been to see after a late-night bout of colic recently.

"Hello, Amelia. How's Sparkie?"

The relief and love on her face was evident.

"He's doing well. He's eating better and pretty much back to normal."

"That's great." I smiled and touched her shoulder. "You've done a brilliant job looking after him."

"I stayed all night in his stable when you left. My mum thought I was mad, but I couldn't leave him."

"It's a good idea to keep a close eye on them when they've been colicky."

"Thanks." Amelia's cheeks turned rosy, twisting her hands together in front of her. "I just wanted to say thank you for saving him. I was so worried and he means everything to me." The girl's voice wobbled a little but she took a shaky breath and carried on. "You see, there're some girls at the stables

saying things about me"—she gestured down her body—
"saying that I'm too fat to ride him, that I'm not good enough
for him, and that the reason he got poorly is because of me."

I gazed into her pain-filled eyes and my heart broke a little.

"Amelia, don't let hurtful people get to you. They're wrong
– you know that, don't you? He got colic because of a build-up
of gas in his intestines, likely from stuffing his face with grass
in his new field, not because of you or because you did
anything wrong."

She nodded but looked unconvinced. I knew how she was
feeling so well. I could see my own teenage self standing in
front of me, struggling to believe in anything but the bad stuff.
I could see the internal war raging inside her, the words of
those around cutting into her self-confidence, the scars so deep
and so real that they physically hurt.

In a quiet voice, I said, "Amelia, I was bullied at school, so I
have some idea of how you may be feeling."

"Really? Why?"

There was a slight look of disbelief, as if any adult could
possibly know what it's like to be a teenager.

"Because of my freckles." Letting my hair fall forwards, I
rubbed my face, covering the freckles on my nose with my
fingers, before realising and forcing my hand into my pocket.
"It's shit isn't it?"

Amelia's eyes went very wide at my swearing in front of
her and then she giggled nervously. "Yeah, it is."

"But Sparkie knows you love him and he loves you back.
He sees you for what you are: compassionate, kind, and
trustworthy. That's worth more than the opinions of some
judgemental teenagers, who likely have some pretty big issues
of their own, right?"

Amelia nodded slowly, a spark of defiance kindling in her eyes.

Attagirl.

"Sometimes we just need to believe in ourselves, block out the mean things people say, and go out there and show everyone what you're really made of, Amelia. That's the best revenge in the world."

"I really want to be a vet too, you know," she blurted out, before ramming her fist into her mouth in horror, as if the admission was a dirty secret that she shouldn't have let escape into the world.

Empathy had never really been top of my emotional intelligence checklist, but the desire to help her engulfed me like a wave.

"Pop in to the surgery after school next week and let's see if we can sort out some work experience for you. There might be a lot of cleaning up of poo and gross things to do, but you're ok with that, yeah?"

The delight in her face shone out.

"Really?"

"Yes, really. Check with your parents, but I'd be happy for you to shadow me to see if it really is what you want to do. And Betsy, our veterinary nurse, is always grateful for an extra pair of hands in the clinic."

"Thank you!"

Tentatively, she stepped forwards and hugged me, and I patted her back awkwardly before she bolted from the queue and back to her family. They smiled warmly as she obviously relayed our conversation to them.

The whole time I'd been talking with Amelia, my mother had stood by, amazingly and unexpectedly silent. When I finally looked at her, all she said was, "You were bullied about your freckles?"

"Yes. The whole way through secondary school."

"Why didn't you tell me? I could have got you some make-up and taught you how to conceal them properly."

"That, right there, is exactly the reason why I didn't tell you," I replied angrily, grabbing my coffee and stomping away towards the dog show ring.

Chapter Twenty-Four

The intensity of the sun was starting to seep into the day. An uncomfortable promise of stickiness and prickly heat beckoned as I sipped my iced coffee, sitting quietly and alone at the edge of the white-roped show ring, slowly letting go of my inner rage underneath a large sign saying "Dog Show" in gold letters. The moment of solitude was welcome, and I was quite sure I was emitting "bugger off" vibes to anyone who looked in my direction, because I had been unequivocally and blissfully avoided for the last five minutes.

Across the other side of the field, in a quiet and shady spot, a battered Land Rover was parking up next to a small gazebo, surrounded by metal sheep hurdles, and my heartbeat spiked in my chest when Teddy got out of the driver's side. He helped Agnes out of the passenger seat and then they went around to the back, opening the door and the distinctive bleating of goats plucked a reluctant smile from my lips. Agnes proceeded to lift the little ones out of the vehicle and place them on the straw under the gazebo, then she turned to Teddy and I watched their exchange with growing amusement as his posture stiffened with what I now recognised as his goat-related anxiety. After a few minutes, during which I imagined Agnes's gently persuasive tone wearing down Teddy's resolve, he reached into the dark recesses of the Land Rover, emerging with Deidre in his arms, his head turned away from her angry bleating, back straining in his shirt as he placed her in the pen with her kids. Agnes gave him a little hug and glanced over in my direction. She waved when she saw me, making Teddy turn as well.

Facing him, even at this distance, made me hot all over – molten lava level hot. His little wave and smile caused a barrage of internal somersaults inside me, and I realised I was nervously jiggling my leg, causing me to spill some coffee on my knee.

"Shit!"

"Hannah? How lovely to see you!"

Mrs Fraser appeared behind me, dressed in a beautiful flowery summer dress and wedged heels and looking like she'd just flown in from a week on the Côte d'Azur. She beamed at me, then waved at her son, who now seemed to be staring in our direction, frozen to the spot.

"Hello, Mrs Fraser."

"Fiona, please," she replied, warmly. "Are you ready for the dog show?"

"I'm judging the first class."

"Oh? I thought you were doing all the classes?"

"No, we have a guest judge who's far more impressive and important." I tried to keep the blade of bitterness out of my voice, but the eyeroll was evident to all around, and Fiona's sharp-eyed gaze was no exception.

"So you're free from about eleven?"

A slightly devious expression crossed her face.

"Er, well, I was going to…" My voice drifted off. What was I going to do? I hadn't planned my next steps after I'd employed advanced level ex-boyfriend-avoidance techniques and secured my exit strategy from this latest shitshow.

Fiona waited patiently for me to carry on.

"Yes, I'm free from eleven," I finished weakly, unable to come up with any viable excuses. My cranium was an empty, echoing void of nothingness, leaving me wondering what the actual use was of a PhD after all.

She clapped her hands together.

"That's great news! We could do with an extra pair of hands in the produce tent at lunch time. Could you come over at about midday?"

I nodded and she practically radiated happiness.

"Thank you so much."

A queue of dogs and their owners was starting to form nearby, and I could see Giles hesitantly wandering our way. Luckily, he was alone.

Fiona contemplated me as I got to my feet, letting out a soft sigh. "You make him so happy – you know that, don't you? I've always worried that he was living in Henry's shadow, but since meeting up with you again Edward has lit up from the inside."

Teddy's treehouse confession rang in my ears. His insecurities had been alive and evident, and yet still so difficult to reconcile with the friendly, charming façade he lived behind. The fact that his mother recognised a small part of this, but was probably not aware of the extent of her son's feelings, made me want to yell and shout at her, shake her until she could see what was really going on with him. I wanted to tell her all the sad truths he kept buried, ask her to believe in him, to tell him that he was as special and important as his twin brother. But I didn't. I kept it inside, unwilling to break his confidence with this secret he had entrusted to me.

Instead, I just said, "Ted's a truly brilliant man in his own right. I'm grateful we've rekindled our friendship too."

"No need to be coy with me, Hannah. I know you two aren't just *friends*," Fiona said with a laugh while patting my arm gently. "I may be his mother, but I see the way you look at each other."

I didn't know what to say. I couldn't exactly relay the fact that he'd spurned my pathetic drunken advances, then essentially ghosted me this week, and it was as clear as day that he didn't want me, not the way I was coming to realise that I wanted him. A quick fumble would most definitely get it out of his system but it would never, ever, be enough for me.

"Fiona!" Giles's outdoor voice, which was loud and intrusive and usually bloody irritating, was like a welcome lighthouse in the fog, saving me from any further squirm-inducing, Teddy-related discussions. "How lovely to see you."

"Giles." A bout of air kissing ensued and I wanted to vomit a little. But instead, I stood like an uncomfortable lemon and pasted a smile on my face as they made small talk.

"Hannah's agreed to help with the judging in the produce tent."

Have I? Crap! Is that what I've signed up for? More bloody judging? In the produce tent?

Christ, it was all Victoria sponges and enormous marrows, wasn't it? What the hell did I know about that shit?

"Has she?" Giles looked as bewildered as I felt, then

gestured at the now very long queue that had formed to our right. "But first you've got to pick the dog you'd most like to take home, and that's going to be tough, isn't it?"

On safer ground with this, I nodded and scarpered into the centre of the ring, pinning my judge's badge to my shirt and swallowing nervously as hoards of my clients entered through the white rope gate, all smiling excitedly.

Then I heard it – the distinctive blood-curdling scream of Bentley Ryan, loudly announcing his presence to the entire field of other canines and their owners, who turned as one to stare at a tight-lipped Mrs Ryan in a floral dress and large straw hat as she tried to drag the reluctant dog towards the ring. The appearance of this pair caused my stomach to drop like a giant leaden suppository into my pants. The animosity in her glare was truly terrifying. It was a laser-like stare that focussed on me with complete and utter disapproval.

Well, isn't this totally splendid.

And then she did something wholly unexpected. Reaching into her handbag, she pulled out a ragged, chewed, and soggy pink tennis ball from a clear plastic bag and offered it to the screaming dog. She knelt down in the grass and stroked his ears as he sniffed this object and tentatively took it in his mouth. The silence that followed was deafening, and the collective dog show participants breathed a sigh of relief, before the furore of excitement from everyone else started all over again.

Dogs of every shape and size were paraded around me, each owner desperately trying to catch my eye. There were purebreds, scruffy mutts, and a fair share of rescues, and the ring was so full it was bursting at the seams. Some of the dogs trotted obediently while others pulled at their leads; some yapped and spun around, and the puppies excitedly jumped up at their handlers; a couple of three-legged dogs and a basset hound in a pram completed the line-up. It's fair to say it was absolute carnage and my frontal lobe went into meltdown. How the hell was I going to choose between them and not piss off a load of people? I was regretting my decision to judge this class because scientific objectivity would not help me here; it was a purely subjective decision. I had to go with my heart on this.

Glancing out to where Giles was standing, I noticed that Jonathan had joined him. He was smirking, arms folded, clearly not oblivious to my discomfort and blatant panic.

Yeah, well, bollocks to him.

With a little shake of my shoulders, I forced my reluctant face to smile as I tried to ignore the horrified looks of some of the dog owners and began to actively peruse each of the contestants.

"Ok, everyone. All handlers under sixteen years old come over here." I gestured to a corner of the ring and noticed with a not insignificant amount of satisfaction how everyone jumped to my command. "Great. Now, all rescue dogs over here." I pointed to another corner. "And dogs under six months over here. Finally, everyone else in the other corner. Excellent, thanks."

Once they were segregated, I went and examined each of the dogs, now in much more manageable groups. From the rescue group, I selected a nervous border collie cross, who wiggled and wriggled around my feet, gently licking my hands as I stroked her, and a beautiful, graceful ex-racing greyhound. I gestured to Giles to bring the rosettes over. I selected a beagle and a Jack Russell terrier from amongst the puppies – these were two pups that I knew were attending training classes and had been particularly well behaved for their vaccinations recently. Approaching the child handlers, I picked a beautiful greying black labrador who gazed adoringly at the small girl who held him, and a mixed breed dog with three legs that was surely the happiest creature I had ever encountered in my years of practice.

With trepidation, I approached the last group, selecting the basset hound in the pram (because how the hell could I not?). Then, bending down to be on eye level with the rest of the dogs, I caught Bentley's attention. His tongue lolled out of the side of his mouth as he dropped the ball on the ground, seemingly smiling at me, and it made my lips quirk in reply. Suddenly he pulled on his lead, slipping from Mrs Ryan's hands, and bounded over, all flapping ears and drool as he launched his barrel-shaped body at me with gay abandon and knocked me backwards.

"Oh! Dr Havens, I am so sorry."

A worried-looking Mrs Ryan loomed over me. Her enormous hat was backlit against the bright sun and blue sky above, while I fought off the slobbery attentions of Bentley.

"It's really ok, Mrs Ryan. He obviously would like to come home with me and the feeling is absolutely mutual!"

I laughed, getting to my feet and placing him on the grass, while I gently rubbed his ears which made him grunt softly in pleasure, his back leg drumming the ground as he enthusiastically scratched at an imaginary itch.

The older lady looked conflicted for a moment, before a slightly haughty expression crossed her face.

"You don't have to give me a rosette just to appease me, you know."

"I know. But Bentley really is a dog I would like to take home. He's so friendly and always happy to see me. He's a pleasure to have in my consulting room."

I paused and took a breath. This might not be the right time, but fuck it, I was going to say it. It was time to be myself and address the elephant in the room.

"The ball works for his anxiety, huh?"

She nodded, uncomfortable for a moment, but I carried on, lowering my voice.

"And his weight is definitely improving too, I can almost feel some ribs in there and I see how hard you're working to keep him happy and healthy."

The tension melted from Mrs Ryan.

"Thank you, I really am doing my best."

"I know you are."

Behind me, Giles appeared with a rosette. "Congratulations, Mrs Ryan. Bentley is looking super now he's dropped a few pounds, isn't he?"

She nodded and looked a little guilty.

"I only want him to be as healthy as possible. He's all I have in the world." She paused and sniffed a little. "Thank you for caring about him, Dr Havens. I'm very grateful, you know."

I smiled and handed her prize over.

"You're welcome."

She graciously took the rosette and then suddenly her eyes went wide as she looked over my shoulder where a cacophony of frenzied barking had begun. Then noise and chaos erupted all around us. I turned just in time to see a blur of white as Deidre the goat raced across the field in my direction, bumping into a few of the dog show competitors, who toppled like felled trees. She bleated in panic as she took a sharp turn around me, with Teddy in hot pursuit. In a rather impressive move, he launched himself at her, but seemed to misjudge, completely missing her surprisingly speedy, zigzagging form. Instead, rugby-tackling me to the ground, landing squarely on top of me and slamming the air from my lungs. His breathless body and startled blue gaze pinned me down completely.

Yes, in a rather unexpected turn of events, Teddy Fraser was lying on top of me, with every bit of him touching every bit of me, and he was panting, more than a little suggestively, in front of the entire village fayre. Which at this moment in time was nothing short of bloody awkward, but under any other circumstances (as my sex-starved brain helpfully added) would have been most definitely hot as hell.

Chapter Twenty-Five

"Sorry, Hannah, are you ok?"

Teddy's lips were mere centimetres from my own mouth, his breath a warm breeze on my skin. His gaze was intense and enticing, as if he were showing me a window to his very soul, and I lay still like a rabbit caught in full beam. We stared at each other, unmoving, for about twelve minutes. All right, maybe not twelve minutes, but there was definitely enough time for my entire visceral system to liquefy inside my body, alongside a few embarrassed-sounding coughs from various onlookers.

"Ummm, yeah, I'm fine, but perhaps you should get up now?" My voice was a little off – breathy, you might say, and definitely not the voice of an ice queen or a prickly hedgehog.

"Oh, yeah, I should."

But he still didn't move. He kept on staring with fascination into my eyes. And all I could think about in the whole wide world was snogging his face off. Once again.

It was only the sudden loud throat-clearing noise above our

heads that made him jolt his gaze upwards, and I followed his line of sight and found I was looking straight up Giles's nose, accompanied by a curious Deidre by his side as she bent down to snuffle Teddy's hair.

"I caught your intended quarry, Ted," Giles said.

Still lying on top of me, like this was entirely normal and comfortable for everyone, Teddy smiled.

"Thanks, Giles. She's pretty fast for a blind goat."

"Quite. So perhaps you could release my colleague now? I'm not sure she necessarily needs holding captive much longer."

Teddy grinned mischievously and said, "Shame. That's right up there with your fireman fantasy, right?"

I snorted and bit my lip, trying not to give him the satisfaction of seeing me laugh, but he knew what he did to me with every look and every comment. He bloody well knew. With a final small smile and eyebrow twitch, he lifted his weight up from my body, a sudden cool flow of air filling the void where his warmth had been, just as a pair of shiny tan brogues appeared in my peripheral vision.

"Get off her, you boorish idiot." Jonathan quickly bent down and grasped my hand, hauling me to my feet as Teddy stood back, frowning and brushing the loose grass from his clothes.

Jonathan continued in a petulant tone, "You really should listen to me and your mother and get away from this joke of a place. You're far too good for these people."

This day was already proving to be longer and more arduous than I could ever have imagined, and I snatched my hand from his.

"I rarely take anything she has to say on board, but I don't know why you're persistent with this, Jonathan. I've already told you my answer. I'm not returning to Bristol with you."

"I do love you, Hannah. I've made mistakes and I regret them more than you know."

He seemed sincere – perhaps even a touch desperate – and my heart began thumping in my ears. I briefly closed my eyes and tried valiantly to stop the explosion of emotions that was threatening to erupt.

"Why are you doing this?"

"I want you back, obviously."

"No, Jonathan, the real reason. Why are you here?"

He shifted uncomfortably on his feet, refusing to meet my eye. Instead, he cast an appraising glance at the crowd still milling about in the show ring. He opened and closed his mouth a few times before finally speaking in a hushed tone.

"The funds from that large Horserace Betting Levy Board grant have been frozen. The first results we presented to the panel last week were inconsistent." He gave me a beseeching look. "Some of the team have left in the last few months and the students haven't been able to replicate your findings."

I stared blankly at him.

Right. Yeah, of course.

No one in the world would be so hopelessly in love with me that they would show up and beg me to return. Not someone like me. No, he just wanted my lab notes and for me to tutor some fucking students. He wanted me to be his skivvy to do his experiments so he could keep his bastard funding. Reality slapped me across the cheek like a solid, wet fish, and some of the icy ire left my blood so that my shoulders noticeably sank.

"I see."

"So, just to recap, you need Hannah to swoop in and save your research group who are dropping like flies? Because you're too incompetent to manage your own experiments?" Teddy asked through gritted teeth.

"Well, I er—"

"And you're saying that you need her superior intellect and ability to cover your arse?"

"That's not quite how it—"

"But the only thing you're prepared to offer is her old job back and a half-arsed declaration of love to sweeten the deal?" Teddy's voice was steely. "Unbelievable."

"I wouldn't expect someone like you to understand," Jonathan sneered.

"You're right. *Someone like me* would never be able to understand how *someone like you* could treat someone as amazing as Hannah so fucking appallingly."

"You don't know anything about it, so I think you should just piss off, you clueless meathead."

Teddy lurched forward, hands already forming fists, but I grabbed his arm.

"Stop! Teddy, don't. He's not worth it."

Jonathan smirked triumphantly at him, but Teddy turned to me, whitened knuckles resting lightly under my chin.

"No, he's not worth it, at all, but punching his lights out in front of all these people would certainly make me feel better." He paused and brushed his thumb across my mouth, grazing the pad over my lower lip so that my breath caught in my throat. "All that crap he put you through … you know you're worth so much more, right?"

I went to shake my head, the inner confidence I held on to with a narrow thread fully deserting me. Honey-badger

Hannah retreated into a safe, dark hole, hidden from view once more. But with a soft smile, Teddy gently tugged my chin, forcing me to nod my head, a reluctant twitch pulling at the corner of my lips.

"Good," he whispered.

"Touching, really. But sentimentality isn't going to get her a professorship at any of the major vet schools. Only I can do that for her."

He was talking about me as if I wasn't even here. Again.

Yep, still a total and utter dickhead of epic proportions, the honey badger whispered from her hiding place.

"I think you should leave now, " Teddy said.

"I'm the head judge and guest of honour," Jonathan replied with a self-satisfied smirk.

"Actually, with all due respect, Professor Pierce, I'm not entirely sure I'm comfortable with you being here, and I don't think Hannah is either." Giles paused and looked to me, questioningly, and I shook my head. "I thought so." Turning back to Jonathan, he squared his shoulders and took a deep breath. "I regret to inform you that I've decided to withdraw the support of our practice from your research project. I should never have agreed without discussing things with my colleague first."

"What? Now, Giles, wait a min—"

"No, actually, I think I'll manage the rest of the judging today, so you're no longer necessary and should definitely just leave. Right away, actually, if you wouldn't mind. Thank you." Giles had seemingly grown a massive pair of balls all of a sudden, and I was stunned into silence as I watched him hand over Deidre (who he'd lassoed with his leather belt) to a rather reluctant Teddy.

"Don't waste your life on something so completely beneath you," Jonathan called out as Giles firmly ushered him away.

"You ok?" Teddy asked, his voice low and calm.

"Yes, I think so."

"Good." He paused. "Right, I should get Deidre back to Agnes. Will you help me?" His tone was beseeching, nervous, his swagger lost for a moment as he realised he was now in sole charge of a goat.

My rational brain was running the show again since I'd gained a little space and was no longer drowning in the depth of Teddy's pupils. Instead, conflict raged inside me and I knew I should be distancing myself from this twist of emotions, not tangling them up further so they became irrevocably knotted up in my very being. Logic was clear in this case: it was too risky to let my guard down and give in; too messy to contemplate spending any more time in his company. Love and romance were not destined for me. I could see that now. Plus, I was mad at him – mad that he'd not bothered to stay with me the other morning and mad that he'd avoided me all week. And really bloody mad that he'd turned me down and not succumbed to my epically awful seduction techniques. I should most definitely run in the opposite direction and save myself from any more embarrassment. Yet, the lure of him was intoxicating. He exerted a magnetic pull, as if he possessed gravity of his very own, and I was just inconsequential space debris hurtling towards him and my own destruction.

"Sorry, Ted, I think you'll have to manage on your own."

And before he could answer, before I could register the surprise that I knew would be there in his expression, I ran away into the growing crowds of people without a backward glance.

As midday approached, I wandered towards the huge white marquee that held the produce to be judged. I'd spent the last hour or so judiciously avoiding the hay bale tossing – an event that Teddy seemed to be running – and lurked in the shadows of multiple local craft stalls and the large fun fair that was in full swing, keen to avoid running into anyone I knew. But I couldn't put it off anymore, and as I neared the entrance, a panicked Fiona Fraser came trotting over.

"Ah, Hannah, I was worried you'd run off!" Little did she know that I had perfected running away just recently.

"Nope, here I am."

"Excellent, excellent."

"What am I judging?"

"I've put you on the kids' entries with—"

At that moment, Teddy appeared from the tent entrance, rolling his shirt sleeves up to reveal his corded forearms, long fingers flexing around the folded linen at his elbows. "Mum, what have you roped me into…"

His voice trailed off as he saw me, darting his gaze away when he met mine.

"Edward, there you are. I've put you and Hannah together on the kids' entries. Won't that be nice." Her eyebrows lifted and she reached up to pat his cheek.

"Well, that's probably not a good idea," I said just as Teddy muttered, "Umm, no, I don't think so."

With an irritated look, he ran his hands through his hair. "Do you really need us both? I'm sure Hannah has better things to do."

There was a subtle barb there, a little dig, aimed at me. I

knew I deserved it but it caused a little frisson of annoyance to tingle up my spine. I was avoiding him, yes, but why did it still hurt that he was now trying to avoid me too?

"No, I promised Fiona I would be here." I let my hair down out of its ponytail, allowing my curtain of defence to fall free and partially cover my face. "But, Ted, as the chief tosser at the hay bale tossing stand, aren't you missed back there?"

Hedgehog Hannah was coming to the rescue, covering up my hurt with prickly retorts. Normal service had resumed.

"It's finished for the day. Anyway, given your speed when you ran away earlier, I was sure you'd be entering the charity running race this afternoon. It certainly looked like you were in training for it."

Teddy's posture was rigid, his arms folded, and his fingers were drumming an angry beat on his bicep.

Fiona's head bobbed backwards and forwards between us, like she was watching a tennis match.

"Perhaps, with your great disappearing-act skills, you should offer your services to the magician in the children's entertainment tent?" Hands on my hips, I glared at him.

Mirroring my expression, he loomed over me. "Perhaps, with your complete lack of communication skills, you shouldn't be tasked with judging anything."

"Well, clearly my recent judgement of your character is pretty abysmal – I'll agree with you on that."

The hurt and rejection in my tone rang through, stinging my lips with their venom, even though my heart unexpectedly ached as I spoke.

"Thank the Lord, she agrees with me about something!" Teddy said petulantly.

"Ok, ok! Stop! Stop it, you two! *J'en peux plus!*" Fiona said, exasperated, her French accent thickening in obvious frustration. "I don't know what's going on here, but you're behaving like small children. You are both judging and that is final. Sort out your differences, like adults. Kiss and make up or something, but stop being so ridiculous! *Non mais ça va pas, vous deux!*"

Then she stalked away towards the Victoria sponges, shaking her head, and leaving Teddy and me desperately looking anywhere else but at each other.

"She only ever shouts at me in French when she's really pissed off," Teddy said, kicking his toe into the dusty grass.

"It's a first for me to be shouted at in French. Madame Jourdan only ever told me off in English at school, even when she caught me staring at the rugby players in Year Ten rather than working out how to ask for twelve baguettes and a cabbage at the local market in Rouen."

A small smile quirked over Teddy's lips.

"I can't believe you called me a tosser in front of my own mother."

I fought my face, determined to keep the grumpiness, but it wasn't working. "If the cap fits."

"You're not going to run off again, are you? I'm not qualified to judge the best animal made out of vegetables on my own, you know."

"Neither am I."

Teddy chanced a look at me.

"Don't we make a good team, usually?"

I couldn't hold his stare and I focussed instead on the long lines holding the marquee in place, fixing my gaze on where the metal peg protruded from the ground.

"We have, on occasion, been known to work well together."

"On occasion?"

"Yes. When you don't abandon me like a regretful one-night stand the morning after rejecting me because of my complete lack of attractiveness and seduction skills."

There, I'd said it. It hung in the air between us, a blackened piece of my soul suspended on a silken thread, fragile, waiting for his affirmation of what I already knew. I held my breath, waiting to be destroyed.

"You think I rejected you the other night?" he asked slowly.

"Yes."

"Because I didn't think you were attractive or sexy?"

"Yes."

Was he going to make me spell out the whole disastrous debacle again? My cheeks flamed with embarrassment.

Should have kept your mouth shut, the tiny, mean gremlin sneered in my head.

"And then you think I abandoned you the next day? That I didn't want to see you again?"

"Yes! Yes, all of this, Teddy, but it's fine. We should just leave it, because we're good as friendly acquaintances, aren't we? That's best?"

"Don't give me that bullshit, Hannah." He was bristling.

"It's not bullshit if it's true, Teddy, and you haven't given me any reason to think otherwise."

"Hold on, didn't you read my note? I left it for you the other morning, by the bed?"

My mind flitted back to Aphrodite and the orange juice fiasco, the sodden notepad on the bedside table.

"No."

He blew out a long sigh. "Well, this explains a lot."

"It does?" I wasn't sure what could possibly be in the note

that would explain his ghost-like avoidance behaviour. But, whatever.

"Why do you think so little of me?" Teddy demanded, rubbing his hands over his face and through his hair.

"What?"

"Why do you immediately jump to the conclusion that I'm some complete arsehole of a human intent on dumping you at any given moment?"

"Because we're in different leagues. Men like you aren't seriously interested in women like me. I'm not stupid."

"That's debatable."

"Hey!"

"Do you want to know what was in the note?"

"Does it matter?"

"It matters to me. Maybe it will matter to you, if you just hear me out."

"All right." I folded my arms protectively over my chest. "I cannot wait to hear this ground-breaking and poignant prose. Go for it."

Teddy shot me an irritated glance. "If you'd bothered to read it, you would have known that I had an early flight to Edinburgh from Bristol that morning, to work on the designs for a new visitor centre near Loch Leven, and that the phone reception was really patchy on-site."

He raised an eyebrow, challenging me to disbelieve him.

"Ok, fine, that's plausible."

It was, I suppose.

"And, if you'd not jumped to conclusions that I was such a fucking bastard, and read my words, you would know that I decided not to wake you at 4am because you looked so peaceful and beautiful asleep in my bed. So much so, that I wanted you to stay there forever. That I nearly missed my flight because I didn't want to leave you."

He scrubbed his hand up his neck and through his hair again, mussing it so much that my fingers were biting into my arms in an effort not to run my hands through it.

"If you'd actually looked at the carefully written prose, you'd know that turning you down was the hardest thing I've ever done in my whole life, when all I wanted was to tear your clothes off and devour every inch of you." He paused and swallowed. "If you'd only taken a moment not to run away from me at every opportunity since we first met, you'd know that I fell in love with you when I was eighteen years old, and not a single other person has held a candle to you since."

I was aware I was staring.

"Your mouth is hanging open, Hannah."

With deliberate slowness, I pursed my lips together.

"Any questions? Or should we get on with judging the creations waiting for us in there?" Teddy gestured over his shoulder and into the produce tent.

"Why did you turn me down?" My voice was little more than a whisper. I wished my honey badger would bloody well make an appearance in this, my hour of need, instead of the funny little softly spoken fairy creature I seemed to have become.

"I only turned you down because I don't want the first time we sleep together to be some drunken fumble on my couch. I want you fully aware of what you're doing, of what I'm doing to you, and what the hell that means, because"—he leant in close, his breath a soft caress over my skin—"once we do it, I'm never ever letting you run away from me again."

Chapter Twenty-Six

As if in a daze, I followed Teddy into the marquee, alive with tumbling feelings that were rocking me off my axis. I stumbled along behind him, barely aware of the stifling heat and press of bodies around us. The brush of his fingers against mine lit up my skin. With a quick glance down, I watched hypnotically as Teddy wrapped my hand in his and guided me through the throng of people towards the far end of the tent. And I was grateful. I felt grounded to this point of contact, the radiation of warmth, the steady stroke of his thumb over my skin, the gentle reassurance as he squeezed my palm.

We stopped in front of the lines of children's entries – three tables full of gardens on a plate, artwork, flower arrangements and animals made of vegetables – and not for the first time I was immensely glad that Teddy was the one who was in this with me. Expectant parents and wide-eyed youngsters stood around, watching our every move as we perused the offerings, and Teddy murmured things like "What a lovely replica pond in this one, with the little pebbles and the painted waterfall"; or "How about this wonderful drawing of a pony"; or "What an amazing vegetable hedgehog, such inventive use of carrots as spines".

And I nodded and smiled along with him, agreeing and trying to look as if I was paying attention and not just fixating on how his mouth moved as he spoke, or on the occasional glimpse of his tongue and the salacious memories it evoked, which completely derailed my train of thought.

"What do you think?" Teddy asked.

What I was thinking was not really appropriate for a family audience, so instead I inclined my head and said, "The hedgehog has to win, obviously."

"I agree. Hedgehogs are definitely my favourite of all animals and are even better in vegetable form. Well done, Oliver, aged four." Teddy placed the small red card with "first prize" next to the hedgehog, and a squeak of excitement erupted from a blond-haired little boy to his left. Teddy's answering smile was dazzling. "It's a great hedgehog, buddy."

I didn't know how it was possible for him to become any more attractive, but in that moment he was elevated to top-tier, bestselling romance novel hero, like the most swoonworthy Regency duke you could imagine, and I had to put my hand on the table to stop my knees from buckling. And wasn't that embarrassing? Because Teddy noticed and gave me a sexy little half-smirk, which didn't really help matters.

When we had dished out all the certificates, and some special prizes for some particularly young competitors, we finally escaped the tent, stepping back out into the sunshine and leaving the claustrophobic hustle behind.

"Well done, you two." Fiona appeared out of nowhere. "Glad to see you're getting on again now."

"You're welcome," I replied, subconsciously stepping away from Teddy, trying to feign indifference. After all, old habits die hard, but I was fooling no one if the smile behind her hand was anything to go by.

Teddy leant down and kissed his mother lightly on the cheek, and she patted his face affectionately.

"You should bring Hannah home for dinner and let us all get to know her a little better."

"Perhaps."

He was being cagey, the sideways glance he gave me was anxious and questioning, and I didn't know how to respond. My whole body was awkward. We hadn't talked about this, I hadn't really thought beyond the very real desire to rip his clothes off.

And despite his earlier admission, some little niggles of doubt remained.

"Always so evasive." Fiona sighed and rolled her eyes. "Don't ruin this, Edward. She's an exceptional woman and she's not going to wait around forever." And with a smile at me, she turned on her heel and headed back into the marquee.

"I should go."

"Not unless you have a genuine reason to leave. You're not running out on me again." Teddy grabbed my hand. "We've been through this."

"What?" I laughed nervously. "I wasn't running away."

I totally was.

"You totally were." His eyebrows knitted together and his voice took on a growly, seductive tone. "Please don't run from me."

"But—"

"I know what's happening here. My mother inviting us for dinner has fried your brain, hasn't it?"

"No." But my head was nodding all the same.

"I thought so."

Stepping into face me, he ran his knuckles softly down my cheek, his thumb dragging over my bottom lip, his other hand holding me tightly.

"We're going to do this our way, just you and me. No one else is going to interfere, right?"

"Ok."

I was being drawn in, leaning forwards, unable to resist, despite all of this being a bad idea.

"Including the little voice in your head telling you that this is a bad idea."

How does he know about that?

"Because it's not a bad idea, us being together. It's the best fucking idea of my whole life, Hannah."

"Ahh."

The ability to speak was gone. Kaput. I was just a wobbly mass of feelings and squishy internal organs. So enraptured in the ferocity and heat of his gaze that I couldn't back away. I couldn't bring myself to do anything other than stare back into the dark pools of his eyes.

"Edward?"

The quiet, quavering voice nearby broke the spell, and we both turned as one to see Agnes, looking confused and a little fearful. Her usual twinkle was missing and her body was stooped and frail.

"Have you seen Frank? He said he was coming back, but he hasn't. I don't know where he is and I need him."

"Agnes, it's me, Teddy. Are you ok?"

He dropped my hand and stepped towards her, touching her shaking shoulder, his large hand dwarfing her thin frame.

"Where is he?"

"Shall we head back to the goats?" I suggested gently, and it was then that Agnes noticed me behind Teddy. A little spark of recognition lit up behind her eyes.

"Hannah?"

"Yes, Agnes. Shall we go and find Deidre?"

"Deidre? Yes." The vacant look began to dissolve, and the Agnes we knew, the shrewd and intelligent woman with her bright, sharp gaze, returned. "There you two are."

"Here we are. Is everything ok?"

"Yes," She replied unsteadily. Perhaps she was still a touch uncertain, fighting through the fog of confusion as she looked at us.

Lacing my arm through hers, I started to steer her back towards the goat stand where a number of children were clambering on the fence and reaching in to pat Deidre. With some of them precariously close to falling into her pen.

"Come on. We'll help you sort through this rabble, then get you home later. Is that ok?"

"Oh yes, dear, I'd be so grateful. Some of those children are really quite delinquent."

Teddy laughed and took her other arm in the crook of his elbow, and together we walked back to rescue the goats from being mauled by sticky fingers, and to ensure that Deidre didn't manage to eat everyone's ice creams.

As the end of the day drew to a close and the crowds began to disperse, we tidied away the gazebo and loaded the goats into the back of Teddy's Land Rover, hefting Deidre's sizeable bulk into the vehicle alongside her kids and closing the door securely.

"Are you coming, Hannah? I can give you a lift back to the surgery." Teddy opened the passenger door, and I slid across the bench seat and into the middle where I had to, unavoidably, place my legs either side of the gearstick, while he helped Agnes up next to me.

When he climbed into the driving seat, Teddy's thigh was very firmly pressed against mine, and with a delightfully naughty smirk, he started the engine and reached between my knees to put the car into gear.

"I really love this car."

Agnes chuckled softly to my left, and I felt myself set on fire every time Teddy reached to change gear on the fairly short trip back to Abbots Lane.

We dropped Agnes at her house and ensured she had some dinner and all was well again with her, then settled the goats back into the shed, before heading back outside, where the warmth of the day was now more tepid and bearable.

Leaning languidly against his Land Rover, Teddy studied me intently.

"Do you want to come in for a drink, and maybe a bite to eat?"

"Ummm…"

Noticing my hesitation, he smiled and stepped forward.

"It's up to you, but it could be really *nice*."

"*Nice*, huh?"

His intonation did not go unnoticed and my heart began to thud wildly in my chest.

"Oh yeah. I've got a few advanced lessons on how to be nice that I want to show you."

"Oh."

"Oh?"

"Umm…"

Teddy laughed, heading for the front door of The Old Rectory.

"You coming?"

I dithered, hopping from foot to foot. I knew this was a pivotal moment. A point of no return. I was either going to throw myself into this head-first or run away and hide, and until my feet began to move, I wasn't sure which way it would go. But the relief that washed over me as I took Teddy's hand and stepped over the threshold was all-encompassing.

Teddy closed the door behind us, while I caught sight of myself in the large floor-length antique mirror in the hallway, its scrolled and gilded frame twinkling in the low light of the lamp that sat on the console table by the door. And I was hit with a sudden burst of disgust, the large and uninhibited view of my whole body causing a ripple of revulsion and self-loathing to radiate through me.

"Perhaps this was a bad idea." I turned my head away, certain now that there was no way that Teddy was being honest with me. This could not be real. It wasn't possible.

"Look at yourself, Hannah," Teddy whispered, moving in close behind me, close enough that I could feel his warmth, but not touching me.

"I can't," I replied, my eyes cast down to the flagstones at my feet. I scuffed the floor with my sturdy ankle boots.

"Why? What do you see?"

"I don't like what I see, so it's better not to look," I murmured.

My inner turmoil was raging and bubbling intensely.

"Then look at me instead," he answered softly.

Gently he laced his fingers with mine, holding my left hand tenderly and using his right hand to sweep the long curtain of my hair back. He caressed his way over my shoulder, across my collar bone, the rough pads of his fingers brushing the skin at the opening of my shirt. Slowly, achingly slowly, he inched his hand up my neck, the side of his face now close to mine, breathing softly in my ear, he tipped my chin up with his thumb.

"Look at me, Hannah."

I glanced up at our reflection, taking in my awkward gawkiness and his glorious self-assuredness as he stood behind me, the breadth of his shoulders against my slim ones, the difference in our height, the slight downward tilt of his head, and the way he pressed his nose into my hair. Our eyes met in the mirror.

"Good. Now keep looking at me, whatever happens, ok?"

"What's going to happen, Teddy?" I asked breathlessly.

"I'm going to tell you how beautiful you are, and you're going to believe me," he replied. "But you're only to look at me, ok?"

I nodded, captivated by him, by the insistent and persuasive tone of his voice, the feel of his hands on me, and the warmth of his body now pressed against my back.

His hand moved down the column of my throat, his eyes holding mine.

"Your skin is so soft here. I've never forgotten how you felt under my lips, how you tasted, Hannah, even after all this time, and the other night only whetted my appetite to taste more of you."

I swallowed nervously, but I could see no mischievous glint in his expression, only sincerity.

Pressing his nose more firmly against my ear, he nuzzled in, his eyes closing briefly before he glanced back into the mirror.

"And the way you smell, like fresh morning rain, it has me totally spellbound, unable to think of anything else at all."

His hand was on the move again, upwards, so that he was now caressing my jawline, his thumb brushing my chin, then smoothing over my lips. He let out a little groan, and the noise was soft and sensuous.

"Your lips are incredible, so full and sweet. How you used them to kiss me, Hannah. Better than any porn star, I imagine," he murmured with a cheeky, lopsided grin, and I couldn't help but smile, a quiet huff of laughter escaping.

With a gentle insistence, he dragged my lower lip down with his thumb, parting my lips.

"And your mouth, so warm and seductive... You have no idea of the fantasies I've had about your mouth, Hannah."

I shivered, still staring at his eyes, which met mine unflinchingly. Releasing my mouth, he dragged a light grazing touch over my skin, tapping a forefinger gently on the tip of my nose.

"Your nose is impeccably cute and straight, and these freckles are everything."

"You like my freckles?" I replied, hopeful yet unsure, not wanting to be teased and not yet able to believe.

"Do I like them? Hannah, I want to know every single one. I want to discover every freckle on your body and worship them all. They are unique and beautiful and so perfect that it's almost impossible to believe that they're actually real," he murmured gustily, warm breath tickling down the side of my face as he pressed closer.

"Your hair is the colour of a warm golden sunset, and so soft and silky that I want to run my hands through it all the time. I want to mess it up and feel it fall against my bare skin, Hannah. I want to know how it is to lie back against my pillow and be surrounded by your hair, with you leaning down over me. I want to see how it looks first thing in the morning, when you've just woken up after we've made love all night in my bed. I want to know if it's as wild and untamed as I imagine it to be." Teddy paused and swallowed audibly. "Will you let me see that, Hannah?"

I gazed steadily back at the reflection of his face. His expression was open and sincere, and I saw a deep-seated desire in his returning look. I nodded hesitantly.

"Then, of course, there are your eyes."

Gently, Teddy used his fingers on my chin to twist my head up and around to the side, leaning me backwards against him. His reverential expression momentarily blinded me.

"I've never seen eyes this green, this enchanting. The colour seems to change like magic, showing me everything you're feeling. Your eyes let me in, even when you try to shut me out. They sparkle with intelligence and kindness, and I don't think I'll ever tire of staring into them."

An infinitesimal movement of his head brought our noses close together. Our breath mingled, lips parting.

"Your face is the only one etched onto my memory, your scent the only one I've ever yearned for, your kisses the only ones I've replayed thousands of times in my mind. You will never see yourself the way I do, Hannah, I know that, but you should also know that, to me, there is no one more beautiful than you."

I think it's safe to say that I was a complete puddle of goo at this point. A person made entirely of liquid and no solid components. Did I think I was beautiful? No. Not even close, but that didn't matter because this man thought I was. He'd said it. And he meant it. And for this brief moment in time, I'd felt it. I'd actually felt desirable and attractive. I was totally about to jump his bones when suddenly the front door opened and Henry and Clara walked in, and we sprang apart like guilty philanderers caught red-handed.

"Shit, Henry! Don't you knock?" Teddy said, running his hand through his hair.

"Sorry, but you said to just come straight in with the takeaway."

Henry looked really uncomfortable and Clara was just bobbing her head backwards and forwards between Teddy and me.

"Let's put this in the dining room. Come on," she said quickly, looking up at Henry's concerned face and taking his hand to lead him away. The relief and love that poured out of him was palpable. I noticed the squeeze of his hand in hers, the nod and the soft smile that he gave her.

I followed their retreating backs enviously. To be so easy and free in someone else's company, to wilfully, knowingly show how much you are in love with someone by the little gestures. I knew I would always struggle with that, knew that even though Teddy was opening up to me, I would undoubtedly find it difficult to do the same.

Teddy stood woodenly, unmoving except a faint tic in his jaw muscle. His eyes narrowed as he watched me.

"I should go," I said shakily.

I'd been swept away in the moment and my instincts were screaming at me to slow things down. I needed to let myself breathe and get used to the idea that Teddy might actually be interested in me, and possibly not just for sex. And, perhaps this alien feeling in my chest, which was something rather more special than I would care to admit to, was greater than the obvious desire I felt for him, was secondary to something else, something more serious and frightening? Something I needed to become comfortable with before I shared it with anyone else. Especially Teddy.

"Yeah, perhaps you should just leave."

"Are you ok?" I asked, surprised by his curt tone.

"Fine. You can see yourself out, right?"

I nodded mutely as he stormed away after Henry and Clara, so that I was left with only a deep-rooted ache for his company, and the debilitating feeling that I'd unknowingly broken something truly rare and beautiful.

Chapter Twenty-Seven

"There's someone here to see you. She says it's important." Betsy announced, as she skipped into the back office where I was having my lunch.

It had been a very busy Monday morning surgery, and this was my first break since I'd started the clinic several hours ago. My attention was still drawn to the unopened letter that I'd been turning over and over in my fingers for the last five minutes. The stamp had been franked in Bristol and the university crest graced the top corner of the envelope. I couldn't escape the knotty, sick feeling in my stomach.

I waved my sandwich at Betsy. "If it's an emergency, Giles is about somewhere."

"It's not, but she says she has to speak to you. It's urgent."

"What's it about?"

"She didn't say, but was very insistent that she sees you."

"All right, give me five minutes and then show her into consulting room one."

Betsy gave me a little salute and backed out of the room. I glanced at the envelope again. Taking a fortifying and exaggerated deep breath, I ripped it open and quickly read the letter, typed neatly on headed paper, my sandwich now forgotten in its wrapper.

As I skimmed the words, key phrases jumped out:

…vacancy in the equine hospital and research team…
…your academic record speaks for itself…
…always a valued member of the department…
…by mutual agreement Professor Pierce has stepped down
from his post…
…left the university with immediate effect…

I stopped and read this part again. And once more for luck. Jonathan had left. Gone from Bristol. I let this sink in for a moment. I wondered what he'd done this time. Had he got his comeuppance, finally?

Oh, I bloody well hope so.

The letter ended with an invitation to interview for the job of heading up the research group – Jonathan's vacated position. Obviously this wasn't a cast-iron offer, just the chance to throw my hat in the ring, but they had asked me specifically to apply so the chances were good. Stuffing the letter back into the envelope and tucking it safely in the pocket of my jeans, I headed down the corridor, almost running straight into Clara outside the consulting room.

"Clara? Come through." I gestured ahead of me and closed the door behind us.

"Hannah, thanks for seeing me. I hope I haven't disturbed you?"

"No, not at all. Is everything ok? You don't have any pets, do you?" I asked, looking around for a cat carrier or a dog.

"I have a cat, Spencer." Her eyes glazed over with a look of devotion and she smiled. "He's a bit grumpy but I love him. He's actually very fond of Henry though, the disloyal little git."

"Right. Is he ok? Have you brought him? Do you need me to take a look at something?"

I was a little agitated, probably being overly curt, as my mind ran away at a million miles an hour, the letter burning a hole in my back pocket. I was desperate to read it again to make sure it was real.

"Oh, no! I'm not here about Spencer. He's fit and healthy, but thanks."

Clara blushed a little and her eyes darted away.

"Ok, so what is it I can do for you?" I said, aiming for contrite. I liked Clara a lot, and I didn't want her to feel uncomfortable.

"Umm, yes, the thing..." Her voice trailed away and she twisted her fingers together, looking around the room. When she finally glanced at me, I raised my eyebrows and waited for her to continue.

"Oh yeah, right, so, um, here's the thing..." She gesticulated with her hands, as if I should know what this "thing" was. Her brows creased and I sensed that she was thinking pretty hard, caught in some sort of inner turmoil.

"The thing?" I prompted, when she hadn't spoken for a few moments.

"Oh, yeah. Teddy. Teddy is the thing."

"He is?"

Teddy had been conspicuously quiet and absent since last

Saturday despite several of my attempts to reach out to him over the week, and I'd managed not to think about him for the last ten minutes or so, but there he was again, larger than life, at the front of my mind. My confusion about how things had ended after the village fayre started up again, an ache opening in my chest like a wound. But I had a way out now. I had another option, an escape route from all the awkwardness I had inadvertently caused. A chance to start over if things with Teddy had really gone as pear-shaped as I was beginning to believe they had.

"Yes, and Henry," Clara carried on.

"So, twin things?"

I was still no clearer about what was going on.

Clara smiled and blew out a long breath. "I'm just going to get right to it."

"If you would, I have an unappealing and slightly soggy tuna sandwich waiting for me to finish eating before my next appointment."

"Oh, I'm sorry!"

"It's ok, Clara. What's going on between Ted and Henry? Is everything ok?" I gentled my voice, smiling genuinely.

"Yeah, no. Actually, no. And only you can fix it, so I've come here to ask for your help." She wrung her hands together. "To, um, well, you know, fix it?"

"Do you want a seat?"

I gestured to the examination table and propped my bottom against the edge. She smiled and clambered up next to me, so we were shoulder to shoulder, looking at the blank wall of the room rather than at each other.

"Teddy thinks you're in love with Henry," Clara blurted

out suddenly, swinging her stiletto-clad feet rhythmically backwards and forwards.

"What?! You know that's not true, right? And Henry, please tell me he knows that's not true?"

Christ! I was mortified. Where the hell had this come from?

Clara turned a little to face me.

"I know – we both know. Don't worry. We've seen how you look at Ted." She gave me a knowing smile, then continued, "But we can't seem to get that through to him. He's adamant about it. They argued the other night and he said some stuff about being compared to Henry all his life, and he was sick of never measuring up. That he didn't want to see him anymore and Henry is distraught and now they're not speaking. In fact, Teddy won't speak to anyone and has gone completely off the rails."

"What can I do? Ted's not exactly speaking to me either." He hadn't returned a single one of my calls or messages.

"He isn't?" Clara seemed surprised.

"No. After you turned up after the village fayre, he pretty much kicked me out and has been ignoring me ever since. I can see why now."

"What happened?"

"I don't know. We were chatting and, well, um, likely about to kiss or something, when you burst in on us," I said uncomfortably.

"Ah, righto. Sorry about that." Clara's foot swinging ramped up in speed and irregularity. "We need to come up with a plan to get you two face to face, so you can tell him you love him."

I began to cough. "Love him?"

"Yes! It's so bloody obvious that you two are madly in love with each other."

"I don't know about that," I said in a strangled voice. "He's only after a good time anyway. You know what he's like."

Clara let out a long breath.

"You and I both know that he's really not the playboy he wants everyone to think he is. Henry told me that he's barely had any girlfriends his whole life, and that he actually doesn't like parties. Can you believe that?"

"Yes," I admitted.

Clara nodded. Her large blue eyes were bright and shrewd as she gazed at me. "Don't you love him?"

A soft fluttering had started in my chest, a feeling so alien and unknown and uncomfortable that it was more like nausea than anything else I could put my finger on.

"Because he most definitely loves you. He admitted as much to Henry the other night. Which is why he's so hurt by all this, even if it's all just in his own stupid mind," she continued, gesticulating in large circles pretty close to my head.

My internal organs seemed to plummet and then rise, like being in an aeroplane during turbulence. It was simultaneously exhilarating and terrifying, a feeling of imminent death.

"I, um…"

"You don't have to tell me anything – it's ok. But I could really do with your help to patch things up between Henry and Ted. It's totally floored Henry and I can't bear to see him so upset."

"Will Teddy listen to me though?"

"I think you're the only one he will listen to, Hannah."

"But he won't answer my calls or messages. How on earth can I get him to talk to me?"

"I honestly don't know, but you're our only hope." Clara hopped down off the table and reached into her bag, handing me her business card. "My number's on there. Call me if you think of anything."

"The thing is, Clara, I might not be staying around here."

"Oh." Her face fell. "I see."

"I've been offered the chance to return to my research career in Bristol. I'm due to go for an interview in the next few weeks. So maybe this isn't such a good idea."

"Oh," she said again. Fixing her face into the shakiest smile I'd ever seen, she reached over to pick up her handbag. "Well, that's great news. I'm sure the interview is just a formality and you'll sail through it."

"Thank you."

"Oh, while I'm here, I thought you might like this. It's a gift." Digging in her enormous bag, Clara pulled out and handed me a rather tatty paperback with a faded picture of a buff shirtless man in a kilt on the front.

"A romance novel?"

"Yes!" Her face lit up like a firework. "But not any old romance book. It's got this really hot highlander in it. Give it a try."

"Right." I was struck dumb for a moment. "Why?"

"Why what?"

"Why do I need this?"

She grinned. "Fraser is a Scottish name, right?"

"Right," I said again, staring intently at the book in my hands and trying to work out where on earth she was going with this.

"So, read it and see if it helps clear anything up for you regarding Teddy."

"Teddy?"

"Yes." She winked and pointed some finger guns at me, so that I totally forgot why I was perplexed, instead smiling broadly, a laugh bubbling up in my throat. There was something endearingly odd and wonderful about her.

"Have I done a weird thing?" She looked doubtful for a moment and reached over to take the book from my grasp, but I pulled it out of her reach.

"No."

"Ok, phew. Well. Good. Excellent. I'll just go then."

As she turned to leave, I opened the first page and began to read.

He was taller than any man she'd ever seen, broad across the shoulders, dark-haired and charismatic. He drew the eye of every lady in the great hall, and as his laughter lit up his ruggedly handsome face, people flocked to him like flickering moths to a flame. Even at this distance, his presence filled the room like a teacup overflowing the brim, sweeping her along and swirling her ever closer to him.

I didn't read any more because the letters were swimming on the page and merging into each other and my head suddenly erupted with thoughts of Teddy. Everything Teddy and I had experienced together, how is presence filled my senses to the brim, nauseatingly so. And despite my best intentions, a fluttery, flouncy buzz was growing and growing behind my ribs, coupled with a new sick and desperate longing to see him, to talk to him again. To kiss him.

Well, shit.

Clara had opened the door and stepped out into the hallway. She gave me one last saddened look. "Nice to see you again. Good luck with everything."

"Wait."

She paused, hands falling back to her sides. "If it'll change your mind about helping us, Henry can lend Teddy a kilt—"

"No! No, that's ok." Alarmed as to how much Clara was about to tell me about Henry's kilt fetishes, I quickly interjected. "No. Clara. I think I may have a plan."

"You do?"

"Yes."

"What about Bristol?"

"Maybe I won't even get the job." I paused as the cogs of my brain turned, gathering speed. "Or maybe I can do both?" The thought of leaving was becoming like a solid weight of sick in my belly. "But I'm going to need you and Henry to do some things for me. Are you in?"

A luminous mischievousness played in Clara's eyes, and she sidled over to me like a funny cartoon villain, ringing her hands. "I love a good plan. What are we going to do?"

"First, I'm going to need you to get Ted out of his house for a few hours tonight, and then I'm going to need a notepad or something."

"How about sticky notes?" Clara said, producing several blocks of different sized pads of yellow and pink sticky notes from her handbag.

"You came prepared?"

"You never know when you'll need sticky notes," she replied matter-of-factly.

"Right."

"So, what's your plan?"

As I began to tell her what I had in mind, her eyes grew wide. She clapped and squealed and bounced on one leg, and I knew, without a shadow of a doubt, that my plan was a bit mad bonkers, and would either work, or alienate me from Teddy forever.

So, absolutely no pressure whatsoever then.

Chapter Twenty-Eight

After I finished work that afternoon, I shot an email over to the Dean of the Veterinary School at Bristol to request an interview time, then nipped out to the shop to get the supplies I needed for my plan to win Teddy over. I would utilise all the skills he'd taught me in my flirting masterclass sessions with him. As I devised the intricacies of my plan, reliving each of the funny, poignant, and surprising moments of my acquaintance with Teddy Fraser, my heart began to brim with hope and warm feelings, yet a touch of anxiety still swirled in my stomach.

What if I couldn't make this work? What if I just created some ridiculous shitstorm that I had to live with for the rest of my life?

But there was more than just my relationship with Teddy at stake. The thought of the Fraser twins never speaking again didn't bear thinking about, and I knew I had to do this for them as much as for myself. Even if Teddy could never look me in the eye again.

As agreed, Clara had concocted a dastardly plan to ensure

Teddy was delayed at work that afternoon. His father was enlisted to pile extra projects on him and keep him in the office until late so I had time to get everything ready at his house. Then Henry would accompany him back, under the pretence that they needed to try to clear the air, then make sure that when he arrived home he participated in the weird little treasure hunt that I had devised, before leaving the rest up to me.

I only hoped that it would work.

Clutching my carrier bag of props, I headed across the surgery car park, pushing open the rickety gate of The Old Rectory. At the top of the stone steps, I felt around for the spare key that he'd started leaving under the plant pot on the doorstep after the whole cellar incident, and I let myself in, sticking the first clue to the front door next to the heavy iron knocker.

Throw me around and give me a clout, you're likely to find me where the porn stars hang out. What am I?

Taking out an ancient, battered rugby ball hastily purchased from the charity shop in my lunch break, I glanced around the hallway, before placing it at the foot of the mirror where he'd told me how beautiful I was, just over a week ago. And stuck the next note in the centre of the reflective glass and over the pinched and nervous face staring back at me.

Superstition says I'm lucky for some, but perhaps not if you end up with thorns in your bum. What am I?

With Pluto's rather twisted horseshoe in my hands, I was

transported back to that fateful morning a few weeks ago. I'd been so shocked and mortified to see his face again, yet now couldn't imagine not seeing him every day. It was so weird how things can change in the space of a heartbeat, how feelings can bloom out of supposedly nowhere. Looking around, I chose the handle of the kitchen door to hang the horseshoe on and stuck the next note above it.

A feline abscess burst up above, yet you didn't pass out before the goddess of love. Who am I?

My confidence was still shaky, but I carried on into the kitchen, where I selected Aphrodite's cone of shame, with my badly drawn cartoon of her face decorating the plastic shell. I placed it on the table with the next note tucked underneath.

Don't be afraid, no need to cry, you'll find me outside where the devil sheep lie. Where am I?

Outside in the bright, clear sunshine, I began to question again what the hell I was doing. Would this really work? Clara had been adamant and hugely enthusiastic, and even Henry had apparently approved of this insanity, if the excited text messages I'd received were anything to go by.

As I reached the shed, I selected the "I ♥ goats" keyring from the bag, a joke present for Teddy that I'd got when the sales rep from one of the drug companies had come in last week. I hung it on a small nail protruding from the door frame and attaching the next note on the door.

Who lies in wait? Are you sure you won't hide? I am
fearsome, I am terrible, but a softy inside. Who am I?

I pushed open the shed door to discover Agnes sitting in the pen. Her back was to me, and she looked so peaceful in the soft sunshine that illuminated the sleeping kids.

"Hello, Hannah, dear," she said pleasantly without turning around. She carried on stroking the top of Deidre's head as the goat quietly chewed her cud, her jaw working in a circular motion. It was strangely hypnotic.

"Hi, Agnes. How did you know it was me?"

"A sixth sense, perhaps? If you're looking for Teddy, he's not here."

"I know." Swivelling her head to look at me, I saw that the smile on her face was sad and tired. "Are you ok?"

"Oh yes, dear. Just not sleeping so well."

"I'm sorry to hear that." I joined her on the straw bale and affectionately patted Deidre. "Any particular reason?"

"Not that I can fathom. It's a right bugger getting old – I wouldn't recommend it."

"Perhaps not, but it's better than the alternative, right?"

"Right."

Agnes's eyes misted over a little, and I knew she was lost in her memories.

"I need your help with something."

"Oh yes?"

I took a deep breath. "Teddy and I haven't been honest with you, and I'm sorry about that."

Her frail, bony hand covered mine, the crêpey skin over her knuckles translucent, paper-thin and fragile, but the firm squeeze she gave me hinted at the strength I knew she still possessed.

"We aren't a couple, not really, but…"

"But you want to be?"

I nodded and looked at my feet, scuffing my toes in the straw.

"I do, at least."

"It's obvious that he does too."

"It is?"

It was her turn to nod.

"Mmmm, well, I want to be more than friends with him, but I didn't believe that he wanted anything more than, you know…."

I did a weird gesticulation with my hand, hoping not to have to say any more.

Agnes chuckled. "You thought he just wanted to have sex with you? And nothing more?"

"Right."

"What a silly goose you are."

"I am?"

"Yes, you are. That man looks at you with hearts in his eyes every day. Even when he's angry with you he can't hide how much he loves you."

"He does?" My conversation skills were slipping, obviously, as I stared at the old lady next to me, hope blossoming at her words.

"He does. Whenever you're around, you're all he can see. He is so hopelessly in love with you that it radiates off him in waves." She paused and patted my hand again. "For an intelligent girl, you're pretty stupid about some things."

"That's what Teddy says," I muttered.

"So what do you need my help with?"

Here goes nothing, if she didn't think I was stupid before, she definitely will now.

"He's got it in his head that I'm in love with his brother. Which I'm not," I added hastily. Agnes nodded, gesturing that I should continue. "He's not talking to me or answering messages, so to show him how I feel, I've devised a treasure hunt to remind him of our shared experiences and all the little things about him that I love. Is that bonkers?"

"A treasure hunt?"

"Yep."

"What's the prize?"

I pointed my index finger into my chest and cringed. This was ridiculous and would never work.

"I should scrap it. It's a terrible idea."

"No, you shouldn't. You need to put him first. Show him how you feel. He's done it for you more times than you'll care to admit, hasn't he?"

"Yes," I confessed in a sulky whisper, because it was true. He put himself out there for me, regularly, without hesitation.

"So be bonkers and silly for him. Risk embarrassing yourself and then he'll know you really mean it. Step outside your controlled and logical comfort zone, Hannah. Live a little!"

With a sigh, I got to my feet. "You're right. Thank you."

"You're welcome. So, what can I do?"

Digging into the bag at my feet, I pulled out the next note. "Deidre's one of my clues, and an instrumental part of our recent history. Do you mind if I pop a clue in here somewhere?"

I handed Agnes the note and she read it with a smile on her face.

A tool that's useful for the best DIY, I also spin wildly where you let sleeping vets lie. What am I?

"I don't know what this means, but I definitely think you're being bonkers enough."

I winced and handed a little drawstring bag to her. She placed the note inside and tied it on to the thick leather collar Deidre wore.

"If you're sure you don't mind waiting?"

"Of course, that's fine. I'll stay with her and make sure none of them eats it. Goats will be goats, after all. But if one of them swallows it, that's not going to help you snag the sexy architect."

Bending down and folding my arms around Agnes's thin shoulders, I gave her a little squeeze.

"You're my people, Agnes. I hope you know that."

"Silly goose," she murmured, but couldn't hide the flush that bloomed over her cheekbones. "Now get on with it. He'll likely be back any moment and you need to get home and put on a peephole bra and crotchless knickers."

"Agnes!" I coughed. "I will absolutely not be doing that!"

She tutted. "Some prize you are." But she was chuckling to herself and waved me away. "Go on, leave this old woman in peace with her goats."

I headed back to the house and up the stairs, via the back passage where a bucket and the plaster mixing drill had been stored. Still unable to suppress the bubbly snigger when I thought of that epically disastrous plastering session (and not at all thinking about the Mr Darcy-esque climbing-out-of-the-pond moment), I placed these items by the bedroom door, the next note stuck to the handle of the drill.

> *I'm prickly and spiky and grumpy as hell, but fundamentals in flirting have treated me well. What am I?*

In the bedroom, I assessed my attempt at a vegetable animal again. I wasn't too proud to admit that it wasn't a patch on the one Oliver, aged four, had made for the village fayre, but it still looked vaguely like a hedgehog, so it would have to do. I snuggled it down happily amongst the bedclothes and alongside the next note.

> *I glitter and shimmer and I'm crap in a tree, but you love her, I know it, when she's down on her knees. What am I?*

On the windowsill, I placed the silver sandals that I wore to the garden party, tucking the next note inside and wistfully thinking back to the treehouse – the first time he'd really let me see him, and see into his heart – regretful that I'd not had the right words to say to him then, or since. I hoped he'd give me the chance to make this right.

> *Oh, would you look, in the car park no less? An arrow, a marker, what does it confess?*

Leaving the house, and locking the door behind me, I trotted along to the surgery, conscious that Henry and Teddy would be arriving back here soon, when a text pinged in my phone.

Clara: They're heading back, he's pissed off
and has had a massive row with Henry
outside the office. ETA 20 min. Brace yourself.

Excellent. Well, this might turn into a monumental shower
of shit after all. But I was committed and there was a whole
load of people involved – not least of which was Agnes who
was still sitting in the shed and making sure that none of the
goats ate my note. So, no turning back now.

In the car park, I organised some sawdust into a large
arrow in the gravel, pointing towards the door of my flat, and
placed the penultimate note on the ground at the head of the
arrow with a rock on top.

Follow this arrow to find a tool of this vet, and I'm honestly
(possibly) never meant as a threat. What am I?

With a large, fortifying breath, I hung my last prop on the
door handle, with the final note, before heading inside to await
my fate.

Chapter Twenty-Nine

I paced about my flat for about twenty minutes until I saw Teddy's Land Rover pull into the drive of The Old Rectory, closely followed by Henry's red Jaguar. I wanted to look away, to step back from the window, but it was like some kind of car crash television show that I couldn't not watch, even though my brain was yelling at me to go and sit down, to wait and try to act cool. But I was too entranced, inextricably drawn to this, mesmerised and helpless to look away.

Teddy marched up the front steps, his pace hurried. He was clearly irritated, but he stopped short of the door, clocking the note stuck there before turning to Henry, who shrugged, hands in his pockets, attempting nonchalance. My heart was in my mouth as he read it, and when they both glanced up at my window, I reflexively dropped to the floor like a fainting goat, hoping that neither of them had seen my illicit voyeurism.

Lying on the carpet and staring at the circular patterns on the Artex ceiling, I pictured in my mind Teddy walking through his house and finding all my notes and props. I hoped he got the clues. I tried to imagine how he would react, and what his face would look like. Would he laugh? Would he be annoyed that I had been in his house without permission? Would he feel that same dull ache behind his ribs that I felt when I thought of him? Or the fluttering of butterflies when he smiled because of something I'd said? It was hard to let go of the niggling feeling that he was playing a game and stringing me along.

Perhaps he was just very good at luring women in and would still turn tail and dump me when he'd finally got his end away?

Shaking this from my mind, I tried my best to believe the good in him that I knew was there. I focussed on my breathing, letting the anxiety flow out in cathartic waves, attempting to manage the tempest that putting my vulnerability on show had created.

I had started to calm down – ten minutes or so of deep breathing had definitely helped – when through the open window, I heard the distinctive rumble of men's voices in the surgery car park below. My pulse peaked and sweat beaded on my palms, undoing all my attempts at mindfulness in one quick swipe.

Excellent.

"Look, we're here now, right at her door, and she's gone to a lot of trouble, so just stop being a dick, Ted, and go and talk to her," Henry grumbled, his voice wafting in through my open kitchen window.

"Why don't you talk to her?" Teddy's voice was petulant, but I could sense that he was wavering. His resolve was weakening, that maybe he didn't quite have the conviction in this line of thought anymore.

"It's not me she wants to talk to," Henry said. There was a pregnant pause. "Look, here's another note. Read it."

I heard Teddy's long sigh. "It says 'Look in the bag'."

"Well then, look in the bag, Ted, for Christ's sake."

I could hear the rustling of the plastic bag that I'd hung on the door handle. Now my heart rate really went into orbit, hammering a pulse through my whole body and thudding in my ears like a military tattoo. This was it, the biggie, the baring-my-soul moment, and I didn't know how he would take it. Once it was all said, it could never be taken back or hidden by a prickly overcoat ever again, and that was terrifying. I was itching to close the window and not hear any more, because letting someone in to my inner sanctum, the squishy marshmallow centre that I kept protected and secret, really was unfamiliar and uncomfortable territory for me. Plus, my ability as a poet was monumentally shit, and the thought of a public recital made me a bit sick in my mouth.

There was silence outside.

"Well?" Henry sounded impatient.

"Maybe it's private, you dickhead."

"Oh no you don't. You'd not have done any of this without me pushing you along. I'm far too invested now, so I'm not leaving until you tell me what's in the last one. Give it here."

There was a slight scuffle, and I couldn't help sniggering as I thought of two grown men fighting over my stupid little sticky note.

"Fine. Get off, Henry. All right. I'll read it."

He paused, and my breath stuck in my throat, heart stuttering to a stop, balanced on a knife-edge of uncertainty. Like how I imagine that moment of weightlessness before you plunge into a bottomless crevasse.

"'These are my emasculators, but never fear, you've moved up the scale from possibly to nowhere near.'"

"Emasculators?" Henry sounded a little funny. I wondered if his skin had actually turned a particularly lurid shade of green. Probably. This was a comfort to me.

"Yes."

"You've talked about this before?" Silence for a beat. "Actually, I don't want to know."

"There's more."

"About emasculation?"

"No."

"Thank fuck for that."

"Do you want to hear it or not?"

"Yes, hurry up. I'm meant to be picking Clara up in ten minutes."

"Right, it says:

'I'm caught in your spell, not able to run,
your masterclass in flirting has left me undone.
I've listened to my heart and it's you that it chooses,
I'm sorry that it's stroppy and covered in bruises.'"

There was a pause, before Teddy carried on quietly, barely audibly.

"'But luckily for you this treasure hunt is now done,
so come on inside and see what you've won.'"

Another moment of silence stretched on, only my increasingly noisy hyperventilating filling the space in my head.

"Well, what are you waiting for?" Henry asked, quietly, reassuringly, the whisper of their unique brotherly bond feathering the edges.

"What if this wasn't meant for me?" Teddy's voice was still almost a whisper as he looked to his brother for support.

"Come on, Ted. In your heart you know it's not me she wants. It's *you*. You're so mad for each other – it's obvious."

"Hmmpph. Well, what if she leaves after all?"

"She hasn't gone to all this trouble just to leave. Now, I will fucking well carry you inside if I have to."

Ah, no-nonsense Henry was back. Excellent.

The squeak of the door opening carried up the stairs and I got up from my position on the floor, perching on the arm of one of the chairs and trying to calm my insides, before they conga-danced out of my skin. But when Teddy appeared in the doorway, nervously clutching all manner of weird paraphernalia from the treasure hunt in his arms, I couldn't help a breathy little gasp escaping.

He glanced at me, but not for long, seemingly unable to keep the eye contact.

"Hello."

"Hello."

"Hello." Henry appeared behind Teddy, grinning, his thumbs stuck up in a nerdy little salute.

"You can go now." Teddy shot an irritated glance over his shoulder.

"Righto."

"Wait," I said softly. "I want Henry to hear this too."

"I see." Teddy seemed to stiffen.

"Don't be a dick, Ted," Henry said and shoved his twin's shoulder, so he stumbled over the threshold and into my flat.

"He's right. You're being ridiculous."

"Am I." It was a statement, not a question. His tone was defensive. He was hurt.

"Yes, you are. Where on earth did you get the idea that I fancy Henry?" I asked. Teddy shrugged, but kept quiet.

"I mean, he's nice enough, but, well, he's *Henry*. What were you thinking?" I carried on, exasperated and waving my hand in his twin's direction.

"Er, thanks, Hannah." The crease between Henry's eyebrows deepened and he pouted a little.

"But the way you look at him…" Teddy's voice was so unsure. "You never look at me like that."

"Like what?"

"Like you *yearn* for him."

"When have I ever looked at him like I *yearn* for him?!"

I was baffled and glanced at Henry, who rolled his eyes, and mouthed "dickhead" behind Ted's back.

"He was all you wanted to talk about when we first bumped into each other, remember? Then, the other night when he and Clara burst in on us, and when we all met in the pub a few weeks back, you couldn't stop staring with moony eyes," he replied bitterly.

"Moony eyes? What are you talking about?"

I racked my brains, trying to remember what I had done with my face and my eyes. I tried to rekindle whatever feelings I had experienced in those moments, but the only thing I could think about was how I had coveted the ease with which Clara and Henry loved each other. How their obvious affection and loyalty was evident, how safe and secure they were, like no one else needed to exist. I remembered envying their sense of comfort and acceptance, their unwavering love in the face of all adversity. That was what I longed for – someone who wanted me just the way I was, prickles, freckles, and all. And that was when the realisation dawned.

"It wasn't *Henry* I was yearning for when I looked at them."

"Clara?!" Henry and Teddy both said in shocked unison.

"No, you idiots. Not Clara." Pinching my nose and closing my eyes briefly, I sighed and tried to gather my thoughts. "I've never seen two people who are so obviously meant to be together, who so obviously and unashamedly love each other. That's what I yearn for, what Henry and Clara have together, Teddy, not an illicit lesbian affair with Clara."

"I think I should leave you to it." Henry flushed a little and backed away, giving me an encouraging smile, before disappearing down the stairwell and leaving us alone.

"Do you mean that?" Teddy said.

"Yes. Clara's beautiful, but I'm definitely not yearning for her."

"No, not the lesbian bit, although that thought is quite hot." Teddy seemed to drift off somewhere, a dazed expression on his face, until the coaster I lobbed at him caught him on the arm.

"Focus!"

"Sorry." He pulled out his top-tier sexiest grin, blinding me with teeth and dimples, and mischievousness. "I actually meant the bit about wanting to be unashamedly in love with someone?"

"No."

"No?"

307

"No. Not just someone. Someone who unashamedly loves me back."

"I see."

"And I was hoping that might be you."

The weight of this confession tentatively stretched between us, a thick thread of hope and anxiety, vibrating with doubt, a moment stopped in time as I waited for his answer.

"Were you?" He was quiet. His eyes were impossibly dark, his whole body still, except for a slight flexing of his fingers where he held the emasculators.

"Yes. But…"

"But?"

"But if you only want a quick fling, then…"

"Then?"

I sighed and felt myself start to crumble inwards. "Then I'm not sure that's something I could do."

"I see." He stepped forward and placed all the objects he was holding on the dining table and closed the door to the stairwell behind him. "That's not something I want."

"Oh."

"Oh?"

"Ok." Fiddling with the slightly frayed hem of my shirt, I focussed all my being on not crying, and on rebuilding my defences, prickle by painful prickle.

"Don't look like that, Hannah. I thought you knew me well enough by now. I thought I'd made it very clear what I wanted?"

"Right." I kept my eyes trained downwards, not really taking in what he was saying, hoping to hold it together for a few more moments. Until he left, until I was alone with this humiliation and could unleash the devastation that was wrecking my whole body from the inside.

"Please look at me, Hannah."

I chanced a glance in his direction. My vision was swimming with unshed tears, but he smiled a soft, sincere smile.

"I don't want a casual fling. I want *you*, all of you, with my whole being. Completely. Forever." He paused and swallowed. "You should know that in every moment of every day, you are all I want and all I can think about. You drive me crazy." Running his hands through his hair, he glanced nervously to my feet and then back up to meet my eyes. "I love you, unashamedly."

"You do?"

"I do."

Right, well thank the actual fuck for that.

We stared at each other, and I began to unwind, my body thrumming with a different intensity now. Anxiety and humiliation slid away to be replaced by a swirling maelstrom of desire and something else, something wholesome and fulfilling, that wrapped around the spiky bits, softening the barbs almost unrecognisably.

I brushed away the single, static tear that decorated the corner of my eye and with a wobbly smile I said, "Unequivocally unashamedly?"

"I am completely unequivocal about my unashamed loving of you, Dr Hannah Havens."

"Mmmm-hmmm."

"Do you unequivocally and unashamedly love me in return?"

"Undoubtably."

"Thank fuck for that." Blowing out a long breath, Teddy ran his hands over his face. His arms flexed as he leant backwards. "But…"

Ah yes, there's always a but.

"But?"

"But I don't want to be the one to stop you following your dreams. I don't want you to commit to something with me and give up your chance of the research career you deserve."

He was being sincere, willing to walk away so that I could be the best I could be. "Who told you?"

"Clara."

"Let's see what happens after the interview. Bristol isn't a million miles away, and I'm not even sure if I want the job, even if they do offer it to me."

Getting up from my seat, I padded over to him, only stopping when we were almost touching. When he moved to close the gap, I placed my hand in the centre of his chest and pushed firmly. A little huff of air escaped his lips as he hit the door behind him with a thump.

"But before we go any further, let's get something straight here, Edward Fraser." He gulped, his eyes widening in shock. "I promise not to get those emasculators out, if you promise never, ever to mess me around. Deal?" He nodded. "Then we're good. Now, let's get to the *nice* stuff, shall we?"

And I finally did what I had been dying to do since that very first kiss fifteen years ago. I pressed my body firmly against his and ravaged his mouth like a porn star possessed.

Chapter Thirty

There was nothing sweet about this kiss. It was all grasping hands and hot, wet mouths, frantic teeth and tongues, and it left me breathless and gasping. It was fraught and messy, and bordering on violent. It was chaos and carnage, yet it seemed to calm and soothe me at the same time. And Teddy met me every step of the way, pushing and moaning against my lips, his hands reaching down and firmly gripping my backside, hoisting me off the ground.

Wrapping my legs around his waist, I held on with a monkey-like death grip, roughly ripping open his shirt, popping a few buttons clean off. I pushed it down his arms and feasted on the skin of his neck and shoulder, sucking and licking and biting.

Was it wrong that I wanted to devour him? That the feel of his pulse hammering under my tongue, his breathing quick and erratic in my ear, were the hottest things I'd ever experienced? Or that I was acting like a rabid badger in heat and running on pure instinct? I had never in my life wanted to actually climb inside someone else's skin, but in this moment I couldn't physically get close enough to Teddy.

"Shit, Hannah. Is this your porn star A game? Fuck!"

I huffed a laugh against his throat, fascinated as his Adam's apple dipped and bobbed.

"Yeah, who'd have thought someone like me could kiss like this, Ted?"

"Oh, I always knew you'd kiss like this, Hannah. And I've thought about it a lot." He paused to nibble my ear. "Mmmm, this is so fucking *nice*."

"*Nice*, huh? You've not seen anything yet, sunshine," I replied, burying my hands in his hair and tilting his head backwards, running my tongue over his chin and along the seam of his lips.

"Fuck me," he groaned.

"I fully intend to."

Sliding back down his body and out of his grip, I prised his shirt off over his hands and stood back to admire him. He was beautiful, as I'd imagined he would be. Chiselled and firm, and quite hairy, which I was definitely down with.

"You're looking at my chest like you might be having me for dinner."

"Is that a problem?"

"Definitely not."

"Good."

"But we should remove your top too. Fair's fair."

I made a non-committal noise and glanced up at him, allowing my hair to fall across my face, before slowly and deliberately undoing each button of my shirt. I watched his breathing hitch as the swell of my breasts in my new lace bra came into view, just a tantalising glimpse as my shirt fell open, his gaze tracking my fingers as they worked. When it was completely undone, I dropped it to the floor with a stripper-inspired flourish. And a wink. Yes, a full-on, face-creasing, lip-lifting, cringe-inducing wink.

For fuck's sake.

If I'd performed such a thing under any other circumstances, I'd be praying for an immediate sinkhole to appear to relieve the world of my sub-par seduction techniques. But the amused twist of Teddy's lips and returning eyebrow twitch dissolved any hint of my winking regret, and I continued my nerdy little striptease with renewed vigour.

I didn't look down – I didn't want to end the spell by seeing myself. Instead, without breaking eye contact and biting my bottom lip to stop myself thinking too hard about this, I unbuttoned my shorts, wiggling my hips as I slid them down my legs and then kicked them off, standing before him in my brand-new seduction-level red underwear. And, although the crotch was well and truly present and no nipples were peeping out, it was like nothing else I owned – and pretty bloody slutty, to be honest.

"Well?"

"Well, I know what I'm having for dinner." Teddy's voice was hushed.

In two strides he was on me, pushing me backwards, twisting his hands into my hair, and reinitiating the ferocious kissing so that we fell together, tumbling over the armchair, which tipped onto its side. Hitting the floor with a bump, his arms cradled my head to protect me from the impact.

"I've wanted this for so long," he groaned.

The rough scratch of his beard and the burn of his jeans against my bare skin seemed to awaken something feral inside me, and with a growl I pushed him over onto his back and then straddled him, leaning down and possessing his mouth without restraint. His hands roamed every curve of my body, squeezing and exploring, the slight callouses rasping across my skin and making me shudder and press into his touch. But in a flash I was back underneath him, and we were rolling across the carpet in a primal dance, locked together in a passionate struggle, pushing and testing, teasing and exploring each other's limits.

As we writhed and fought each other, a side table was knocked over, the lamp falling to the floor with a crash.

"Shit. Should I fix that?" Teddy asked breathlessly.

"Don't you dare."

I barely felt human anymore. The animal part of me had been unleashed and I was ferocious and wriggling, until I was once again rocking back on top of him. I unzipped his jeans and reached down inside, making him hiss out a breath as my cool fingers delved inside the waistband of his boxer shorts.

Grabbing both of my wrists he held them over my head and pivoted me back underneath him, trapping me in a firm grip, his mouth searing a path of fire down my throat. The sounds I was making were foreign and unfamiliar, matched only by the racing of my heart and a deep bellyache of desire that was stoked by every touch and kiss, alive and responsive to Teddy's masterful manipulation of my body.

With a snap my bra was undone, and he quickly descended on my newly exposed skin. One large hand kept my wrists tethered while the other cupped my breast, his thumb expertly flicking the tip until I was moaning and arching against him. Letting go of me momentarily, he sat back and kicked off his boots, then removed his jeans and socks. The whole time, he never took his eyes off me. But I made the most of the opportunity, and with a devilish sense of glee, I launched myself at him, catching him slightly off balance, so we collided in a heap against the dining table, knocking the treasure hunt props everywhere, and I ended up sat astride him.

As if in slow motion, the emasculators slid off the edge, narrowly missing Teddy's head as they hit the floor. Picking them up, I spun them around, blew the end, and pretended to holster them on my thigh like I was starring in a spaghetti western. Why was I being such a twat? Excelling at being the nerdiest of nerdy nerds, rather than the queen of seduction that I had been aiming for.

Excellent.

"Despite your obvious prowess with such an offensive weapon, I'm not sure I'm entirely comfortable with you holding on to these in my current state of undress," Teddy said, propping himself up on his elbows.

Raising an eyebrow, he gently took the cold metal implement from my hands, placing it out of reach, back on top of the table.

"Now, where were we? Ah, yes, you'd just thrown yourself at me like you were practising for a wrestling smackdown. Shall we continue?"

"Only if you're sure you can handle it?"

The look Teddy gave me was devastating. There was a temptingly wicked curl to his lips, a blush feathering his cheekbones. "Why don't you try me, cowgirl?"

Still sitting conveniently on his hips, I wriggled seductively, riding in circular motions over the very hard contents of his shorts. He blew out a breath unsteadily, just as my own breathing began to quicken. Sitting up so we were face to face again, he took my hands in his and then quickly snaked them around my back so he was holding me captive once more. I arched my spine and pushed my breasts towards him, the abrasive rub of his chest hair on my nipples a delicious sensation. Teddy began to gently bite a line across my collar bone, soothing each sting with a soft kiss and blowing cool air over my fevered skin, my head thrown back, eyes closed, alive only to the feel of his mouth on me.

In my daze, I barely heard him murmur, "Perhaps we should get up off the floor?"

"Mmmm?"

"Find somewhere more comfortable?"

"Sounds like a good idea."

"I'm full of those."

Hoisting me off his lap, he stood up and pulled me to my feet, while in a swift and surprising manoeuvre he slid my lace knickers down to the floor, lightly holding my hand as I stepped out of them. On autopilot, I began to cower inwardly as he perused my naked body, my anxiety urging me to fold in on myself and shy away from his red-hot gaze.

"Don't overthink this, Hannah. Eyes on me." His voice was so deep and commanding that I involuntarily snapped my gaze back up to look at his face. I saw the wonder, and the hunger there. "You are beautiful. Every single last bit of you."

Trying to dodge this comment and expel it from my brain, Little Miss Logical made an appearance, her tone prim and haughty. "I am naked and you are not."

"That's true. Would you be happier if I were?"

"Yes," I choked out. "Fair's fair, Teddy."

With a nod he reached down for the waistband of his boxer shorts and quickly divested himself of them. He stood before me in all his glory, and he was a sight that made my mouth (and other parts) water. I'd never seen anyone as thoroughly breath-taking as him before, and certainly not naked. All previous lovers faded into insignificance, leaving me feeling like an inexperienced virgin all over again.

"My eyes are up here." Teddy laughed, and for the second time in as many moments, I was forced to meet his gaze.

"You're magnificent." As the words escaped, I was already trying to suck them back into my mouth and unsay them. I wanted to try and hide behind my usual air of cool indifference and not let all this naïve honesty spew forth embarrassingly into the ether.

"Thank you."

If I thought he would tease me about my stupid comment, I couldn't have been more wrong. If anything, he looked pleased, and relieved. I was left stumped again to see this difference in the real Teddy, to see the inverse of his confident, slightly smug outward persona, knowing now that his overt alpha maleness was just a cover for his own insecurity. But here, now, vulnerable together, the vestiges of the façade had been stripped away, leaving his soul as naked as his body. And he really couldn't have been any more magnificent to me.

Stepping forwards, he scooped me off the ground and carried me to the bedroom, peppering gentle kisses all over my face and neck until I was squirming and giggling, breathless in the face of his attack. Lowering me onto my back on the bed, he relinquished his hold, running hot fingers from my thighs to my knees. The pads of his thumbs drew small circles on the soft skin on the insides of my legs, applying an insistent pressure until I opened them for him, and he knelt at the edge of the bed.

"Teddy, you don't—

"I do. I have to, Hannah. I'll die if I don't taste you."

Pressing my head back against the covers, I closed my eyes and stared at the reddened insides of my lids. My other senses now fully tuned into the warm breath and soft kisses that were decorating my inner thighs, to the glide of his palms, and to the tickle of his beard as he climbed and climbed. And when his hot mouth was on me, I nearly came apart on the spot, his talented lips and tongue flooding my body with sensations that were almost too much to comprehend. I threaded my fingers into his hair and rocked my hips in time, glancing down and meeting his gaze. There was a wicked glint in his eyes as his hands gripped my backside, his fingers digging in and upping the pressure until I couldn't take any more and an orgasm hit like an explosion. My heart practically leapt out of my chest as my body convulsed, shaking with such intense pleasure that I could no longer work out which way was up.

Crawling up my trembling body, Teddy carried on kissing everywhere so that no part of my skin was left untouched by his lips. Meanwhile, I floated back down to earth, merely a tingling, boneless, weightless creature made entirely of stars and butterflies.

"Pretty *nice*, huh?" Teddy whispered against my lips, kissing me with such fervent desire and need that my body was already gearing up for round two.

How does he do this?

"Oh yeah, that really was *nice*," I replied when he finally let me come up for air.

With a not-so-gentle push, he was on his back and I was on top, leaning down to the drawer in the bedside cabinet and reaching for a condom.

Sitting back up, the golden evening illuminated us both, leaving no shadows for me to hide in. My body was on display, my insecurities pushing to resurface. But there was luminosity in Teddy's eyes, his hands were resting on my waist while his fingertips were drumming a quick-fire, impatient rhythm against my skin, his desire so obvious it drew me ever closer to him, bringing me back to this moment and out of my own head. I ran my hands up and down his chest and abdomen, following the ridges and furrows, tracing an old appendix scar that was still a little pink. I felt emboldened, allowing my hands to dip lower. "Now then, we should do something *nice* for you too, right?"

"I only want you to do what you want to do," he whispered.

"What I want is you. Now. Completely."

I'd never been so sure of anything in my whole life.

"Me too."

With a smile, I continued my journey south. I gripped both hands around him, encasing my fingers along the hot, hard length of him, before bowing my head and swirling my tongue around his tip, tasting and teasing him, before taking him into my mouth and watching with satisfaction as his eyes rolled up into his head, and he gripped the bedclothes as if his life depended on it.

"As fantastic as it is, Hannah, I don't want to come in your mouth," he rasped, gently pulling my head away after only a few moments, allowing me to sit back up and roll the condom on.

Teddy held me around the waist which helped me to balance as I slid down onto him, our bodies fitting together as if carved only for each other, as if hewn from the same piece of stone. The stretch and pull, the glide and heat, all of it was so right, so entirely needed, so perfect.

Why the hell had I put this off for so long?

"Fuck, Hannah. You feel amazing," Teddy groaned, his hands cupping my arse while I moved my hips as he thrust up towards me.

Bracing against his chest, I established a punishing rhythm, riding him until the build-up of sensation low in my belly already started to unravel, my breaths turning to pants. But it was the sight of the man beneath me coming undone that really switched things up a gear, his moans and tightening grip indicating to me that he was getting close. His eyes never left mine. He remained fixated on my movements. Observant and committed, he matched me, the continuing battle of our bodies getting close to their final crescendo. This push and pull between us was so vital, so consuming, that I leant back, letting go and releasing the cacophony of fireworks in my brain, surrendering to the total oblivion of everything other than the pulsating pleasure coming from our point of contact. At the same time, he arched up into me, climaxing with an incoherent shout, every line of him taut and unyielding. And I collapsed on top of him, my limp body against his damp chest, his heart thundering in my ear as he cradled me in his arms.

Well, that was pretty bloody epic.

And yet, not entirely unexpected. Eighteen-year-old me was correct all those years ago, my naïve little heart having seemingly picked an absolute corker of a lover after that first, devastating kiss. But this time there was no doubt in my mind about how I felt. No doubt whatsoever. No, this time I knew with absolute certainty that I was truly, hopelessly, and unashamedly in love with Teddy Fraser.

And he loved me back. Which was really quite nice after all.

Chapter Thirty-One

S tretching out under the covers with a sigh, my bed seemed conspicuously empty. There was not a hint of another being – only the rumpled covers, a pleasant soreness between my thighs, and a lingering citrus scent giving any indication that Teddy had been here at all. For the entirety of the previous evening and night, we'd not left the bedroom except for snacks. But where was he now? Had he gone and run away again?

My brain was catapulted into wide-awake mode. The angry honey badger was stirring, growling, and getting ready for defensive manoeuvres as necessary. I sat up and scanned the bedroom, and out of the open door into the living room, which had been tidied after our bout of passionate wrestling yesterday. But there was still no evidence of a six-foot-three architect anywhere. There was no sound of the kettle boiling or the shower running. It was silent. It screamed of emptiness and imminent heartbreak.

While indignation and ire began to burn up my throat, my gaze came to rest on a pink sticky note sitting on the pillow next to where my head had been lying only a moment ago.

Stop freaking out. I have not left you and run away to join a monastery. I had agreed to meet Agnes this morning, and you seemed a bit tired after your exertions (which were spectacularly nice, by the way). Come over to her house if you want? Or I'll call back in to see you later. T x

Then a text came through on my phone.

Ted: Read the note on the pillow, you lunatic.

Shaking my head, I fired off a quick "see you soon" reply and headed to the shower.

It was another glorious summer morning, and a warm, fresh breeze ruffled my hair as I made my way up the path to Agnes's house. The side gate was open, and I followed the sound of music and laughter round to the back of her quaint, tumbledown cottage, ducking under trailing honeysuckle and avoiding the snagging brambles that reached out trying to catch my clothes like grasping fingers. From my secluded spot, half-buried in the hedge, I had a prime view of the garden, and I took a moment just to observe.

"Teddy, you waltz very well." Agnes was beaming and her diminutive frame clutched onto him as they spun in circles to the crooning and slightly crackling voice of Frank Sinatra coming from a large wind-up gramophone sitting on the picnic bench.

"Well, you do me the honour of being a very graceful dance partner," he replied, smiling down at her affectionately.

"I really do appreciate you fixing that old record player for me. It belonged to my father, a dusty old relic he held on to, claiming it sounded so much better than the modern ones. But I'm coming to think he may have been right after all."

"You're welcome. It was a fun little project to keep my mind off things."

"Things?"

"Hannah," he admitted sadly, and my stomach dropped.

"But you two are good now, right?"

"Yes, I think so. I just…"

"Just what?"

"I just don't want to mess things up, Agnes."

She tutted loudly and smacked him on the arm.

"Now stop it. You're not going to mess anything up. You're too hard on yourself, young man."

He smiled. "I really do love her."

"And she really loves you too. That treasure hunt of hers was quite nauseating, actually."

"Wasn't it just?" Teddy snorted. "But I absolutely bloody loved every single second of it."

"And that's because you're just as bonkers and nauseating as she is."

I couldn't help the bubble of laughter that escaped, causing Agnes and Teddy to turn and spot me, partially concealed by shrubbery, arms folded, leaning against the cool wall of the cottage.

"We really are pretty bloody bonkers, aren't we?" Teddy said.

My gaze locked with his and a moment seemed to pass between us, that now familiar invisible force drawing me towards him, charged particles pinging around us, as if we'd created our very own Hadron Collider.

"Ah, there you are. Let's have some tea." Agnes stepped out of Teddy's arms and headed into the kitchen, seemingly making a lot of unnecessary noise for preparing some tea. She crashed around inside and sang loudly, in an obvious effort to give us some privacy.

"Hey, you." Teddy seemed shy all of a sudden, quiet and pensive, which surprised and thrilled me. I wondered if he could read my thoughts as a reel of naughty images flashed through my brain as his cheekbones coloured a little red.

"Hey, you." Hands in my pockets, I sauntered over to him, nonchalantly. "How you doin'?"

He laughed. "I'm doin' ok, thanks. You?"

Fuck it. I couldn't keep my hands to myself any longer, and in two strides I was launching myself at him, attaching myself to his face like a limpet. His groan of desire reverberated through his chest as he kissed me back, wrapping his arms around me tightly and pulling me in closer and closer until I could hardly breathe. The singing and pot clattering from the kitchen grew louder and Teddy smirked against my lips.

"Perhaps we should take this somewhere a little more private, snuggle bun?"

"Oh, sexy monkey features, you read my mind."

"I didn't have to read your mind. Your actions spoke loudly and clearly."

"Tea!" Agnes shrieked, walking backwards out of the kitchen, a tray rattling loudly with crockery. "You can stop your canoodling now."

Reluctantly disentangling myself from Teddy's grip, I took the tray out of her hands and placed it on the table, taking a seat in the middle, next to the gramophone, just as Teddy's phone began to ring.

Glancing at the screen, he looked a little confused for a moment, before excusing himself and nipping through the hole in the hedge and back towards his garden next door.

"So your cunning plan worked then, Hannah?" Agnes's voice jolted me back from the lurid fantasy I was having while watching Teddy disappear from view.

"Seems so. Thank you for your help yesterday, by the way."

"You're very welcome. That poor boy has been all over the place about you, young lady, so don't you mess him around now, will you?"

I did the Girl Guide salute. "I promise."

I knew I never would. Because in total honesty, and as scary as it was, I couldn't even imagine myself looking at another person ever again. This man filled my entire mind to the brim, leaving no room for anything else, no capacity for anyone but him.

"Good." With a shaky hand, Agnes poured the tea into a flowery cup, the crazed porcelain wobbling noisily against the saucer.

"How are you feeling?" Taking the teapot, I took over being mother, and Agnes sat heavily on the wooden bench.

"Tired, Hannah," she replied, her voice and the slump of her shoulders confirming the sentiment.

"Do you need help with anything?" Stirring in a lump of sugar and adding milk, I handed her the first cup. "Teddy and I can do bits with the goats or help with the garden? Give you a break for a bit?"

She looked defiant for a moment, and I recognised that expression, that need to be self-sufficient. I understood the desire to be independent and the refusal to ask for help in case it was construed as a sign of weakness. But then it fizzled away, replaced by dejection, and she nodded almost in defeat. And my heart broke a little bit for her.

Opening the packet of shortbread biscuits, I handed her one and then took one for myself, dunking it in my tea and savouring the sweet butteriness.

"Teddy is such a worrier, Agnes. He wants to keep an eye on you. I've told him that you're a tough old bat and don't need us to interfere, but if you could just appease him, it would get him out of my hair and I'd be grateful."

Agnes laughed.

"A tough old bat, huh?" It was my turn to nod and she sighed. "You are so like my late sister. She'd have said exactly the same thing. Fine, I'll do it. But only for Teddy."

"What are you doing for me?" He said, reappearing through the hole in the hedge, looking a bit shifty.

"I'm letting you help me with the gardening, so you can trim that bloody hedge as you wish so you can nosy into my property."

"Right. Good. Well…" Teddy glanced at me, silently urging me for something – what, I had no idea. "Don't be mad, Agnes, but I've got someone here to see you."

We both craned our necks to look as Teddy stepped into the

garden with an elderly gentleman and a tall, young man, who both came into view through the gap in the thick privet hedge.

Agnes's hand began to shake, and I gently took the cup from her, placing it securely back on the saucer.

"Are you ok?" I asked, but she was fixated on the people who had just appeared, ignoring my question entirely.

"Agnes," the older gentleman said quietly.

"Edward?"

Teddy blew out a long breath. "Yes, I tracked down your brother-in-law, Agnes. It turns out he only lives ten miles away with his family and was very keen to see you again."

A young, dark-haired woman appeared too, holding a small, chubby-cheeked toddler and clasping hands with an older child, who hid shyly behind her mother's legs.

"Hello, Agnes. I'm Rose and this is Freddie, my husband, and our children, Benjamin and Elizabeth."

"This is my girlfriend, Hannah Havens," Teddy added, proudly.

Emotion brimmed over in Agnes's eyes. Her lip trembled.

"How did you find him?"

Teddy ran his hands through his hair, before rubbing his chin a little self-consciously.

"It took a bit of effort, but it's amazing the contacts my mother has through the WI."

"It's been so long. How are you?" Edward Timms stepped forward, and I helped Agnes to her feet and she stumbled into his arms, hugging like they were clinging on for dear life.

Edging away from the table, Teddy took my hand and pulled me in under his arm then gently kissed my hair. We watched the Timms family gather around Agnes, bringing her into the fold. Delight was evident on her face and tears rolled freely down her cheeks.

"You're a marvellous man, Mr Fraser," I whispered.

"Why, thank you. What a very *nice* thing to say. Have you been taking lessons, Dr Havens?"

"Oh yes, from a master of flirting. It's been a real eye-opener."

Freddie Timms turned to us and smiled. It was a familiar expression I'd seen in a tatty black and white photo in Agnes's kitchen.

"Thank you so much for contacting us, Ted. Being able to connect with Agnes after all these years has really lifted my dad, and for us all to meet our long-lost aunt has been astounding and wonderful. We have their wedding pictures in an album and my father talks about his brother so fondly."

"You're welcome."

"And of course, Agnes is very much part of our family now she's been found again. We'll help wherever we can," Rose added, the toddler wriggling in her arms and squeaking to get down.

"If you head up into the orchard, there are some baby goats to meet. They love children," I said quietly, indicating the rickety gate beyond the overgrown flower bed, and the Timms family meandered away with a grateful smile, all of them excited as children as they entered the realms of a secret garden.

Meanwhile, Edward had cranked the gramophone up again and taken Agnes in his arms. With overjoyed laughter, the two were dancing together, chatting excitedly and waltzing about the patio, a lightness now gracing their every step.

Snuggling in tighter to Teddy, I slipped my hand into the

back pocket of his shorts and squeezed. "Such a do-gooder, and here I was thinking I'd fallen for the evil twin."

Teddy huffed into my hair, muttering, "You definitely did. All this niceness has just been a ruse to lure you into my lair and never let you escape."

He did a very good imitation of evil laughter.

"Yeah, I don't buy that at all."

"You don't?"

"No, I don't. You may think you're the black sheep of the Fraser family, but I don't agree. If anything, you might be a grey sort of sheep, but definitely not just your average run-of-the-mill white sheep."

"Grey though?"

"A Herdwick, perhaps. Quite rare and imperfectly perfect."

"I see. Thank you … I think."

Giving him another squeeze, I leant up and whispered in his ear, "Teddy, it's fine just to be you, and not compare yourself with anyone else. I mean, if I can love you for all your bits, then everyone else will, right?"

"All my bits?"

"Yeah, the uncertain bits, the funny bits, the silly bits, the sexy bits. They're all really *nice*."

Spinning me around to face him, he tucked a lock of hair behind my ear, fingertips lingering over my cheek.

"Do you know what? Being loved by a prickly little hedgehog definitely has its advantages."

"It definitely does. You'd better not forget it."

"I won't, and I'm going to continue to love you, and all your bits, even your glorious spikiness, until we're old grey sheep together."

"Then we're in agreement?"

"Yes. A devout plan of being a bit kinder to ourselves, first and foremost?" He smiled.

"All right."

"And I'm sorry that my own stupidity nearly caused me to lose you and my brother."

"Yeah, don't be doing that again, ok?"

"I won't be doing that again." He pulled me against his chest and curled his arms around in a protective vice. "Because you're the only person who sees the real me, with no expectations to be anyone else." He kissed my forehead, a lingering gentle brush of his lips over my skin. "And you were right too, you know."

"I often am, but please enlighten me?"

With a chuckle, he said, "I too yearned for the love that Henry and Clara have, but I didn't want to admit it. Although, I'm pretty certain that what we have is actually better, so there'll be no more comparisons." There was a pause, while I breathed him in – his scent, his warmth, his love. "Henry once said that he and Clara were made just for one another, and I completely took the piss out of him at the time, but now I understand what he meant. Because, Hannah, you were made just for me."

He was right, of course, and I felt exactly the same way. It was annoying to admit it, granted, but I was going to have to get used to him being right about stuff. Because, while it was true that I allowed him to be himself, that I loved him for every imperfection and relished the vulnerability and awkwardness he held inside, it was his effect on me that was far more profound. His acceptance of my spikiness without judgement meant the world, and his innate ability to somehow turn my barbs to jelly protected me from hurting myself and other people in the process. I felt surprisingly secure that he truly accepted me for who I was, unequivocally. Unashamedly. Prickles and freckles and all.

Some might say that he had liberated my inner marshmallow hedgehog and showed me how to be a bit nicer all round. Had he? Yeah, probably.

And I bloody well adored him for it.

Epilogue

It was shady in the treeline, and much cooler than being out in the full sun. The freckled skin on my shoulders was already pink and protesting, despite the factor fifty I'd slapped on. To my right was an unobstructed view of the Cotswolds laid out in glorious technicolour – rolling hills that were luscious and green, and a patchwork of manicured farmland as far as the eye could see. Insects buzzed lazily around us, and there was the drone of tractors and balers in the distance and the smell of cut hay providing a quintessentially English country backdrop to the day.

As my body swayed in time with Pluto's steady hoofbeats, an unfamiliar fluffy contentment settled in my chest, like I was being filled to the brim with sickly sweet candy floss. Things were slotting into place, my life having taken such a different trajectory in recent months. The absence of feeling like I was always on the brink of disaster was taking some getting used to. Teddy and I had discussed our future at length: he was supportive of me moving to Bristol and had even offered to try and set up an architectural practice there, but for me it felt like a backwards step to return, so I'd rescinded my request for an interview. In a quirk of fate, a job offer from a local equine referral practice had come through just a few weeks ago, a part-time research position created just for me, which allowed me to stay on as a partner with Giles and build up the practice, yet still fulfil some of my academic yearning. I'd read and re-read the terms of the offer, certain there was a catch somewhere, but it really was as perfect as it could possibly be.

Teddy had been keen that I move into The Old Rectory straight away, but I'd resisted for a while to check he was sincere. Newsflash, he was. And since me moving out of the flat freed up space for a new vet to start at the practice, it did make sense. But when I'd locked my old front door behind me for the last time, and entered The Old Rectory as my new home, a bubble of anxiety and distrust had set my jangly nerves on edge, as I waited for this perfect façade to crumble away to dust. In fact, I'd kept an overnight bag with essentials packed and ready to go, just in case I needed to make a speedy getaway. That was, until last night, when Teddy had found it under the bed, packed a case of his own, and placed them both by the front door, asking casually over dinner if we were going away anywhere nice on a mini-break.

Holding my hands gently, he'd said, "I'm with you, always and forever, but if you feel you need to run away, give me a chance to get my stuff together first, because I'll gladly go anywhere you want."

Pluto flicked an ear to the left in brief acknowledgement of something crashing about in the woods next to us. Picking up the loose rein from his neck, I leant forward. "Come on, fella, let's beat his sorry arse."

Striking into a canter, we set a blistering pace across the edge of the field, aiming for a dip and a small break in the trees ahead, all the while conscious of a brightly coloured shape zipping between the trunks alongside us at an alarming speed. As I urged the horse on, a broad grin stretched over my face, the wind whipping exhilarated laughter from my lips, cast away and lost into the turbulent air behind us.

As we neared the entrance back into the woods, our pace easing back to a trot, Teddy appeared on his mountain bike, blocking the path into the trees ahead. Even after these last few months together, this glimpse of him set my heart rate rocketing. His face was the picture of perfection despite him panting and beaming like a loon.

"What took you so long, slowcoach?"

"Well, fancy running into you today, Teddy Fraser."

He was extraordinarily pleased with himself, I could tell, as he patted his swanky new steed affectionately. The smug twitch of his lips drew my eye straight to his mouth, instantly setting into play an erotic movie reel of what it had been doing to my body when we'd woken up this morning.

"What a piece of luck, huh?" Pluto began sidling up to Teddy, who leant his bike against a tree and reached up to pat the horse's neck, offering him a mint from his pocket. "You ok, mate? Has she been picking on you again? Us chaps really do need to stick together."

Sliding down from the saddle, I stroked my horse's nose gratefully while he snuffled my fingers in search of more sweets, licking his lips and slobbering delightedly at the treat I offered him.

"Yeah, you boys are so hard done by."

Teddy had taken his helmet off and looped the chinstrap

over the handlebars. His hair was dishevelled and standing on end, his eyes twinkling in that gloriously mischievous way that was so familiar to me now.

"I'm glad you recognise this fact. Pluto's had a mint, but how are you going to make it up to me?"

I unclipped the lead rope that was attached to the saddle and tied Pluto up to a nearby tree, whereupon he happily began snacking on the lowest branches, now well used to these impromptu woodland rendezvous.

"I don't know, Fraser, what would be a *nice* thing for me to do to make it up to you?"

The answering grin was radiant. "I can think of a few *nice* things you can do."

"Mmmm."

Closing the distance, I tugged at his fingers until he followed me around the back of a large oak and under its ancient branches, which drooped almost to the ground. We stood together on a carpet of spongey moss, an electric tension palpable around us.

"What could you possibly have in mind, Dr Havens?"

I still had my riding crop, and with an overt flourish I slapped it against my long leather boots, so that his eyes darkened and he swallowed slowly.

"Well, well, well, this is an unexpected surprise," he said in a low voice.

"Am I making you nervous?"

I pointed the whip at his chest, flicking the little leather flap so it smacked against his clothes.

"A little." Stepping forwards, he took the whip gently from my hand and laid it on the ground. "Why don't you show me just how much you've learnt since becoming a fellow in the

Fraser Foundation for Flirting."

Snorting, I removed my riding hat, before tracing a finger over Teddy's tight Lycra T-shirt, my palm resting on his pectorals. I firmly pushed him back against the trunk of the tree and bit my lip while my hand travelled down towards the waistband of his shorts. I didn't break eye contact, noticing with satisfaction the widening of his pupils and the distinctly uneasy bob of his Adam's apple.

Leaning in to nibble his neck and tasting the salt on his skin, I gently sucked and kissed my way up to his ear.

"How about a little role play?"

Teddy sucked in a breath.

"Oh yeah?"

"Yeah."

"What do you have in mind? Brave knight and damsel in distress?"

"While you make a very good damsel in distress, Teddy, that's not what I had in mind."

Our faces close now, he grinned against my lips. "Doctors and nurses?"

I tutted. "So clichéd."

His hands reached up to my hair, grabbing my ponytail so he could tilt my head backwards. Running his nose up my throat, he groaned against my skin, the noise rumbling and reverberating through to my very core.

"I can definitely be a fireman, but I'm not being Mr Darcy again."

"How about you play the sexy architect and I'll be the ravishing vet."

"Sounds implausible."

"Undoubtedly, but let's give it a go."

Acknowledgments

A huge thanks, once again, to Meg Davis at the Ki Agency, and Jennie and all the team at One More Chapter for believing in me and championing this book before you'd even read it. And then loving it enough to publish it and not make me write a different one. Thanks also to all the people who bought and read *The Hot Henry Effect*, and the lovely reviews and messages that I have received. I've been quite literally blown away by them, and may have (more than once) cried some snotty tears of joy.

I am now a fully ensconced member of the Writing Community on Twitter/X and Instagram, and although all the wonderful people who follow and encourage me on there need a mention, there is simply not enough space here. So a huge and collective thank you to you all, for the laughs, for the mental shakes that I sometimes need, and the constant inspiration and camaraderie. I'm forever grateful. For the close friends I've made since embarking on this author journey, you've added more to my life than you know, including opening my eyes to entirely new terminology, the boundless limits of euphemisms, and the confidence to do lip-syncing/dancing videos, the likes of which I'm quite sure the internet will never be ready for. Some of you are really, really special, and I've definitely found my tribe.

Thanks again to my family and friends too, for not minding

when I suddenly go off into a bit of a daze when inspiration hits, or when I just have to run away and write for a few hours. Or if I go on and on about the imaginary people in my head, and particularly if you feel you can't tell me anything in case it goes in a book (I mean, it probably will, fair warning). The support I have received since finally admitting to you all that I am a closet romance writer has been brilliant. Thank you.

To the Smallest Chalice, I'm really sorry that people ask you about me and the books (especially in your piano lessons, I love you too Mimi), and if I ever do get famous I will go on Celebrity Catchphrase at your insistence. Luckily for all concerned the likelihood of this is as close to zero as is possible. By the way, this is another book you cannot read until you are 35 years old, so put it back with the other one and all the Jilly Cooper books.

Thank you to Henry and Clara and Teddy and Hannah, and the bonkers yet wonderful people who talk to me inside me head on a daily basis, I'm less keen on you keeping me up at night with your shenanigans, and If you could reserve your chats for when I'm at my computer and not driving or in the shower, that'd be grand.

I am, as always, astounded by where this has taken me, and the fact I have two books out in the world. So my biggest thanks is to you, the reader, for taking a chance on this unknown author and slightly mad scientist from Devon, for enjoying my stories and wanting to read more. For not judging my weird turns of phrase or slightly flawed characters too harshly. For loving them and holding them in your heart like I do. I am more grateful than you'll ever know.

Read on for an extract from *The Hot Henry Effect*

The Hot Henry Effect: a genuine scientific phenomenon whereby those around Henry fall instantly and helplessly in love with him, the outcomes of which he has remained entirely oblivious to.

Well everyone except Dr Clara Clancy. But when they end up working together, it's not long until they slip into the easy friendship they had back at university. And this time, will Clara really be able to resist the Hot Henry Effect...

Extract from The Hot Henry Effect

CHAPTER ONE

The ridiculous swooning had started almost the instant he set foot in our laboratory. A wave of fluttering eyelashes, a gust of breathy sighs. Astute, intelligent scientists reduced to simpering wrecks. I felt like an extra in the screen adaptation of *Pride and Prejudice* rather than a doctoral student at one of the most acclaimed academic institutions in the world.

And it irritated me to the core.

"Bloody hell, Henry, stop touching the tip of the pipette to the top of the bottle, or you'll get all the cultures infected," I complained, slightly more acerbically than I had intended.

"Sorry," he mumbled, head bent against the glass partition. A faint blush coloured his cheeks and even though he didn't look in my direction, I could see from his perfectly formed profile that he seemed a bit wounded.

Damn it. Must. Be. More. Tolerant.

Tongue poking out in concentration, he tried again. His hand flailing the Gilson pipette wildly around the cell culture hood like he was conducting some kind of scientific semaphore, attempting to locate a fresh new tip from the sterilised box in the corner and suck up the required amount of bright pink growth media.

I couldn't help the impatient little huff that escaped from my lips, and he glanced over distractedly, splattering the once pristine stainless steel base of the cabinet, and completely missing the wells of the ninety six-well plate he was aiming for. I really tried to stop the eye roll, but my eyeballs seemed to be rotating reflexively these days.

"Just try again, with less exaggerated arm movements and you'll be fine," I said in a falsely bright and positive voice that was not well received, judging by the creased brow and slightly pouty look behind the goggles. I wondered if this was his version of Zoolander's "Blue Steel" and had to suppress a snigger from escaping.

It was easy to see why our research group had suddenly become a hive of female activity. I wasn't totally oblivious. Even Prof. Hart from genomics (who was fifty-seven years old and happily married to the dean of the medical school) would waft about in Henry's presence, clutching her pearls and sighing theatrically. In the last month, oestrogen levels had become worryingly high, and we had had an influx of undergrad and postgrad applications to work in our group, ninety-nine per cent of which were female. And, while I was all for encouraging women into STEM research, transferring laboratories or selecting a career just to stare at some guy's pretty face did not seem to be an appropriate or sustainable motivation.

In his defence, Henry Fraser did look like a cover model for GQ magazine; blue-grey eyes, impressively symmetrical bone structure, wavy chocolate brown hair, and at well over six feet tall he cut an impressive figure. Also, amazingly, he seemed blissfully unaware of the effect he had on anyone female. Or male actually; the dead faint that Ben, my undergrad research student, had performed when I introduced them would have made a Regency debutante's mother proud.

But the man was hopeless with a pipette, and at this moment in time I was attempting to teach him the intricacies of cell culture, whilst also frantically trying to finish my final few experiments in order to complete the last chapter of my doctorate here at Oxford. At least Henry's was only a short stint in our lab, just a few months for me to train him before he returned to his engineering PhD in the States.

He flashed a triumphant smile as he finally managed to get the full one hundred and fifty microlitres of growth media into the first well on this plate, and I responded with a double thumbs up and an attempting-to-be-supportive expression, which was probably more akin to a bulldog chewing a wasp.

"Good work, Henry, just ninety-five more to go," I crooned sarcastically.

"Motivational speaking is not your forte, Clara," he muttered, flicking the used tip off the pipette and dropping it into the plastic beaker he was using for waste. Hesitantly he went in for a new one, hand shaking madly causing the tip box to rattle musically as if he was trying to incite a flamenco dance-off.

As his mentor, I could not fault him as a student. Quietly polite, thoughtful and staggeringly intelligent. In fact, the unwavering attention and focus that he gave my every word, studiously copying out my protocols and seeking me out to ask detailed questions on the minutiae of every procedure, was to be commended. I couldn't recall a time when our dingy little office had ever been so well visited, what with Henry regularly dropping off coffees and pastries for me, stopping in for little chats, and then the constant stream of groupies who thought that I was the keeper of his diary, and could maybe guide them on the way into his heart, or his bed (some were more blatant than others), it was like Piccadilly Circus most days.

Staring out of the window, I let my mind wander just a little, the lure of this late summer afternoon providing an enticing distraction to those of us stuck inside. The hum of the strip lights and the astringent, antiseptic laboratory aroma triggering memories of many long and tedious hours spent in pursuit of my research. The constant second-guessing and attempts to do something important, something worthy of publication. And I was so nearly there, so close to getting my thesis written up and finished, after which I was convinced that a whole world of new and exciting opportunities was waiting for me. I just had to get through the viva first. The mere prospect of attending the trickiest exit interview in the world had my heartrate spiking and palms sweating, the multitude of horror stories told to every graduate student the world over flashing through my mind. But I could bloody well do this, I had to, and it was about time I said goodbye to the self-doubt and fear of rejection that had plagued me since I was a child.

"Shit." Henry's voice brought me back to the present day with a sweary little bump.

The tip of the pipette was now aimlessly sinking to the bottom of the container of growth media and Henry was attempting to fish it out, wholly unsuccessfully.

"It's alright, Henry, just leave it in there," I said, closing my eyes briefly, having already decided to write this bottle off and pour it down the sink after our session, convinced that it would have all kinds of funky organisms growing in it come the morning.

"If you're sure…" he replied, turning his whole body to look at me and catching the edge of the bottle with the cuffed sleeve of his university regulation bright blue lab coat, and sending the almost full container teetering precariously. On instinct, I shot my gloved hand into the hood, desperately trying to avert the impending doom of flooding all the plates that we had spent two hours painstakingly seeding with stem cells. But just as I thought I'd saved it, our hands collided, and I watched in dismay as the bottle was flung against the back of the cabinet, and a pink tsunami engulfed all in its path.

"Shit," he said again, eyes wide with horror behind the slightly battered and scratched laboratory goggles he was wearing.

"Indeed."

I wasn't sure how I was staying so calm. Ahead lay an entire afternoon and evening of clean up and decontamination of the cell culture suite before starting all over again on growth and expansion of my diminishing source of bone marrow stem cells, setting my experiments back at least another two weeks.

"I am so sorry," Henry whispered, trying to shrink away to somewhere deep inside the recesses of his lab coat.

"It's ok." A surge of pity and compassion warmed behind my ribs at his distraught face, so I added gently, "Don't worry, we can sort it out."

I have no doubt that some of my fellow graduate students would have considered this turn of events to be a disaster of truly epic proportions. One that heralded the point of no return. The time at which to permanently eject hapless Henry from the lab, while simultaneously lamenting the loss of the cells and crying into a cup of strong tea with Morrissey playing on full blast in the background, all due to the inevitable delay to their thesis completion. And, while I was tempted to theatrically throw my hands up in defeat and run off a string of expletives about what a complete and utter ball ache this was, I didn't actually have it in me to do any of these things. Because, in spite of my initial misgivings and annoyance at having to babysit an engineering student, Henry had grown on me in the last few weeks, and I had begrudgingly begun to like him. Indeed, no one was more surprised than me when we formed an unlikely friendship.

Initially, I had assumed that he was going to be an arrogant prick, a player, a cad, adept at using his handsome face and charm to manipulate those around him. But I couldn't have been more wrong. Even with my almost constant barrage of snarky comments and little digs, his patient kindness and dry humour had proven unexpectedly disarming, so much so that I spent more and more of my time in his company trying not to smile. Plus, while he was undoubtedly dedicated to his own research, he was also hugely generous with his time and insights, often approaching things from such a different perspective that I was beginning to feel as if I was the one getting the most benefit from our mentorship. Although I tried never to let it show just how much value I placed on being with him – even someone as nice as Henry didn't need to have their ego stroked too much.

He also had this particular expression, one he was wearing at this moment, one that he used if he needed me to stay late or help with something, one that he could use to devastating effect. It was hard to discern; a soft light in his eyes, a slight tilt of his lips, open and hopeful, indulgent and encouraging, shy and secretive, all at once. And, despite my best intentions, I seemed to fall for it every single time.

"Shall we clear this up, then perhaps you can buy me a drink and we can work on some theory in the pub?" I suggested quietly, any lingering anger or resentment completely dissolving away as he huffed a sad little sigh.

"Sounds like a good plan," he replied with a dejected nod.

Handing me a spray bottle of seventy percent ethanol, he picked up a full roll of blue paper towel and started to mop up the disaster that was now dripping onto his plastic over-shoe. We worked in comfortable silence for a few minutes, scooping all the mess into the clinical waste bin and systematically taking apart, cleaning and disinfecting all of the equipment.

In general, Henry wasn't a massive talker, particularly in large groups, preferring to let others be the centre of attention, and we had become quite content to just be quiet in each other's company. It was refreshing not to have someone else's opinions foisted onto me all the time, and I also knew that when he did eventually speak, he would have considered what he was going to say very carefully and weighed up the merits of the topic thoroughly, and would not just spout the regular drivel or postgrad posturing I was usually subjected to.

With both our heads close together inside the laminar flow hood, Henry turned to me nonchalantly and said, in a deadpan voice, "What did one stem cell say to the other when it stood on its foot?"

"What?"

"Ouch, that's mitosis."

I snorted with laughter. "That's a really dreadful joke, Henry."

"Yeah, but I know that you're going to pass it off as your own when you see Jo later," he said, a small smile playing over his features.

"I might do," I answered with a non-committal shrug, thinking how my best friend Jo would definitely snigger too. "How many engineers does it take to change a lightbulb?"

"None, that's a maintenance issue."

"Hey, you stole my punchline!" I threw a balled-up piece of sodden blue paper at his head, and it stuck to his goggles with a satisfyingly wet thud.

"Have I got something on my face?" he asked, his tone utterly serious.

"Nope, no, nothing at all."

"Are you sure? Not something around here?" His hand was waving around the blue splat that was now dripping and sliding down the plastic lens. "Because you can't stop staring at me."

"Maybe a little something, but generally I think it's a huge visual improvement on your face."

"Ah, in that case I'll leave it where it is," he said, grinning widely. And my heart stuttered, just a little bit. Christ, Clara, get a grip, they're just his teeth, and lips. And dimples.

"I might have to record this as a cell culture health and safety violation, where's the logbook?" Henry carried on, as he peeled the blue sludge off his plastic glasses and wiped his face.

"I definitely know somewhere that we can put the logbook, Henry, somewhere that the sun doesn't shine, even from you…" I muttered darkly, eliciting a soft chuckle from him.

"I know what will cheer you up – let's listen to some music!" he said brightly.

"Urgh, not your best of Bon Jovi playlist again, Henry," I groaned, trying to hide a smile.

"Jon Bon Jovi is a god amongst men, Clara, the sooner you accept this, the better," Henry replied, fishing out his phone and linking it to the speaker on the back wall of the lab.

Soon the room was filled with the upbeat tones of 1980s soft rock, and I couldn't help tunelessly singing along using the mop handle as a microphone, with Henry right there next to me on air guitar. And even though I knew that it was going to be a very long day of cleaning, that I'd lost pretty much an entire batch of irreplaceable stem cells, and my thesis completion date had likely been delayed yet again, I suddenly didn't feel so bad about it after all.

Available in paperback and ebook now

ONE MORE CHAPTER

The author and One More Chapter would like to thank everyone who contributed to the publication of this story...

Analytics
James Brackin
Abigail Fryer

Audio
Fionnuala Barrett
Ciara Briggs

Contracts
Sasha Duszynska
Lewis

Design
Lucy Bennett
Fiona Greenway
Liane Payne
Dean Russell

Digital Sales
Lydia Grainge
Hannah Lismore
Emily Scorer

Editorial
Janet Marie Adkins
Arsalan Isa
Charlotte Ledger
Lydia Mason
Jennie Rothwell

Harper360
Emily Gerbner
Jean Marie Kelly
emma sullivan
Sophia Wilhelm

International Sales
Peter Borcsok
Ruth Burrow

Marketing & Publicity
Chloe Cummings
Emma Petfield

Operations
Melissa Okusanya
Hannah Stamp

Production
Denis Manson
Simon Moore
Francesca Tuzzeo

Rights
Helena Font Brillas
Ashton Mucha
Zoe Shine
Aisling Smythe

The HarperCollins Distribution Team

The HarperCollins Finance & Royalties Team

The HarperCollins Legal Team

The HarperCollins Technology Team

Trade Marketing
Ben Hurd

UK Sales
Laura Carpenter
Isabel Coburn
Jay Cochrane
Sabina Lewis
Holly Martin
Harriet Williams
Leah Woods

And every other essential link in the chain from delivery drivers to booksellers to librarians and beyond!

YOUR NUMBER ONE STOP

ONE MORE CHAPTER

FOR PAGETURNING BOOKS

One More Chapter is an
award-winning global
division of HarperCollins.

Sign up to our newsletter to get our
latest eBook deals and stay up to date
with our weekly Book Club!
<u>Subscribe here.</u>

Meet the team at
<u>www.onemorechapter.com</u>

Follow us!

 @OneMoreChapter_

 @OneMoreChapter

 @onemorechapterhc

Do you write unputdownable fiction?
We love to hear from new voices.
Find out how to submit your novel at
<u>www.onemorechapter.com/submissions</u>